Grab

Bag

4

FOR LITERARY HEAT

WARNING: This book is for sale to **ADULT AUDIENCES ONLY**. Contains graphic gay male sex, reluctance, multiple partners, anal sex, non-graphic violence, gay sportsmen, gay pilots, gay sailors, gay Australians, and gay romance and gay love, all of which may be considered offensive by some readers. **All sexually active characters in this work are at least 18 years of age.**

This book is copyright © habu 2013
Published by BarbarianSpy in 2013
Cover design © S Bush 2013
Cover image: © Wrangel | Dreamstime.com
ISBN Paperback: 978-1-922187-53-6
All rights reserved

Published by BarbarianSpy
Jindalee St
Toronto, NSW 2283
AUSTRALIA

Grab Bag

4

by

habu

Table of Contents

Introduction 7

Two Men in a Dungeon 11

New Master at Riverbend 23

Swimming Lessons 47

Satin Sleigh Ride 61

Satin Circus 73

Only a Custodian 79

Sailors and Flyboys 89

Solicitous Service 115

First and Only 127

For the Glory of the Earth 151

Snow Trap 181

Arabists' Literary Weekend 195

Friday Nights with Lenny 213

Experiencing Partnered Sounding 243

Porn War 249

About the Author 269

Introduction

This fourth volume of habu's *Grab Bag* collections contains fifteen all-new short stories and continues a series trend of eclectic gay male settings and plotlines presented in the order in which they were delivered for writing by habu's fertile muse within the period of only a couple of months.

This collection, atypically for habu set mostly (but not wholly) in the United States, takes us from one coast to the other and through time from the antebellum period of the American South to the present and from schoolroom to jazz club.

Included, in addition to story ideas just dropping from the sky, are stories inspired by e-mail exchanges with readers, requests for specific fetish stories, the exploration of a rarely written story specialty of habu's—the gay male fetish of sounding—in both story and essay, and stories written specifically for themed contests. As always, though, the reader will also be entertained with representative takes on habu's signature themes; gang banging, double penetration, domination, rough sex, male prostitution, older-younger, big black on small white, humor, bondage, twist endings, and gay romance. There might even be a vampire or two lurking about.

Two of the stories, the initial one, "Two Men in a Dungeon," and the later "Sailors and Flyboys" were inspired by a series of e-mail discussions (accompanied by photos) from a reader, a former Air Force officer and currently serious bodybuilder, wanting to exchange experiences and "interests." Two stories, the Russia setting "Satin Sleigh Ride" and "Satin Circus," were the result of a reader's specific request for stories on a "satin" fetish that he hadn't seen covered in gay male stories before.

Habu has come to specialize in offerings on the rare and extreme gay-male fetish of sounding. Included in this collection is a story on both sounding and drug use, set in a jazz club, "Friday Nights with Lenny," and, by request, an essay, "Experiencing Partnered Sounding," on the research habu did to be able to write these stories.

Two of the stories were written to theme specifications for writing contests. "For the Glory of the Earth," dealing with plans for uranium mining in rural southside Virginia, was inspired by actual news reports, and was written for an Earth Day contest. "Porn War" was written for another themed contest requiring the story's protagonist to be a story writer who experiences the erotic events he writes about.

History, both foreign and U.S., is a frequent setting for habu's stories as are the themes of big-cocked black men dominating small white men and of male brothels, intrigue, treachery, double penetration (DP), and unusual sexual positions. All of these elements come together in the antebellum South plantation life story "New Master at Riverbend."

Among the favorite foreign locales of habu stories (e.g., Southeast Asia, the Middle East, the Mediterranean) Australia ranks high. Not only has habu traveled there and found the men there open and inviting, but it's also where the publisher of the *Grab Bag* anthologies lives and works. Therefore, there's almost always an Australia setting story or two in his *Grab Bag* collections. There are two in this collection, although the first, "Swimming Lessons," doesn't say it's set in Australia. However, the beach behavior observation that inspired the story was set on an Australian beach. Other inspirations for this story were the longstanding habu writing fetish of DP and a reacquaintance during this period of writing with the positions of the male Kamasutra. Habu was first initiated into these exotic positions when he was introduced to male-on-male sex—by an Indian doctor in Bangkok. An illustrated discussion of these positions popped up during the months of writing the stories in this collection in an Internet search and the positions have been used in several of habu's recent stories. The "sex in the surf looking back at a beach crowd" theme is also one that recurs occasionally in habu stories, being brought back by memories of beach play he enjoyed in Cyprus.

Another story connected to Australia, "First and Only," set in a gay district of Sydney that habu frequented when he traveled down under, was inspired by the intersection of discussions with his publisher on finding books of nude male art for the publisher's drawing classes and the scintillating image of a male model sent to habu over the Internet.

The other international-setting story in the collection, "Arabists' Literary Weekend," also relates to a recent habu trip abroad—this time to the Forest of Dean area of England. The setting of this story is an ancient manor house habu lived in for a week while sightseeing around southwest England and Wales. The setting was married to a theme stemming from habu's reading "binge" on Arabic authors of historical Middle East novels.

The remaining three stories are set in the United States in present time. In "The Custodian," high school teacher Blake is looking for a hookup with a professional man, but that isn't who he is drawn to. In "Snow Trap," set in a snow-bound mountain home, the young protagonist, Boyd, is trying to escape the man he is attracted to but who should be taboo to him. And in "Solicitous Service," a young congressional intern,

Tyler, is getting an unexpected kiss off from an unclassy political leader in a classy suburban Washington, D.C., restaurant.

Two Men in a Dungeon

The Hulk crouched near the bolted heavy oak door, eyeing Rab, ready to pounce, trying to anticipate where Rab might try to scurry next. The stone-walled chamber wasn't small, but it wasn't so large that Rab had much of a chance evading the Hulk much longer. Both men were panting, having played this cat-and-mouse game for several minutes, but Rab was more winded than the Hulk was. No one in his right mind would have bet on Rab in these circumstances.

The hulk couldn't have looked any more fierce. His loincloth only accentuated the jungle primeval nature of him. He was more than six and a half feet tall, with a massive, heavily worked musculature, the development of which must have taken up most of his adulthood. Bald and bullet-headed with bushy, reddish-blond eyebrows nearly hiding jet-black, intelligent eyes that darted about, seeing everything at once, measuring the angles and the distances, he was a man to easily strike terror into the heart of a young, small man like Rab. Though beautifully proportioned and handsome of features, Rab was less than three-quarters the size of the man stalking him in the windowless chamber, silent as death other than the heavy breathing of the two men.

The man's chest was massive, set between arms with biceps larger than Rab's waist. Although considering the aspect of hair on the giant brought the observer's attention immediately to the bald head, bushy eyebrows, and the Fu Manchu mustache and extra-long goatee, closer examination revealed that his arms and chest were covered in reddish-blond hair as well, so long and fine that when the light was set behind him his body took on a haloed effect. Blue, green, and red tattoos peeked out through the pelting: oval designs on the forearms and a dragon on the left shoulder and bicep. The nubs on the man's chest were prominent, begging for rings, but, other than the tattoos, the Hulk sported no body adornment. The most dominant tattoo, at least at this moment, was the word "Respect" carved in a Gothic-letter arc following the diaphragm curve below the bulging pecs.

Rab was, at the moment, giving the Hulk all of the respect he could muster by trying to stay out of his grip. The young man, covered only in a gauzy white cotton tunic of sorts, was moving in a semicircle as far on the other side of the stone-walled chamber as he could. The two were eyeing each other warily. The Hulk, grunting, would make a feint in one direction and Rab would quickly dart in another. Then the action would be played out in another direction. Rab knew what the Hulk was looking for in the young man's evasion, why the man was toying with him like this. He could see the intelligence in the Hulk's eyes. He knew the man was mapping Rab's pattern of trying to maintain the distance between them. He knew that the man enjoyed this game, also knowing how it inevitably would end. Rab was trying to change his movement pattern, but he could see by a flash in the Hulk's eyes and a growling laugh that rumbled deep inside the man that his moments of freedom were nearly at an end.

The Hulk crouched on his beefy haunches, ready to spring in whatever direction he decided. A broad, calloused hand went to the string holding up his loincloth. He tugged on the string, snapping it, and the loincloth fell to the floor. He gave Rab a sneery "this is all going to be inside you" smile.

Rab's eyes opened wide and he sobbed. The big cock was already sheathed in erection, leaving no doubt of intent, not that there ever had been doubt of intent from the moment he was thrown into the dungeon with the giant.

The Hulk's groin was hairless to accommodate the most intimidating tattoo of all, the triangle above the cock being taken up with the wings of a bat centered by a hound's head, oversized fangs flashing. Talons reached down from both sides of the wings, perpetually trying to dig into the root of the man's cock. The cock itself, wrapped at the root by a tight leather band was massive in its erection. Not overly long, but thick, cut, and bending menacingly to the right just beyond the glans. And it was sheathed and greased, ready for immediate action.

Rab's entrance had been greased too before he was tossed into the room. There would be no foreplay, no time to adjust.

Rab's hand went to his mouth to stifle the scream of recognition of what the Hulk intended to do with that cock—and how sure they both were that the Hulk would do as he liked. The moment of shock was just what the Hulk had been waiting for. He feinted right but pounced left, springing off the spongy tatami matting of the floor, and was almost upon Rab before the young man could react. When Rab did move, it was in the wrong direction.

The young man slid across the matting toward the far corner of the room. He went down in a heap and was just a second too late in springing back up. There was no place to go but the corner. Which meant there was no place to go at all. Rab cowered in the corner, drawing his knees up into his chest and trying to cover his head with his arms, not wanting to see what was coming. His pursuer hovered over him for a moment, grunting and growling. He smiled, obviously pleased that the new phase of this game was now opening. Reaching down, he grabbed onto the back neckline of Rab's tunic and easily lifted the young man up in the air. He shook his prey, looking at it as if contemplating where to begin. Rab was babbling and pleading, but the Hulk took no notice. With a sweep of his arm, he tossed Rab into the center of the empty room. Rab landed hard on the tatami floor and, with a whimper and shudder, folded himself into a fetal position.

But in three strides the Hulk was standing over the young man again. He reached down and grabbed the neck of the tunic once more with both claws and just ripped it away, off the young man's body, and tossed it aside. Rab lay on the matting below him, trembling and whimpering. His body was alabaster white. He was beautifully formed. Rather than the exaggerated bulk of the Hulk in every dimension, his was a very young, well-muscled, but pampered body, perfect in every proportion for a young man of barely five and a half feet. He was smooth-skinned, and had been unblemished before he had been thrown in the room but would show bruises after whatever happened to him here. His head hair was auburn, with golden highlights, and curled in a thick mop around his head. His eyes were hazel and wide open now in terror.

The Hulk reached down, put a beefy arm around the young man's waist, and lifted his body, bent over, up into the air. Rab struggled, flailing out with both his arms and legs, resisting as best he could the assault on his body. The Hulk turned him facing up and, with his other hand, backhanded Rab twice across the face. Rab wailed and lost a bit of the fight, but not much. He was stunned long enough, though, for the Hulk to work his hips between Rab's thighs and to position his cock so that he could start repeatedly brushing the top of his shaft across the rim of Rab's hole.

Recovered a bit, Rab started struggling harder again, but the Hulk just laughed, retaining his strong embrace with the arm under Rab's waist and holding his pelvis in to where

Rab's cock rested against the hounds head of the bat tattoo. With his free hand, the Hulk slapped Rab's buttocks several times, eliciting little cries from the struggling young man. The hulk went down on his knees on the Tatami and slammed Rab down on his back in front of him. As they reached the flooring, he pushed his knees under Rab's buttocks so that the young man's pelvis was elevated above his torso, his legs were spread on the outside of the Hulk's meaty thighs, and his channel offered a straight shot for the Hulk's thick, curved cock. Winded, Rab didn't struggle as the Hulk pulled the smaller man's torso into his, jerking Rab's legs up on his thighs. And then, pressing down on Rab's sternum with one hand and grabbing his own cock with his other hand, he started to stuff the head of his cock into Rab's hole. This produced louder cries and increased flailing of Rab's arms and shaking of his head.

The Hulk lowered his mouth to Rab's nipples and sucked and bit those as he pressed his cock slowly home, stretching Rab's channel to accommodate him ever so slowly as there had been no preparation other than that Rab had been greased up before being tossed into the chamber.

Rab was still struggling, trying, without success, to move his legs into some position from where he either could attack the Hulk or push away from him. He was beating with his fists, again without effect, all over the Hulk's torso, trying to push him away. His head arched back and he cried out at the rough treatment the Hulk was giving his nipples. He also was giving a babbling commentary of the movement of the cock down his channel.

Bottomed, the Hulk raised his head off Rab's chest and gave the young man a smile of victory. He reached for and imprisoned the wrists of the flailing arms with his fists and forced them down on the tatami flooring out wide on either side of Rab's head. Chest heaving, Rab stared back up into the giant's face with an expression of wonder at all that was inside him, throbbing, stretching. They held there for a few seconds of recognition that they now were one, unified, connected in some primeval way and that the reality was that there was no going back to a moment when Rab was not fully possessed by this man—and one, slight moment of acceptance on Rab's part of what *was* and would not ever again be otherwise. Miraculously, Rab's channel walls had stretched to accommodate the pulsating shaft. For no more than a slight second Rab was struck with the thought that the victory wasn't all the Hulk's. The man was panting for him, deep inside him, his cock throbbing, beyond his control in wanting him. In some way this was Rab's victory too.

The moment did not last, though.

Giving a knowing smile, the Hulk moved his hips back, just once at that moment, withdrawing his cock half way, and then moved forward again, slowly, deliberately, pushing deep inside Rab's channel. The moment of accepted connection was broken. In a whimpering voice of resignation, Rab spoke coherently for the first time. "Please, just go slowly, Please don't hurt me."

Whether it was that the Hulk didn't hear him or that he didn't understand or that he simply didn't care, he smiled cruelly, reared his hips back and thrust forward hard. Rab's body jerked and he threw his head back and cried out. The Hulk thrust hard and deep inside him, again and again and again. Rab did not plead again. He was moaning and wailing and whimpering and cursing the man with every foul word he could think of, and the Hulk just smiled and continued pumping the channel hard. And as the time passed, Rab quieted down in defeat and went limp.

Laughing, the Hulk released the young man's wrists and raised up a bit, giving him an inch more in depth as he pumped. He had stopped the pounding, though, and had started all over at a deliberate beginning, working the channel in a slow pump, which steadily but not too quickly picked up speed again. He ran his hands over Rab's chest as the young man panted a shallow pant of resignation. The Hulk moved back on his haunches, which brought Rab's torso off the tatami, the Hulk supporting Rab's torso with hands on his waist. But Rab just lay back, arms akimbo at his side, head flopped back, the only motion in those being the slight jerks, accompanied by a moan or a groan, marking the relentless thrusts inside his channel. The Hulk leaned over and nibbled at Rab's nipples, but the young man gave no response; he just lay there, limp.

Tiring, the Hulk's pumps slowed down again and set into a regular pattern of a few short thrusts, followed by some bulb work on Rab's prostate, and then a few long, deep strokes. Rab's channel had opened fully to be able to take the cock even though it was still a tight fit.

And then, slowly, the Hulk's eyes opening in amazement, something was going on inside the channel. The muscles of Rab's channel walls were starting to undulate over the cock, and Rab was sighing and moaning. And then his hips started to move, revolving and moving up and down and back and forth, forming new patterns of pleasure for the Hulk's movement inside him.

Rab reached for one of the Hulk's hands and moved it to Rab's cock, encouraging the giant to start stroking. In utter surprise and delight the Hulk fell into this enthusiastically. Rab reached up with his hands and ran his fingers through the Hulk's chest hair. And his fingers went to the prominent nubs and made them plump up even more than they already were. Rab was purring, and, in as far as a monster man like the Hulk could do, he was purring as well.

The young man raised his torso, with no objection from the Hulk, and moved his mouth to that of his assailant. He then opened his lips to give entry to the Hulk's tongue. Now the Hulk definitely was purring.

Rab shuddered and gave a couple of little jerks and ejaculated up the Hulk's flat stomach, the cum reaching for the arced "Respect" tattoo. The Hulk trembled, amazed that Rab now wanted him. Rab cooed and moved his hips, signaling that he loved the fucking the Hulk's cock was giving him.

Then nudging the Hulk toward one side, he tried to turn them into another position. At first the Hulk didn't understand and he gripped Rab hard, but then he began to realize what Rab was trying to do—and he was grateful, because he had been crouched over Rab's body and pumping his channel for what seemed to be an eternity. As Rab had become not just accepting but also a partner in the fuck, the adrenaline had started to flow out of the Hulk's body and he was tiring.

He allowed Rab to turn them onto the side and then, nudged further, turned onto his back. Rab was on top of him now, saddled on his pelvis. And it was Rab who was moving his channel on the cock, fucking himself.

The Hulk ran his hand up and down Rab's sides as the young man arched his back and rode the cock. A look of amazement came over the Hulk's face as he jerked and fired off deep inside the young man. Giving him a saucy smile, Rab came off the cock and wormed his body down until he could roll the sheath off, clean the cock in his mouth, and continue to make love to it for several minutes.

When he rolled off of the Hulk's body, the giant stumbled up onto his feet and looked down at the curled-up Rab in wonder. He had conquered in a way he'd never imagined. The Hulk had not, in a thousand years, thought that he could make a forced conquest like this want him. He had been told he was being given a fresh one to do what he wanted with. He had planned on breaking the young man and leaving him incapable of serving another man for some time to come. And he had done damage; he was sure of that. But no conquest had ever grown to want the cocking as this small man had. He had always fully planned to fuck the young man again, but this new experience was giving the Hulk pause to consider what was happening here.

He walked around the perimeter of the chamber, close to the walls, keeping his eyes on the collapsed figure of Rab. The young man was still breathing. The Hulk could hear the rasping breaths slowly becoming controlled, and the young man moving to where he could watch the Hulk pacing around him. The Hulk wasn't sure what to do. He was still randy, already reengorging. Would he be restalking the young man again in a few minutes? Would he fuck him more brutally this time to break him, find the key that would terrorize and break him? He always had to reestablish his control before, but this one was different. This one had come to act like he wanted it. Was it all a ruse—to hold off on a second fucking? If so, it wouldn't work.

The Hulk pulled the spent condom off his cock and threw it to the side. There were other, new ones, in various sizes, scattered around at the sides of the tatami mat. He reached down and retrieved a Golden Ticket Magnum packet, split it open, and rolled the condom on his cock. All the time he was watching the young man, expecting him to cower and to start moving away from the Hulk in realization that his ruse hadn't worked, marking the start of another pursuit.

But Rab didn't cower or retreat. As the Hulk was rolling the condom on his cock, Rab went up on his hands and knees and started crawling along the floor toward him, his eyes pleading. "Fuck me again, daddy. Please fuck me again. Fuck me hard," he murmured, raising an entreating arm toward the big bruiser.

With a roar, the Hulk stepped to Rab and scooped him off the tatami. He fucked him this time standing up in a crouch, with Rab's body draped down toward the floor of the chamber, held in front the Hulk with hand grips on both sides of Rab's waist. The Hulk pulled the young man's channel onto his cock with a long, fast jerk that had Rab crying out, "Yes! Yes! Fuck me hard!" And then the Hulk just pushed and pulled Rab's canal off his cock in strong, deep motions that got more and more rapid until the Hulk had filled the bulb of his condom again. Rab's cries of taking subsided in whimpers and the blowing of bubbles from his lips as his body limply arched back to the floor. When he was done, the Hulk let Rab's body slowly sink to the floor. Trembling, Rab encircled the Hulk's beefy thighs with his arms, lifting one hand to roll the spent condom of the Hulk's cock, and then cleaned the cock with his mouth. Still confused, the Hulk stood away from him, listening to Rab whimper, "Again, daddy, again. Fuck me again. Fuck my brains out," in a small, distant voice.

But the Hulk was spent. For the first time in his memory, he was totally drained of cum and the energy to fuck. And he was confused and amazed. This one had been turned to wanting him. The beautiful young man wanted the Hulk's cock.

Still pondering his new-found talent to make such a perfect young man want him, the Hulk slowly backed to the door. Rab dragged along, clinging to his legs, pleading, "Fuck me. Please do me again." The Hulk pounded on the door to signal that he was finished, and then disappeared on the other side, leaving Rab moaning and panting heavily in a pile inside the door.

At length, Rab slowly sat up, checked his body for damage, and shook his head to clear it. Giving a little smile, he stood up gingerly and opened the door. It had been shut but not locked. On the other side of the door, he opened a closet and took out another cotton tunic and pulled it down over his head. Then he padded out to the reception area.

The house pimp was sitting at the desk, smiling and shaking his head.

Rab walked up to the desk and collapsed into the chair beside it.

"I don't know how you do it," the pimp said. "You pushed him to over an hour and a half so he had to pay for two hours and even then he left a hefty tip for you. Each time you go back there with a big bruiser like that, I expect to have to send medics and a shovel back there to scoop you up, but here you are, walking out on your own two legs. He had a monster cock; I saw it; not long but extra thick. And he said he wanted to pay the rough fees and did. And he wants to come back tomorrow. He even asked what the rates were if he wanted to take you to a hotel room for the night. How do you do it?"

"I was trying to push him to over two hours to get an even higher rate. Managing bruisers like him is all in the timing," Rab answered. "They want to be shown they are the scariest thing in the West and then, whether they know it or not, they want to think they are the world's greatest lover. I just help them to think both ways. It was a little rough, though. I'm not sure I could have taken him again. Is it possible to call it a day? I've had three of those today already, although that one was, by far, the most taxing. What a magnificent body that bruiser had on him."

"Would you go with him overnight?"

"Sure, if the money was good and the hotel had strong beds. God, he could fuck. And his body was magnificent—much better than trying to pull the cum out of some of the ugly old men who come in here. So, can I call it a day?"

The pimp pursed his lips. "Gee I don't know. You're down for another one in an hour. Same plan."

"What is it with the business now?"

"The fleet's in. Another couple of days and it will be dead again."

They both looked up, sensing that something overpowering had just moved into the reception area. It was a big black bruiser, and even with what had already walked through the doors that day, he qualified as big. And he looked mad at the world and ready to kill something—and fully capable of doing so just with his hands.

"That the next appointment for the dungeon?" Rab asked.

"Yes. Early, probably anxious, but he looks bad. If you don't want to—"

"Naw, it'll be a piece of cake," Rab said. "If it's the last one I have to take today, of course. A piece of cake. All you have to do is cower for them and then make them think they're the world's greatest lover. Some of them are actually pretty good. That last one was hung and could fuck forever. I was having trouble not enjoying it from the beginning and was thinking of taking him home."

New Master at Riverbend

Jerome stood just inside the doorway at the shadowed end of the room. He should have just turned and gone down the stairs and out to the carriage to tell Thomas that Master John wasn't ready to go yet. That's all Thomas, Master John's carriage driver, had told him to do. But the shock of what he'd found when he'd entered the house on Decatur Street and been waved to the second door down the hall on the second floor held him plastered to his shadowy vigil spot long enough to engage his curiosity.

He was old enough to understand this between a man and a woman—he'd been fucking cook's daughter, Macey, long enough in the smoke house himself that she was waddling around supporting her belly with both her hands and with a big smile on her face. And he did the field hand Lottie regularly out in the cotton field too. She was too old to bear, he thought, but she knew what to do with a young man's cock. She'd been riding his since he became a grown man, old enough to go to the fields. These things Jerome already understood in his nineteenth year on this earth. But this. This was not something he had considered possible.

When Jerome had quietly pushed open the door and stolen in, he was suspecting something like this was going on. Everyone knew what went on in the Decatur Street house. But he didn't expect this. He didn't expect this at all.

A small black man of not more than Jerome's age was lying on his side on the bed—naked. He was up on one elbow and his back was turned to Jerome. Young Master John, also naked except for the billowing white cotton shirt with the flounces on it, open so that Jerome could see his hard-bodied chest, had the fingers of one hand buried in the black, wooly hair of the black man's head, holding the head to his groin. The black man was moving his mouth down and up on Master John's cock. The white man's other hand was reaching down and gripping the black man's cock and was stroking it.

Jerome hadn't ever seen anything like this at all. He should have turned and run out, but this was something entirely new to him, and Jerome was the curious type, especially where it came to sexual activity. And not knowing any better, the old master not having pushed the Riverbend plantation slaves to attend church, Jerome had no internal prejudices set on things such as this. Slave row at Riverbend was an earthy place. As soon as he had become aware of his sexual nature, Lottie was showing him how it could give him pleasures that transported him from the hardships of plantation life. She didn't tell him that it was only something that men and women did.

Still, it had not occurred to him that there were other couplings possible such as this one.

Before Jerome could get the notion to leave and go tell Thomas that their new master, John, didn't appear to need the carriage any time soon, the tableau on the bed was changing. Master John was standing on the floor on the other side of the bed and had turned the black man on his side and lifted the man's left leg to rest his ankle on John's shoulder. The black man's plump buttocks were plastered to the white man's pelvis, and the white man was fucking the black man's ass with long deep strokes. Master John was still fisting and stroking the black man's cock, and the black man was moaning and writhing against the deep stroking inside him. He had his left arm raised and a black hand palmed on the white chest, whether to try to push the white man away or to establish a connection to the man fucking him, Jerome couldn't tell. His other hand was stretched out across the bed and he was clutching the bed cloth in a fist. It seemed to Jerome that he was bunching and releasing the material in the same rhythm that Master John was stroking him with his cock. Whether or not that was so, Jerome saw it as so—and it aroused him.

The black man's face was turned toward Jerome, set in an expression of almost pleading. Jerome wondered if the man could see him there in the shadows. Possibly so. There was little danger that Master John could see him, though. White slaveholders rarely saw their slaves even in broad daylight; they looked right through them as if they weren't even there. The black man's eyes were opened wide, glittering, and his mouth was slack. He was moaning and groaning.

Master John turned him again, to his back, his buttocks at the edge of the bed. The white man grabbed the black man's ankles with his fist and brutally jerked them wide. He was leaning over the black man's chest, growling and grunting. His hips were pistoning fast and hard. The black man was clutching at the bed cloth with both of his fists and writhing under the white man and babbling incoherently and crying out at each deep, rapid thrust.

Master John tensed, abruptly stopping the thrusts. His body jerked and his head turned up toward the ceiling. Jerome saw in his face the same ecstasy he saw in Macey's when he released his seed in her. One, two, three more pumps and

Master John let out a long sigh and collapsed on top of the black man, who just lay there, moaning.

Jerome realized that he had wet himself with his own sticky manseed. He hoped that Thomas wouldn't notice that when he returned to the carriage. Master John's ejaculation, though, broke the spell, and Jerome realized that he had been away from Thomas too long. He withdrew quietly and then clattered out onto the street.

"I do believe Massa John be ready soon," he said breathlessly to Thomas when he arrived back at the carriage. "But he ain't ready now."

"Why you be so long in findin' that out?" Thomas asked suspiciously. "You find some pussy to poke for yerself while you in there?"

"No, no. They's not want to tell me where he was. Took me a time to get them to check on him. You know I can't 'ford the pussy they got in there."

"You such a handsome stud, I figure they give it to you for free just so they can watch. Nice big cock like yours and fine body."

Jerome blushed—if a black man can blush. Thomas had been talking to him like this for some months. It was only now that Jerome could come to the point of considering what Thomas might be meaning about that. True that often when he was sluicing himself down, having come for the fields, Thomas was there to jabber with him while he was naked. Jerome would need to give that some thought now. Now that he knew that men did it with men too.

Fifteen minutes later, Thomas gave Jerome the evil eye. "Thought you said the massa was about done."

"That's what they tell me in the house," Jerome answered defensively.

"Best I go check, I guess," Thomas said, moving to get down from the driving box.

"No, I'll go," Jerome answered.

He went quietly back upstairs. Although patrons and servants of the house were moving about, no one saw him or challenged him. There were advantages to being invisible to the whites, Jerome thought as he approached the second door down the hall.

The black man was on all fours in the center of the bed and Master John was crouched over his pelvis, fucking him in long, fast strokes. He was cupping the black man's throat from behind and arching his back up. The black man had a wild-eyed look in his eyes and his tongue was lolling out of his mouth. That's how Jerome liked to fuck Macey. Lottie liked that position too, but she preferred Jerome fucking her in the ass when he took her this way. He never realized that it could look so arousing. Master John was leaning well forward on the black man's buttocks so that Jerome could clearly see the thick white cock burying itself in the black asshole and then sliding out and then in again. He focused his attention on that action and felt chills running up his spine. He envisioned himself as poking a white man like that—maybe even Master John, although that gave him a start and a jolt of fear—and maybe even being poked like that.

He was surprised at the thought—but he was even more surprised that he didn't shrink from the thought.

He did, however, step out of the room and down the stairs and out to the carriage.

"I reckon Massa John won't be ready for a time yet," he told Thomas.

Thomas didn't bother to ask why. It wasn't the lot of a slave in the plantation world to ask why, just to stand by, invisible, until some white person told them what, where, and when.

* * * *

The various strata of the Riverbend plantation community had been living carefully and on the edge of concern for several months now, since even before young Master John came to take up residence. The Rembeaus, the family that had owned and lived at Riverbend for generations, were almost all gone now. Master John was the last of the lot, and he was just a cousin to Master Edward, the patriarch of the family last in residence here. But Master Edward's family had, to a member, been taken by the fever while visiting a plantation farther down the Mississippi, and Master John had inherited.

The big concern was what Master John was going to do with Riverbend. There were rumors that he would break up the place—sell the land and sell the slaves too. Neither the slaves nor the next strata up, the overseers, liked this thought one little bit. For the slaves, it inevitably meant a breakup of a community that had lived here for some hundred and fifty years, including, probably, family units. To the overseers it meant new, quite possibly less-desirable, employment needing to be found.

Nothing had transpired yet, but everyone was living in fear. Some, the customary leaders of the slave community, a small network of the older women who were house or kitchen slaves, were not content with sitting and waiting.

"How long has your Adelle been housemaiding at the big house, Naddie?"

"Ever since the young massa arrived. She done everthin' I told her to do—leastwise she claims so—and still he not taken her to his bed."

"Ever thing?" Zumma Mae said, with astonishment. "She a right tempting morsel. I can't see no white man not wanting inside that if she be shashaying around his bed already."

"I don' know what else to try, Zumma Mae. We always have someone in the massa's bed to give us some voice in how things run around here. We gotta do somethin'. I can't live with the thought of being parted with any of my kin. Thas happenin' elsewhere, but we don wan it happenin' here."

Jerome, who was standing in the kitchen doorway and watching Macey move around, putting pots she cleaned away and moving things back and forth into and from the larder room, muttered under his breath, "Usin' wrong bait, I'se supposing'"

"What's that you say, Jerome?" Naddie asked, turning to him. "And wha ya doin' sniffin' around here for, anyhow? Don't think like I don know what you after. Well, you already

28

seeded up Macey here. You can just take it on out to the field. I think I hear Lottie a'callin' you."

The women sitting around the table cackled and Macey looked embarrassed and went into the larder room and didn't come right back out. Jerome didn't budge from the doorway.

"Nothin'. I was saying nothin'." But he sure was thinking about it.

"Might not be nuff on this problem anyhow," Zumma Mae picked up the discussion. "The man could plow Adelle from sundown to sunup and still come away and sell her momma on the auction block. Thas just the way white man do it."

"I suppose," Naddie said, but she added with a determined voice, "But someone gotta do somethin' about it."

The women were deep in conversation, so Jerome took his chance and slipped by them and into the larder. He came up behind Macey, who was facing a shelf, and embraced her, putting both arms around her and cupping one full, ample breast with one hand and her bulging belly with the other. Macey gave a low cry, but nuzzled back into him like she'd both expected and wanted this.

"What you doin' here sniffin' round me, Jerome? You already did your bizness here. You don't want no fat woman."

"I always want this woman," Jerome whispered. He sniffed at her hair, "You always smell so fresh and flowery."

"Flowery, eh? You can't even pick out a flower and bring it to me if you gonna try that silliness on me?"

"It don' matter. I figure you like my dick as well as the next man's. A hard dick is as much flower as I need bring you, I figure."

"More. You know that. You my master. You know that. You git that dick up inside me and move it and you know you my master. That I do anything for you. Ohh, Jerome. You shouldn't . . . not in here. They's busybodies just in the other room."

Jerome had hiked up her gunnysack dress, finding, as he expected, no clothing underneath, and was cupping her

29

triangle and working a finger inside her, looking for the spot that made her moan.

She moaned.

"Let them find their own dick," Jerome murmured. "If you promise not to make no noise, I'll promise not to either."

"You stop that now, boy. You know this tain't the time nor place."

"With you any time or place is right."

She moaned again as, having bunched the dress up around her waist, Jerome unbuttoned and released himself. He covered her mouth and nose with his hand to muffle her cry as he pushed up into her and started to pump slowly.

When he felt she could control herself, he dropped the hand back to her breast. "You still think we shouldn't be doin' this, sugar?"

"Jus' be good to me, Jerome. I tole you already. You get that dick of yours up there and I'll do anythin' you want."

He proceeded to be good to her.

A voice floated in from the kitchen. Naddie's voice. "Don't ya think I don't know what ya doin' in there, Jerome." The voice wasn't angry though; it had a tinge of laughter to it.

Jerome wasn't just fucking, though. He was also thinking. What had she said—twice? Get that dick up in her and he could do anything he wanted with her. There was something to think about in that. And what Jerome was thinking was that just maybe Naddie had the right idea but was looking at it from the wrong direction. When he thought of "the wrong direction," he gave a little laugh.

"What you find so funny?" Jerome, Macey asked in a breathy voice.

"Not a thing, sugah. You just keep pushin' back on it like that, and we do just fine."

* * * *

Jerome stood inside a two-walled isolated area set off behind a shed near the end of the Riverbend slave row, sluiced the first bucket of water over his body, and followed the rivulets of water down his torso and on to his thighs with his hands. He sensed that Thomas was nearby, watching him, and he smiled. This was working as he meant it to. He turned three-quarters sideways toward where he presumed Thomas was standing and moved a hand down to his basket, first cupping his balls and the underside of his cock and then moving his hand to his cock and giving it a few languid strokes.

He lifted his eyes and looked into Thomas's eyes. Yes, there is want there, he thought. Now that he knew that men did it with men as well as with women, he could clearly see the want in Thomas's eyes. It wasn't any different, really, than the want he'd seen in Macey and Lottie's eyes—indeed, in the eyes of most of the slave women. He just hadn't looked for it in the eyes of a man before. He smiled at Thomas, and Thomas gave an embarrassed start.

"You wanna lift the other bucket over me, Thomas?" Thomas, dressed only in his breeches, came slowly forward. He was trembling as he lifted the bucket of water over Jerome's head and let the liquid roll down his body. Thomas was a massive man, standing a good head taller than Jerome and with bulging arm, chest, and thigh muscles. Jerome felt diminished in his presence, needing to act carefully, because if he gave too much too soon, the man would overpower him and just take what he wanted and walk away. Jerome needed him to want him so badly that the massive man would follow his lead.

"Umm, feelin' good," Jerome whispered, running his hands down his torso to his thighs again. He could hear the catch in Thomas's breath, and before the man could move away from him, Jerome reached back and took Thomas's hands, bringing his arms around his body. He held one hand to his breast and moved the other one down to cover his genitals. Thomas was trembling. He asserted some control, however, pulling his hands away and running them over Jerome's body as he wished, but when the hands stopped roaming, they were back where Jerome had put them. Jerome was fighting hard the moan his throat wanted to give in response to the feel of the massive cock running up from his waistline. If the man wasn't so much taller than Jerome, Jerome was afraid that the cock would be in place already and that Thomas would just hold Jerome in a tight embrace and enter and take him right there.

"Me bein' wrong, Thomas? Does you not want to fuck with me?"

"Yes, I want to fuck you. Very much. But you only lie with women."

"I was thinkin' that to. But do you know what Massa John was doin' in that Decatur Street house?"

"Yes, I know well."

"And that he was doin' a man?"

"Yes, I know that too. White massas do what white massas want to do—with who they want to do it to."

"I watched. I be gone so long because I watched."

"Ah. And you be curious now, be you? How it feels to have a man inside you? Or you inside him?"

Thomas wasn't trembling as much. He was holding Jerome closer to him, with a stronger embrace, and he was starting to work Jerome's cock. It was dawning on him that perhaps this really was an opportunity. Jerome could feel the hardness of the man in the small of his back. And now he was the one trembling a bit.

"Yes, I be curious. Havin' another man inside me. But I be also a little afraid. How can I tell it will give me pleasure?"

"There is a way I see that tells," Thomas whisper. "I always find that if a man can suck a cock, he can enjoy it up his ass."

"So, you think . . . ?"

Thomas was already gently turning Jerome's body and pushing the young man down onto his knees closely in front of him. His hardened cock was now pressing into Jerome's cheek, and Jerome just opened his mouth and took the bulb of it inside. Thomas sighed and shuddered, and Jerome showed that he needed little instruction to do what came naturally.

Lifting him back up, Thomas placed his lips on Jerome's and, though it surprised him, Jerome went with the kiss.

"Kissin' be as good a buildup to a fuck as anything else—as with a woman," Thomas said. He went in for another kiss, and while they were engaged in this, Thomas took both of their cocks together and stroked. Jerome was trembling again and released a moan.

"You can suck the cock and you can moan to a kiss," Thomas whispered. "I think you can moan to a cock inside you too. Is it what you want to try?"

"Yay, it is," Jerome murmured. He wasn't fully convinced himself, but he wanted to try it with Thomas first to see if he could endure it—at least whether or not he could convince another man he wanted it and then could take it with a smile.

Thomas gently turned Jerome around, facing away from him. "Bend over. Bend over and spread them legs," he said. And as Jerome did so, Thomas knelt down behind him, snaked a hand between his thighs, and grabbed Jerome's cock. Then Thomas's mouth went to Jerome's ass.

"What?" Jerome asked in surprise and half shock as he felt the wetness of the tongue at his channel entrance.

"Hold still. You be unused and I be big. We need to get you more open or you not bein' enjoyin' this much."

Jerome found himself sighing and moaning again as new sensations of pleasure rolled in waves over his body. The stroking of his cock didn't hurt either.

At length, Thomas stood, bidding Jerome to stay as he was but to spread his legs even further, and Thomas was slowly working his cock inside Jerome's ass, as the young man panted and grunted and groaned and tried his best not to scream out or try to escape.

"Let your body go limp and breath regular. I be in now. We rest and then I take you to glory. Your doin' good. The hurt will go in a bit. You need to be stretched to fit."

Jerome whimpered, "Be good to me," and then almost laughed, as that was what Macey had said to him right before he had fucked her good and hard in that laundry room. And hard had seemed good enough for her to hear her comment on it while it was happening.

Then Thomas fucked Jerome good and hard and took him to glory, and by the time he was finished, Jerome was feeling more pleasure than pain. Half way through the fuck, Thomas pulled Jerome's shoulders up into his chest, and Jerome turned his head and they kissed deeply and shared in whispers how good the fuck was going. And Jerome proved he could take sex this way by shooting off into one of the buckets.

"You done good," Thomas said. "I knew you liked it when we kissed and you began fuckin' me back with your hips. You be made for this."

Jerome didn't love it yet, but he liked it well enough to continue with his plan.

"I been tole if I take a cock and love it, the man is my master."

"I been tole that too," Thomas answered. "I'd like to fuck you nuff to master you, but I'se not sure you'd be letting me."

"How can the man tell he is accepted as master?"

"If a man will fuck hisself on the cock is a clue."

"Fuck hisself? I don't understand."

"I can show you."

Thomas sat on a bench, holding Jerome's waist, as Jerome sat in his lap, facing him, and on the cock and, at Thomas's direction fucked himself on the hard shaft by leveraging off the soles of his feet.

Jerome thought he had gotten the idea by the time they both had come again—and he now thought he had enough understanding and preparation to work out his plan.

While Jerome absentmindedly worked a plan in his mind, he remained sitting on Thomas's cock, and Thomas glided his hands over Jerome's body, kissed his neck, and moved a hand around to play with the his balls and cock. Jerome barely discerned when Thomas's cock was getting big inside him again. It was a jolt when he realized it and he moved as if to rise.

"Go down on your all fours on the grass," Thomas growled.

Jerome did as he was told and Thomas crouched over his hips, grabbed his waist in his hands, and began the fuck again. It was only later that it dawned on Jerome that Thomas

34

had commanded and Jerome had simply complied. Thomas hadn't even asked if he could fuck him again, and Jerome had no idea what he would have answered if Thomas had asked. Was this, he wondered, what being mastered meant? If so, it was a powerful weapon.

Thomas settled that. He laughed and said, "See it works. You fucked yourself on me and then jus' did what I told you to do afterward. So's I's master of you in the fuck now. You gonna let me fuck you again when I wants to?"

"I guess so," Jerome answered.

"I guess so too," Thomas said. Then he laughed again.

* * * *

"Did you feel what your muscles down there were doin' this time?"

Thomas had become more inventive with Jerome over the past two weeks. Jerome had confided part of his plan to the carriage driver. Naddie's plan of Master John bedding the housemaid Adelle and then Adelle having some sway over the master couldn't work because, as Jerome and Thomas knew and Naddie didn't, Master John preferred lying with men. Thus, part of Jerome's plan was to seduce Master John so that he could carry on with Naddie's plan. Thomas had told Jerome that Master John would be a sophisticated and demanding lover, so that Jerome should gain more experience and more knowledge of the various positions himself.

Jerome half expected that Thomas's main purpose in that was to continue fucking Jerome, but it fit in with Jerome's plans, and he had to admit he was increasingly falling under the mastery of the carriage driver and was becoming increasingly interested in being fucked by men—and by Thomas, in particular. That didn't mean he was any less interested in fucking women too. And as a reaction to all of this, he was broadening his own pursuits of the young slave women of the plantation and was almost always well received because of his good looks and well-built body. Slaves could not help but think of themselves as breeding stock, because their masters certainly

35

did, and Jerome was seen as a prime breeding stud. Even the overseer would look the other way and forgive both Jerome's unfulfilled work and that of the young Negress when he saw Jerome's rump between two chocolate thighs in the cotton field. Jerome was producing slave babies, which added to the wealth of the plantation.

This had been a new position. Thomas had been sitting on the grass, legs stretched out, and Jerome had been skewered on the cock facing away from Thomas with his legs stretched back past Thomas's hips and his torso careened out over Thomas's legs. Thomas had held Jerome tight by the wrists, bowing the young field hand's chest out. It was hard for Thomas to stroke in this position, so he had instructed Jerome to fuck himself. Frustrated with getting enough leverage on his knees and toes to create the desired friction on the cock, Jerome's channel had improvised its own solution. The muscles of the channel walls had made love with their undulations on Thomas's cock all by themselves. Both men had enjoyed that.

"Yay, I felt that," Jerome answered.

"Well, keep a doin' that. A man will go wild with your shaft makin' love to his dick like that."

It was after that, as they lay in each other's arms and Thomas was talking of exotic positions they had not tried yet that he brought up the special act that the truly jaded man who was fucked by men got excited about and sometimes dared. Jerome's breathing became labored at the mere thought of it, but he was sure he could never go to that extreme. And he said so. Thomas's reaction to his response seemed one of disappointment, and Jerome became afraid that maybe Thomas was proposing such an arrangement. But he didn't bring it up again.

While Jerome trained in male seduction and the satisfaction of a male partner with Thomas, he was biding his time. He needed something to happen. And then it did.

The house waiter's arm was scalded in the kitchen one day, and it was clear that it would have to remain dressed and the waiter resting for days if not weeks.

"I don' know what is to do," Naddie spoke in concern. She was merely the head cook, but in reality, at least on this plantation, that also made her responsible for the serving slaves. "He will not have a woman serve him his dinner."

"Let me do it," Jerome piped up to say. He had just fucked one of the laundresses behind the hanging sheets and Macey had heard of it and was giving him the cold shoulder in the kitchen. He had come here, though, to jolly her out of her funk. She was too far along for him to be fucking her, and, when she thought about it, she would realize that he had to be fucking and impregnating some Negress—that the economy of the plantation dictated that. And he continued to show Macey in many small ways that he was truly most fond of her.

"You?" Naddie said as if she had never heard such a preposterous thing. "You is jus' a field hand."

"Yay, but I be workin' with Thomas on the carriages long time now too, and I be picking up the ways of the house. Somebody got to do it. No reason it not be me."

He knew he was the favorite of all her sons and he gave her his best smile. If need be, he'd tell her how important this was for his plan—for all of their futures—but only if he had too. He didn't know how she would react to a man lying under another man.

The look worked. That evening, dressed in a white, billowy cotton shirt, a black velvet vest, and very tight black velvet breeches, Jerome was serving at table.

There were no guests. Master John was supping alone. There was only Jerome in the dining room. Master John insisted on only having one servant serving the table when he dined alone.

Jerome moved as gracefully as he could about the room. He had cleaned himself well and been given a musky cologne to use by Thomas, who said it was a particularly popular one used in male brothels. And Jerome looked as shy and docile as he could and did what he could to leave the impression that he was in awe of the master of the plantation and was attracted to Master John. He smiled a shy smile and took demure looks at Master John whenever it would seem

37

that he didn't want the master seeing him do that—when it was exactly the impression he wanted to leave.

He was standing close beside Master John's chair at the table, serving dish in hand, when it happened. His crotch—on purpose—was on the level of John's face and close to it. John suddenly could not take any more of the dance of enticement. He turned his head toward Jerome's crotch, took in a heady, deep breath—undoubtedly breathing in the musky scent of the handsome young black buck—and put his open mouth on the bulge in Jerome's basket. At the same time he snaked an arm around Jerome's hips and clutched at a butt cheek, pulling Jerome in closer to him. He turned his head up to Jerome's face and Jerome smiled down at him what he hoped would be a smile of acceptance. The master-slave relationship being what it was, John wouldn't have expected rejection, but he might have expected a moment of surprise. Not receiving that caused John to shudder in pleasure. Jerome leaned over and placed the serving dish on the table and then he moved his hand down to his waistband and unbuttoned the top two buttons on his fly.

Master John unbuttoned the rest and pulled out Jerome's cock, swallowed it almost down to the root, and began to stroke it with his mouth.

Victory one, Jerome thought. He remembered the theory that Thomas had told him: that if a man will suck another man's cock, he also will take that cock in the ass.

A bit later Jerome was kneeling on the floor in front of John's chair and between the man's legs and sucking on the master of Riverbend's cock.

And later still, Jerome, sans breeches, was sitting in the dining chair himself, his legs hooked over the arms and a pillow at the small of his back rolling his hips up, and Master John was crouched over him, his hands on the back of the chair and his cock jackhammering Jerome's ass channel, while Jerome moaned and groaned and held John's waist in his hands.

Jerome was flat on his stomach, stretched out on the carpet next to the dining table and John was riding his ass, when Master John leaned down, putting his mouth close to

38

Jerome's ear, and whispered, "You cannot be an innocent. No innocent knows how to do that with his channel muscles. You will be in my bed tonight."

"Yes, Massa. Whatever Massa wants," Jerome purred. And then he gave a big smile. Victory in phase two.

God, the man could fuck, Jerome was thinking as Master John mounted him for the third time in his bed that night. But then Jerome knew that was the case already, having again had to wait for Master John for a couple of hours at the Decatur Street brothel not many days earlier. Master John was on his knees on the bed, with Jerome's buttocks resting on his thighs, Jerome's legs bent, and his feet flat on the bed next to Master John's hips. John was clutching Jerome's waist and pulling his channel on and off the cock, having tired of keeping his own hip action in motion to help him ram the cock home repeatedly.

He had been explicit in telling Jerome how much he liked the young black slave's body and that Jerome would be sleeping with him for the foreseeable future—all good portents for the success of Jerome's plans.

But the key thing was that the man seemed to be tiring, and Jerome wasn't, having made the man do most of the work. At the point of Master John's ejaculation and as he was allowing his body to relax and fall onto Jerome, the black slave took his chance. As John came down, Jerome turned both of their bodies so that Master John was still on his knees, but Jerome was on top of him, pressing his chest down on the surface of the bed and rubbing his own cock up and down in the crease between John's buttocks. Weak from the night's exertion, John hunched there, panting. He was saying something, but Jerome wasn't listening to him. He grabbed John's wrists to help keep him immobile and moved his mouth to the puckered hole between the butt cheeks.

John squeaked and moaned as Jerome's tongue did its magic of opening the hole and lathering it up. Satisfied he could get in and just a bit surprised at how quickly it opened up and that Master John wasn't fighting him hard enough, Jerome mounted the man's hips and worked his cock into the channel.

The white man bucked and writhed and cried out within Jerome's grip. Jerome started stroking, running the thought over and over again in his mind that a man who will suck the cock will take the cock in the ass. And the master is the one with the cock in the other man's ass.

He fucked fast and hard, reasoning that if he was going to master John, it couldn't be a tentative matter.

Somewhat to his surprise, when he starting listening to what Master John was sounding off about, it turned out to be exclamations of passion. "God yes, fuck me! Deeper! Harder! Faster!"

The man was happy to be fucked. It was a revelation to Jerome and one that immediately endangered his plan. How easy would it be to master a man by the cocking if he was well used to being cocked. And a further revelation to Jerome was that he was enjoying fucking the man. So, there were men who could genuinely enjoy both fucking another man and being fucked by another man. Jerome marveled at all there was about the mysteries of life and fucking that he had never known.

Still, he fucked on, and Master John encouraged him to do so.

The next afternoon Jerome appeared in the kitchen house decked out in the white shirt, velvet vest, and tight black breeches he'd spent several hours putting back into order. At first the laundress he'd been fucking, who already was beginning to show the evidence of another of his children, was helping him. But she also wanted him to take time to give her a fuck, and he was much too spent to do that, so she'd deserted him to finish his own repairs.

"Ya can take those right off," Naddie spat at him when he entered the kitchen.

"I be serving Massa at supper," he said. "I have to wear these."

"No ya don't have to serve Massa at supper. He sent word you to be excused. That you got other duties. That you gotta rest. I'm using Nathan."

"Nathan be an old man, Naddie," Jerome said.

"Right. Thas right," Naddie retorted. "Seems only an old man is goin' be able to serve twice in the dining room when Massa sups alone. Don't try to hide from me what ya doin' with that man. Sound gets outta that dining room just fine."

"I'se a plan, Naddie. Now you know why Adelle didn't work. Now you know a man's got to do it. We has to try to keep the fambly together here. I'se jus' doin' what I has to do."

Naddie began to cry. She collapsed in a chair and Jerome went over and stroked her hair.

"You tell me to stop and I'll stop, Naddie. But it's for the fambly. Should I stop?"

Naddie didn't answer, but when Jerome reached the door, she mumbled. "Jus ya all be careful. Them white men is mean bastards."

Jerome would take whatever blessing he could get. So, this was enough for him. He wouldn't tell her all of it. He wouldn't tell her that he enjoyed both fucking men and being fucked by them. That didn't mean he enjoyed fucking women any less. And Naddie hadn't said all that much about the big stomachs being seen on the young Negresses of the plantation. Naddie liked her grandbabies well enough.

That night was the test of the next strategic phase of Jerome's plan. Master John fucked him just as he had observed John fucking the male prostitute at the Decatur Street house. First sidesplitting him and stroking his cock and then like a dog, crouched over Jerome as he was on all fours on the bed. But then Master John asked for the fuck himself.

This was the most dangerous point of all of this.

"I be tired. I don' think I can fuck you as long as you want."

"It's what I want. You were supposed to get rest today. I heard you were in the field. I don't want you using your energy in the field anymore."

I be in the field fucking Berta, Jerome thought, and almost laughed. Making more babies for your wealth. But that's not what he said. He had been building up to this moment.

"I be tired, but my cock still be strong. If you want it, you can ride it."

Make them fuck themselves and then you are master, Jerome heard Thomas saying to him.

"Lie on your back," Master John said.

Exhilarated, Jerome turned onto his back. Just as he had promised, his cock was hard and erect. John straddled his hips, facing him, and slowly descended on the cock. He rode the cock hard and wild like he was a ship being tossed on a stormy sea. Jerome came first and then John moved up to straddle his chest, and Jerome sucked him to an ejaculation.

They settled down, stretched along each other's bodies, and dozed. Jerome awoke with the sensation of Master John stroking his cock. This was the next danger point. Would John want to fuck him or be fucked.

"I want your cock again," John murmured.

"I still be tired."

"I want the cock." It was almost a whine.

"You be havin' to ride it yourself."

This time John rode the cock in the opposite direction, facing Master Jerome's feet. He asked the young black man to raise his knees, and he clutched them in his arms and pushed them out and in to match the rhythm of his rise and fall on the cock.

After several minutes, deciding that he had made his point and that he could acknowledge he was rested enough, Master Jerome rose and pulled John over to the side of the bed, with Master Jerome standing on the flour between John's thighs and pounded John's ass, while the white man writhed and cried out in ecstasy and clutched the bedspread in his claws.

Jerome sensed victory, but he didn't feel he could risk yet making the demand he was building up to. That John let men fuck him—and therefore at least partially master him—before Jerome had was disturbing. Perhaps the fucking didn't completely subjugate him.

But then Jerome remembered what Thomas had said some days before about some special act—that if a man experienced that and was one of the few men who loved having it done, that it was the ultimate leverage over a man who wanted to be fucked by men. It might be too much. It might destroy all of the work Jerome had already done. But if Jerome could think of one man who would melt to that act, it would be this man, John Rembeau.

The next night he had Thomas waiting in the shadows of the bedroom, just another invisible slave, when he entered the bedroom. John was there before him as well. He was wearing just a robe, open to reveal the well-muscled line of his body and a half-erect cock. He was standing in the center of the room, reflected in the dim, dancing light from the fireplace and holding a snifter of brandy. He had already been drinking heavily.

"Strip down and come here," he commanded, and Jerome did so, a bit worried that the man was going to reassert control. Perhaps even send him away as a threat to the man's authority. He put the snifter down on a table as Jerome approached. Jerome, like all of the slaves, wore a leather collar. That was all he was wearing now, but it clearly marked him as the slave. As he reached John, the white man grabbed the collar from behind and pulled Jerome's lips up to his—Jerome being shorter and trimmer than John—and took him in a brutal kiss. As they were kissing, he reached down and grabbed Jerome's balls and squeezed them until Jerome's eyes watered. He refused to cry out, though.

There was an ottoman right behind where Jerome was standing, and John pushed Jerome down in a sitting position on that. He reached over, picked up the snifter, took another deep drink, and then put it back on the table. He moved his legs between Jerome's thighs and Jerome reached out and cupped John's balls and brought the cock to his mouth and sucked it. John picked up the snifter again, while moving his hips in a face fuck of Jerome's mouth. Nothing was being said by either man. All that could be heard was heavy breathing. John didn't seem to notice, though, that three men, not two were breathing heavily in the room.

The brandy finished, John pulled his cock out of Jerome's mouth and went down on his knees between Jerome's thighs. He took Jerome's cock in his mouth, while he fingered Jerome's balls and rimmed and invaded Jerome's ass with his fingers when he got tired of the ball work. Jerome laid back on the ottoman, his head dangling off the other end and his arms dangling off the sides.

Moments later John was fucking Jerome's ass and Jerome was giving appropriate moaning and groaning sounds. But this didn't last long. This wasn't what John seemed mainly to be interested in, although he thrust to an ejaculation that Jerome felt flow deep inside him. Withdrawing his cock and moving his legs over Jerome's hips, John descended on Jerome's cock and started fucking himself, leveraging his rises and falls off the soles of his feet. Now he was the one moaning and groaning.

Master Jerome was smiling an inner smile. What John wanted most from him was his cock, and he was willing to fuck himself to get it. Jerome was the master. But there was one last act to try to drive this home.

Thomas was stealing across the room. Big, hulking Thomas. Thomas of the monster cock. When he reached the ottoman, he grabbed John by the hips and pulled him off Jerome's cock. Surprised, John let out a shriek and went pale in terror as he turned his head and saw the other, giant black man.

Wasting no time, and standing right there, crouching a bit down, to give him a good center of gravity, Thomas just lifted John up and set him down on his erect, upturned cock. John's cries of violation and fear quickly turned into those of passion and ecstasy as Thomas began to pump John's channel up and down on the massive cock. As John settled down, Thomas turned him around so that they were facing each other, and John locked his fists behind Thomas's neck and began to move his own pelvis in counterthrusts to take as much of the big cock inside him as possible.

The time of reckoning, Jerome thought, as he rose from the ottoman and approached the two men. Thomas, seeing Jerome coming and knowing what the plan was, slowly bent backward, shifting weight here and there to maintain his balance. Jerome came up behind them, pulled John's butt cheeks wider, and positioned his cock head at the place where John's rim stopped and the top of Thomas's embedded cock began.

There was no room there to squeeze anything in, but, slowly, to the tune of John's cries, Jerome made room for his cock to slide in on top of Thomas's cock. And then, Thomas holding his cock still, Jerome started to pump. John was writhing and clutching as Thomas's biceps and bulging pecs and flopping around and crying out.

The first time Jerome heard the man screaming "Fuck, yes. Plow me. Fuck me. Harder. Deeper!" he knew that he'd guessed right.

Thomas laid John's body on the bed. The man was sobbing. But it was a well-fucked sob, and he was babbling. "The . . . best . . . damn . . . fuck . . . I've ever . . ." He looked up at Jerome and whispered, "Thank you."

"It's just the first of two," Jerome said.

John whimpered and began to pant.

The second time, Jerome laid on his back on the bed for a while and let John fuck himself on the cock, facing Thomas who was kneeling over Jerome's legs and feeding his cock into John's mouth. After a while, Jerome pulled John's back down into his chest and Thomas grabbed the white man's legs behind the knees and spread him and worked his cock in above Jerome's. And this time it was Thomas slow pumping his cock. Both Jerome and Thomas managed to come together inside the stretched channel and John seemed quite pleased.

Later in the night, in the darkness, with John and Jerome stretched out together and in an embrace that was marked by brief dozes and short sessions of kissing, John spoke for the first time since Thomas had left them.

"He was magnificent. Where did you find him?"

"He Thomas, your carriage driver," Jerome answered. He tried to keep the sarcasm out of his voice, although he was thinking, he's driven your carriage since you came here and he's just another invisible black slave to you?

45

His restraint apparently worked, as, oblivious to the insensitivity he'd shown, John whispered, "Please bring him back from time to time. I have never been as satisfied as I was with what the two of you did. Not every night, but every so often."

"As long as I be in service to you. Yes, I be your slave. I do whatever you want, of course."

"My slave? No, you are my master. I want you here with me forever."

Jerome's heart leaped. Was he on the brink of the ultimate victory?

"I can't be here forever if you might sell the plantation and break up the slave community. I be but a slave. You own me."

"No, as I said, you own me now. And I will never sell you—and I won't sell this plantation either."

"The slaves, though. They all be my fambly."

"And they will all stay."

Master Jerome sighed a sigh of victory and happiness and moved slave John onto his side and slowly entered his channel with his commanding cock.

There was a new master at Riverbend plantation.

Swimming Lessons

"I'd like to make an Australian Crawl." Stan gave a hearty laugh and acknowledged an empty glass up the bar. While he was gone, Keith, in turn, acknowledged that his own beer glass had miraculously filled on its own. He didn't have much doubt that Stan was trying to get him drunk so that Keith would go in the back room with him. The burly barkeep had been putting the moves on him for some time now. Keith had to admit, though, that he came back because he was getting a lot of free beer—and also because he was getting closer to giving in to Stan.

It wasn't that Stan was bad looking, in a big bruiser, boxed-a-bit-too-often way. And it wasn't because he was old.

He probably wasn't older than about forty and obviously still went to the gym, although the bartender was putting a bit of a paunch on him. It was more because Keith had heard that Stan fucked a bit rough. Keith didn't mind getting fucked; he just didn't like to be manhandled all that much—or so he thought. He'd shied away from it enough to only know it as a concept.

"And I kinda like the touchy-feely sound of it," Stan said. He was back, looking straight in Keith's eyes to hold the younger man's attention, while he deftly topped off Keith's beer. "The back stroke. The breast stroke—particularly like that one. The side stroke. That's not bad either. And the butterfly. They got an interesting fuck position called the Butterfly in that Indian shit—the Camera Suitable, or somethin'. You ever try that? Ever thought of tryin' that? Now the free style, that would really be something I could get in to; I've wrestled semi pro in my day—maybe with some diving. Get it?"

He laughed and was off again to serve another customer. But Keith knew he'd be back. This was how Stan moved toward a more direct proposition. And Keith knew Stan had been asking around about him and knew he took cock. So there wasn't much subtle about Stan's propositions when he got down to them.

They had been talking about swimming and who at the bar had and hadn't had swimming lessons. It turned out that only Keith had. And he'd also made the mistake of saying that he went to Larson's pond most Saturday afternoon's for a swim. Larson was a rich guy into both nudism and gay sex. He'd opened his pond to nude sunbathing and anything else guys might want to do. All you had to do to get an invitation was to either let Larson fuck you or, if you were a top too, bring Larson someone he could fuck.

The latter was what had happened with Keith. Chris, who Keith had been shacking up with at the time but didn't know liked fucking around a lot, had wanted access to Larson's beach. He had taken Keith to the beach and turned him over to Larson while he cruised the other guys. Larson had fucked Keith silly for nearly three hours straight. Keith resented being used by Chris like that and gave him the gate, but he had enjoyed Larson's cocking enough that he continued to come to the beach and let him do him when he wanted to. Larson liked fresh meat, though, and had ready access to it, so he didn't bother Keith much.

Stan was back, standing in front of Keith, and leaning into him. They could have easily kissed, if Keith wanted to—and he thought that's probably what Stan wanted. But Keith didn't take the hint. "Wouldn't mind getting some lessons like that down at Larson's pond. Especially if you was the one who was teaching me. What say when I get off work here, we trot on down there and you can teach me some strokes and I'll teach you the Butterfly—you know the Indian one?" He was leaning over the bar toward Keith and leering to beat the band.

"Uh, I don't teach swimming, Stan. I can barely remember which stroke I'm using when I'm swimming. And right now I have some place I need to be. Sorry, but—"

A beefy hand shot across the bar top and grabbed Keith's forearm. This was what Keith was a bit afraid of. Stan was quite a bruiser and Keith was wary of being alone with him and in his grip. The grip didn't quite hurt, but almost. Keith wondered if Stan realized when he was hurting a man. He looked down at the forearm. A colorful tattoo of some sort of dragon. Keith wondered if Stan had other tattoos—and where. Keith got a little extra aroused by a man with tats. And he couldn't say that Stan didn't arouse him. He just scared him a bit.

"Come on, man. You know you want it. And I know you put out. I don't know the names of the strokes I use either, but I can stroke real good. Right here in the back room right now, or I'll meet you down by the swimming pond. I'll teach you the Butterfly. I can dick you deep with that. Chris Tucker told me you go wild with the deep diving. And I got a cock ring. You ever been fucked with a cock ring?"

"I really do need to be someplace, Stan." Keith managed to pull himself off the bar stool and out of Stan's grip. What he was thinking mostly was that he'd like to beat Chris Tucker to a pulp.

"But you will let me do you sometime, won't you?" Stan asked. There was an intense gleam in his eye.

Keith was trembling a bit. He'd thought about it and had decided that, yes, under the right circumstances he'd go with Stan just to see what it was like. One of his friends one night at a party had regaled the guys he was talking to about that cock ring Stan had and how different that felt. That's when Keith had first come in the bar. So, he couldn't say he wasn't interested. He had been wondering for weeks how it felt with a cock ring.

"Yeah, sure, we can hook up sometime, Stan," Keith said as he backed away from the bar and acknowledged the good-bye waves of a few of the other patrons, some of whom had been campaigning to get in his ass almost as much as Stan had been. "Just that I have to be somewhere else now."

As he left the bar, he tried to review in his mind what he'd told Stan about his visits to Larson's pond. He hadn't actually told Stan when he usually was there swimming, had he?

* * * *

The sun was out strong on Saturday afternoon and Keith was out on a blanket by Larson's pond working on an all-over tan. He had his Kindle and a good stash of GM action/adventure e-novels he'd downloaded the previous evening, so he was good to go for a while.

He wasn't the only one there, and there wasn't the normal crowd for a Saturday, but there was activity enough for him to glance away from the Kindle occasionally to take in the action. Between the fiction and the real, he was managing to keep at least half hard. He was putting off doing anything about that. He'd usually rev up for a while, jerk off, and then take a dip in the pond. If there was time, he'd repeat the cycle. He liked his Saturday afternoons at the pond.

The action, now that he thought about it, was actually very low for a Saturday. Off on the sand below Larson's vacation house, an area of the beach he reserved for himself, Keith could see Larson's bare rump between two bent brown legs. From the tightening and loosening and forward and backward movement of Larson's buttocks and the way the feet on the legs of the black guy were raising and lowering on the sand, Keith could tell that Larson was giving his usual good fuck. Keith didn't mind Larson fucking him, even though he took a lot of time doing it and left a guy wiped out; it was how Keith kept the welcome sign out for his own pond visits.

Larson fucked deep. Chris hadn't been wrong about that; Keith liked that.

Nearer, on the same side of the pond where Keith was staked out, two college-type hunks were playing a pass-the-beach ball type of slow-moving game out on the sand. Keith had seen these two out on the beach before. They usually played around like this until someone showed up they liked and then they shared him. And by shared, Keith meant that he had seen them do a guy together a couple of times. Keith had never done it that way, and although he thought about it, it scared him. He had been pretty standoffish with these guys and usually there were a lot more here on the beach when he saw them. He was usually just part of a crowd. If it looked like they were zeroing in on him, he'd look away or strike up a conversation with another guy. Today, other than Larson humping the guy on his own beach, it was just these guys and Keith here so far.

Keith actually thought about retreating for the day when he saw that no one else seemed to be showing up on the beach. He shuddered at the thought of these two working him over. They were both studs and appeared to be about the same age, twenty or something, like Keith himself, but they were quite different in their physical perfection. The guy Keith had named "Thick," was Nordic, blond and hairless. He was on the short side and compact, heavily muscular. Not fat, but solid and on the bulging side when it came to muscles. A ruggedly handsome face. A buzz cut for hair. He was the boisterous one, all smiles and laughter and jocularity. Keith had noticed that when they zeroed in on a guy, he was the one who took the lead in getting a guy interested. The name Thick came, naturally, from what was between his legs. Average in length, but thick.

He contrasted with the other guy, who Keith thought of as "Long." He was more the Mediterranean Mafioso type. Swarthy and brooding. Handsome in a dark, silent, sensuous, dangerous sort of way. He was hairy to Thick's smoothness, with intriguingly curling hair on his pecs and down his sternum to his bush. And on his forearms too and his legs. His head hair was curly and a lock fell almost over his eyes. He wore a permanent five-o'clock shadow, and Keith got the impression the guy probably had to shave three times a day to keep it cut back to the exact length. He was taller and thinner than Thick, but still well-muscled, and he, too, got Keith's name for him from what he was swinging. Not thick, but longer than average.

Keith thought arousing thoughts of being fucked by them individually, but he wasn't all that sure about this doubling stuff he'd seen them do.

And right about now, they were forcing him to make a decision on whether to pack up and leave or stay and take his chances of maybe taking two cocks at once. He usually let someone fuck him here on Saturdays, but this doubling business still had him unsure. Their game was moving closer to him, and the blond was flashing him smiles, working on making contact. Keith had seen this before and knew that this was how they moved in on a target.

Keith was about to make a decision when he saw both of them turn and look up at the wooden stairs leading down from the parking lot next to Larson's summer home on the bluff. He let his attention sweep that way too—past the tableau of Larson now being on his back and holding the waist of the young black guy riding his cock—to the top of the stairs, where a young Asian guy—probably Indian—was standing, looking tentatively down at the beach. He was wearing baggy swimming shorts and had a towel and what looked like a pair of water wings tucked under an arm.

After a few hesitant moments, he started to come down to the beach. He was wearing flip-flops on thin legs with strongly defined muscles. They had strength in them; they just looked sinewy.

The two hunks conversed between themselves momentarily at a volume that Keith could almost, but not quite, hear, and then, the blond having given Keith a wink and a "later" smile, they recommenced their beach ball passing game and moved back along the beach, getting closer to where the Indian was spreading out his towel.

The new arrival wasn't tall. Certainly not as tall as Long; more the height of Thick. But he was even thinner than Long was. Keith thought more in terms of wiry than thin, though, as the guy had real good muscle tone. He just was willowy and had long, thin legs, with little meat on the bones.

He was standing below his blanket, nervously eyeing the water and letting his hands prod and knead the inflated water wings like he wasn't really sure how to put them on. He did have inflatable plastic things around his ankles, though, which made him look like a gangly kid. Long had the beach ball and was going back to sit on his towel, arms hugging knees, and watching Thick go to work.

Thick sidled up to the Indian. "Going for a swim with those things?" He was gesturing at the water wings.

"I want to swim, yes," the Indian answered in precise, but somewhat accented English. "But I've never lived near the ocean. I can't swim."

"This isn't exactly the ocean," Thick said with a broad smile. "I think you'd have to get all the way out to the middle before you couldn't touch bottom. You don't really need those wings."

"I think I would be scared without them. There may be deeper places. And I might not be able to float."

"Yeah, you don't look like you have an ounce of body fat on you and might not float too good," Thick said. "Nice body, though. But you're wearing a suit. Do you know what kind of beach this is?"

The Indian was shaking his head back and forth in little dips, which Keith could tell was confusing Thick but that Keith knew was an Indian gesture of "yes." "Yes, I know. Mr.

Larson invited me. He has known me." Considering the strange word arrangements of his sentences, Thick probably couldn't be sure that this meant what he'd literally said either. But the way Thick's body relaxed told Keith that this admission was all the permission he needed to target the guy.

The mention of Larson caused both of them, and Keith too, to look over at Larson's private beach. He was embracing the black guy's back close in to his chest, and, with the black guy raised a bit on his knees, Larson was fucking up into his ass at a fast pace.

As the Indian was looking at that too, Thick chose to more assuredly interpret what he said and gestured as acknowledgment that the Indian knew what this beach was for—and that he took cock.

"Maybe you'd have enough confidence if you had a few swimming lessons," Thick said.

"I have thought of taking lessons, but I never have had the time," the Indian answered.

"Well, if you have the time today, my friend over there and I could maybe give you lessons in a few basic strokes." Thick drew the Indian's attention to Long and smiled and waved, and Long raised his hand and gave a minimal response. Keith could see the Indian's eyes slit when he saw Long, who was sitting with his legs bent and was squatting close enough to the towel that his cock head reached the towel and turned up, almost winking at the Indian.

Maybe the Indian isn't as innocent as he's coming across, Keith thought.

"I think my friend and I could teach you a few good strokes," Thick said. He had an arm around the Indian's shoulders and they were walking slowly toward the water. The water wings had dropped to the sand next to the Indian's towel. He still had the bloated anklets on, though. They were orange. Keith almost wanted to laugh.

Keith watched for a bit, as Thick and the Indian stood in water up to their knees and Thick was showing the Indian how to position and move his arms in swimming strokes. There was a lot of hands-on work and Thick had gotten hard.

The Indian couldn't have not noticed that. Well, he's on his own, Keith thought, and went back to reading his Kindle and turned onto his belly, facing away from the water, deciding that it was time for sun on the back.

When he turned back to lie on his back and took his attention away from the Kindle, he saw that Thick was in business. The Indian was floating on his back—his torso actually looking like it was floating, but from Thick's stance, it was possible that Thick's arms were under the Indian's back, supporting him in the water. The Indian's arms were spread straight out from his side and they, at least, looked like they were floating. The Indian's legs were spread and floating on top of the water—at least the inflated anklets were working a charm. Thick was standing between the Indian's thighs, and from the wave patterns in the water, it was fairly evident that Thick's cock was buried in the Indian's ass and that the blond was pulling the Indian on and off his cock. What was doing the best job of floating were the Indian's baggy swimming shorts. They were floating on the surface of the pond all by themselves and off to the side, remaining afloat with the big air bubble inside them.

Keith wondered what stroke Thick had told the Indian this was.

He noticed movement out of the corner of his eye up the beach and saw Long languidly unfolding himself, rising, and slowly sauntering toward the water line. He was at least half hard. In following Long with his eyes, Keith's attention went to Larson's private beach. It was empty now except for a mussed-up beach blanket. But up on the bluff on the house's porch overlooking the water, Keith could see that Larson was sitting on a chair and the black guy was in his lap, facing away from him, and moving his hips up and down on Larson's cock with the leverage of his feet. Larson had an arm around his waist and both appeared to be watching what was going on in the pond.

Keith tore his attention away from that action and went back to reading his Kindle. He was a little concerned for the Indian, whether or not this was really what he'd come here for, and whether he was getting into more than he bargained for, but Keith didn't want to get involved. He thought he really should just pick up his blanket and leave, but he had just a bit more to read in this chapter. He got to the end of the chapter and it had one of those cliff hangers that bugged him about what a character he liked was going to do to get out of trouble, if, indeed he did, so Keith kept on reading.

It was the sounds coming across the water that arrested Keith's attention and made him look up. The Indian was being quite vocal. At first Keith thought he was in distress as he was using curse words that Keith wouldn't have thought an Indian would even know. But as Keith paid more attention to the words, he realized that the Indian was enjoying himself and most of what he wanted his tormenters to do with themselves, he wanted them to do to him.

The three were plastered together in the water, the surface level of which reached just below where the obvious action was taking place. The tableau was familiar to Keith. Long was behind the Indian, leaning back, his arms crossed and embracing the Indian under the Indian's pecs. Keith had no doubt that Long had his cock snaked up the Indian's channel. Thick was plastered in front of the Indian, holding the Indian's thin, long legs up and spread from his body. Thick's buttocks were making waves in the water behind him as he took long, slow strokes inside the Indian's channel on top of Long's stationary cock. The Indian was clutching the tips of Thick's shoulder blades with his white-knuckled hands. His head was thrown back into Long's shoulder, and his mouth was hanging open. He was practically yodeling.

Up on the bluff, the young black guy's back was arched down to the floor of the porch, with his arms spread on the porch over his head. Larson was gripping his waist and pulling him on and off his cock.

Keith had enjoyed Larson using that position on him. With a sigh, he went back to his chapter in the Kindle. The character he identified with had been trapped by the villain and was being rough fucked. Other members of the villain's gang were gathering around, watching, talking dirty about what they were going to do when they got their turn. Keith's hand went to his cock and enclosed it. He squeezed it and rubbed a thumb on the piss slit. He could feel himself going hard.

He had no idea how much time had transpired, but it came as a shock when he felt a hand brush away the hand he was encasing his cock with and felt the sensation of a warm and moist mouth coming down over his cock and hands clutch his buttocks. He looked down the line of his body and saw the blond buzz cut. Thick was sucking his cock. Thick's hands glided up his torso and latched onto his pecs.

The head Keith was getting was good immediately. Very, very good. There was no fighting it. He let his arms flop to the side and his Kindle sank into the sand next to him. Looking over toward and beyond it, he saw that Long and the Indian were on Long's blanket. The Indian was on knees and elbows, chest pushed into the blanket and his head turned toward Keith, his eyes wide open. Long was crouched over his hips and feeding his cock inside the Indian in long, deep strokes.

Keith was no longer watching the story or even reading a story; he was part of the story. Up on the bluff Larson and the black guy had disappeared. Maybe into the house to rest and then start again. Keith had every reason to believe that Larson could stroke all day.

Moaning as Thick pushed a rolled-up towel under the small of his back, turning his pelvis up, and started to lick from his balls down his perineum to his hole, Keith's hands went back to his own cock. He arched his back and groaned as Thick's tongue pushed into his channel, moistening and opening him. One of Thick's hands was scrounging around inside a beach bag laying off to the side and came out with a small bottle of lubricant and a bundle of condom packets that were attached in a string. He raised the bundle before Keith's eyes and let it open and cascade down.

Thick lifted his head up, smiled, and whispered. "All of these. We've been saving you. By popular vote, this is your day."

Keith groaned again. That was so much like what the villain in his novel had said as he was tying the protagonist's wrists to posts. "All of these," the villain was saying, sweeping his hand in a gesture that took in all of the salivating gang members hunched around them and pulling at their cocks.

Thick was standing in a crouch, lifting Keith's pelvis to his and fucking Keith in quick, efficient strokes when the Indian came over and crouched down at Keith's side and gave him a look of sympathy or some sort of brotherhood. Long was settling on his haunches nearby and watching. The Indian encased Keith's cock in his hand and then leaned over and took it in his mouth. After a few minutes of what Keith considered very expert sucking, the Indian murmured something to Thick, who went down on his knees, bringing Keith's back down on the ground, but not skipping a beat in the stroking. The Indian rolled a condom on Keith's cock; straddled Keith's belly, facing him; skewered himself on the hard dick; and raised and lowered himself on the staff as he leaned over, put an arm under Keith's neck, palmed his cheek, lowered his forehead to Keith's, and looked intently into Keith's eyes.

Keith, who had never been particularly fond of Indians, was embarrassed at the intimacy of this, and would have shrunk away from the Indian when he began kissing him on his face—his cheeks and eyelids and ears—and tried to groan disapproval when the Indian reached the mouth, but he found his tongue being sucked into the Indian's mouth and sucked there just like it was a cock. The sensation was so sensual and such a surprise, that Keith's hips jerked and he ejaculated in the Indian's channel.

Sometime during all of that the thick cock was replaced by a long cock, and Keith realized there had been a change of the guard. Whereas Thick fucked in short, staccato bursts, Long fucked in long, deep strokes.

After Keith had come in the Indian, Thick pulled him off Keith's cock, swung the Indian around by his belly, crawled off a couple of yards with him in tow, and started doggy fucking him. Long was crouched over Keith and looking down into his eyes, giving him a dark, sensual half smile while he stroked. He gripped Keith's knees with his hands, pushing them out and bringing them back in the rhythm of the fuck. Then he went back on his haunches and pulled Keith's buttocks up on his thighs, with Keith's torso streaming down in front of him. He was reaching deeper inside. Keith groaned and crossed his legs behind Long's back, holding him as deep inside as he could.

The deep fuck. What he melted to was the deep fuck.

Keith looked over at the wooden staircase up to the parking lot. Larson and the black guy, still naked, were at the bottom of the stairs, arms around each other and starting to move up the beach toward him. There was also someone new there—a man, a bulky body-builder type—at the top of the stairs. He too appeared to be naked. Keith closed his eyes and turned his head away, wanting all of his senses to go to Long's cock working deep inside him.

He felt Long jerk and shudder and come deep inside him. When Long withdrew and was rising from the sand, Keith opened his eyes and watched him move away, toward Thick and the Indian. Thick was on his back, under the Indian, fucking up into him from behind. Long crouched between the Indian's legs and was rubbing his cock on the Indian's balls, perineum, and inner thighs, waiting for it to engorge enough to double the Indian again. When he moved out of the way, another man was standing there, leering down at Keith and snapping the latex edge of the Maxim condom encasing a huge cock crowned with a thick cock ring. A leather strap tightly bound the root of the cock.

Stan. Stan, the bartender, had shown up.

Stan was sitting, leaning back on his elbows on the sand, legs slightly apart. Keith was sitting on his cock, the two facing each other, his legs on either side of Stan's torso, knees bent, leveraging off his toes. His arms were stiff-armed behind and under him, the heels of the palms buried in the sand on either side of Stan's slightly spread legs. Stan was holding Keith's body suspended over his with strong hands gripping his waist. Both were rotating their pelvises, in opposite

59

directions, Stan's cock ring kissing every part of Keith's undulating channel walls.

Stan was teaching Keith the Kamasutra Butterfly position.

He had already told Keith he'd be taking him home to show him so much more that night. Keith had moaned but had not objected. He loved the feel of the cock ring inside him.

All of the others were gathered around them in a close circle on the otherwise deserted beach. Thick and Long had the Indian between them, both of their hands fondling his cock and balls as he had the cock of each in a hand. Across from them, Larson and the black guy were stretched out in reverse, the black guy on top of Larson, and 69ing.

Keith couldn't shake the sensation that they were all in a waiting pattern. Waiting for the end of the Butterfly lesson so that they each could have another go at Keith. He moaned at the prospect that Thick and Long's specialty was yet to come for him.

Satin Sleigh Ride

(A requested fetish story, written for James A.)

Count Gregor Arninov towered over his elegantly dressed host and hostess in the foyer of their winter dacha as his sleigh was being brought around. He was leaning over them and holding the admiral's wife's small silk-gloved hand in his appreciably larger satin-clad one while he murmured how wonderful their ball had been and that, yes, he had enjoyed dancing with their daughter immensely. The hostess was lost to his charm—and to his handsome face and broad shoulders and slim waist. He was elegantly dressed in evening clothes with satin lapels and finishes and gave off the aura of a powerful, sensual man, whose well-developed muscles were barely contained by the confines of the formal attire. Some who knew him well likened him to a wolf—intelligent, handsomely and powerfully built, but with a dangerous, wild, loner, almost ravenous streak in him that lent an incongruity to wearing the formal attire of Russian winter balls. In the realms of ambition, money and power, however, he was seen to fit right in. Any family seeking what he had to offer—and there were many—held its daughters out to him; the ones that didn't have such ambitions hid their daughters whenever he was nearby.

He could have told them all that they needn't have bothered.

The admiral, also looking at Gregor with both admiration and speculation, asked yet again if perhaps the count should not spend the night here considering the blizzard that was raging outside. He was only slightly reticent in doing this, having given in to the scheming of his wife and daughter to bring their campaign to a close to entice the count into marriage by bringing the daughter and count in close proximity at night under one roof, their bed chambers just a few steps down a deserted hallway from each other. The count had somewhat of a reputation for his nocturnal activity—quite a varied reputation actually—and every noble family in the region had taken notice of his physical beauty, his standing at court, and his large fortune. And most of the young women and even some of the young men dreamed of lying under him.

Citing pressing business at home, Arninov politely demurred again. He gave a slight start as, with the opening of the front door to the swirling snow and howling wind outside, his sleigh driver and new footmen came into the foyer and the candles in the chandeliers overheard flamed up.

But then the host and hostess were returning to the ballroom and their other guests, and the sleigh driver was holding a massive mink coat open for the count to slip into. The young footman, on his first outing and nearly overwhelmed at coming to grips with his duties, stood trembling, ready to open the door and then rush out to the sleigh to let the steps down and take his perch beside the driver. He was a beautiful young man, diminutive for his age, with alabaster skin and dark curly hair framing a face with full lips; a shy smile; large, dark pupils; and thick, curly eyelashes. Although slight of build, his body was perfectly formed, as demanded by the physical fitness championing count. In fact, the footman was of much the same physical presence as all of the count's man servants, save the sleigh and carriage driver, who had been with the count's family for several decades and who saw and knew all—and did whatever the count asked of him.

The count gave the footman a piercing stare as he shrugged into the mink coat. He accorded the young man a slight nod of the head, and, after a moment of trying to match his employer's stare, the footman cast his eyes down in filial obedience. It was a momentary check in the levels of status and privilege of the nobleman and two servants in the foyer, but just a moment. At a signal from the sleigh driver, the footman threw open the door to almost be tossed back immediately by the howling wind and then thrust himself out into the night to reach the sleigh before the count and driver did.

As the count reached the sleigh, the footman let down the steps. The count paused there for a moment, gaining his balance and reaching for the handholds to help pull himself up into the sleigh against the current of the wind. The footman placed his hands on the count's leather boot momentarily to help his master steady himself. He shuddered at the feel of the leather. Rich material moved him. Satin possibly the most of all. The count looked down and their eyes met. In the eyes of the footman was slight fear, but also a note of resignation. Once more the footman dipped his eyes in obedience to the master. In the count's eyes, slight amusement, more than a slight interest, and a touch of hunger.

Moments later, the sleigh was lumbering off into the blinding snow, almost immediately lost from sight from the entrance to the admiral's dacha by a swirling white cloud, and on its swift, but precarious journey across the fields to the count's winter dacha.

From where he sat in the back of the sleigh, wrapped in his luxurious mink coat and contemplating the cigar and cognac awaiting him before his own roaring fire at the end of the journey—as well as, perhaps, a bit of dalliance during the journey—all that the count could see outside the sleigh was the unforgiving world of white swirling snow and the blur of passing tree trunks. The moon was struggling to be seen through the cascading snow from above, but was no more than an eerie light giving a hint to the undulating hills the narrow track of the sleigh was shushing through. The moon was trying to valiantly cast light on the activities of the night, but it slipped behind clouds and failed in its own recognition of inevitable events unfolding by forces beyond its power.

Good, the count thought. He much preferred the dark and the pleasures of the night.

Looking ahead, the count observed the backs of the two heads, the driver, in a fur hat, with puffs of gray tumbling around his ears. The driver was hunched over and snapping the reins of the four black horses, their heads rearing as they pulled the sleigh through the almost-frozen mud and over snow and ice and snorted their billows of breath clouds. The driver was the ultimate servant. His eyes would ever be forward directed, checking the horses, and ever watching the approaching road, no matter what happened inside the sleigh during the precarious journey.

Next to the driver, bareheaded and shuddering, not only from the cold, sat the young, virginal footman.

Save for the snorting of the horses, the occasional crack of the whip, the shushing of the sleigh runners, and the jingling of the sleigh bells, serving the purpose of warning of their approach to any other sleighs out on this dark, snowy night, all was silent as the grave. But it was a silence full of tension, waiting for something momentous to happen, like the long, drawn-out, shimmering note from a violin.

The count leaned forward and touched the shoulder of the footman, who jerked in surprise, but who nuzzled into the satin of the count's glove as the count caressed his cheek. The count pulled back his hand and the footman turned and looked back at him. His eyes were big, his pupils bright, whether with anticipation or fear, it was not known. And, on his part, the count didn't care.

The footman climbed over his seat and into the back of the sleigh. The count, smiling broadly, opened his mink coat up wide and spread his legs. The satin-lined fly of his dress trousers was already open, and a long, thick, erect cock curved up from the opening. Resigned, but trembling, the footman sank on his knees between the count's thighs, and the count closed the mink coat over him—over both of them. Inside the covering mink, the count reached down and took the footman's head in his satin-gloved hands. For several minutes, he rubbed the young man's cheeks on his erect cock until he had turned the footman's face so that his cock slid between the young man's full lips. The satin gloves moved the footman's mouth on the cock.

The smooth satin gave solace to the young peasant who had known nothing of such finer fabric but who had known he would do what he must to be close to it. His hands roamed on the powerful, elegantly clad body of the count as his mouth gave suck. The lining of the trousers was satin, a strip running down the side of the trousers from the waist was satin. The count's cummerbund was satin, as were the lapels on his jacket. The lining of the enveloping mink coat was satin. Even the count's shirt was white satin. The footman took comfort in running the smooth, cool satin fabric through his fingers while the count moved his head on the cock, holding his cheeks in the satin-gloved hands.

The count leaned down and voiced a command, and the footman, fully embraced in the warmth of the mink coat, slowly shed his clothes without losing contact of his mouth with the hard cock. When he was naked under the mink, the count moved the satin-gloved hands to the young virgin's waist and pulled him up onto his lap, facing him. The count's suit coat had spread so that the footman's chest was rubbing on the white satin of the count's shirt. The footman moaned at the feel of the fine material on his bare chest. The count had palmed the footman's buttocks and was kneading and separating them with his satin-gloved hands. His long, hard, thick, curved cock had snaked into the young man's crack and the upper side of that was rubbing across the footman's hole. Kneading the plump, white buttocks with satin-gloved hands, the young man's entrance was stretched and rubbed across the bulb of the cock again and again. The virgin moaned, mewed, and breathed heavily as his entrance slowly opened to the intention of the cock.

The footman's cheek and hands went to the comforting satin of the count's coat lapels, and he panted quietly and whimpered, knowing what was coming but taking comfort in the feel of the rich fabric. Even the satin of the gloved hands rolling and squeezing and separating his buttocks cheeks was arousing to him. He could do this. He had known this would be expected of him.

But he had not known everything.

The count squeezed and parted the buttocks cheeks and rolled them up so that the bulb of the upcurved cock was throbbing at the entrance of the hole. The footman whimpered his fear, feeling the bulb in position.

The storm outside the sleigh had not abated. It had picked up and the wind was howling. The sleigh driver cracked the whip, knowing there were miles to go and that the landscape was becoming more threatening, the swirling snow more enveloping.

The footman howled too and clutched at the satin lapels as the bulb of the cock moved into him, stopped, pulsing, to permit his channel to open further to the thick shaft. But the footman's howls were taken away by the wind. Three inches inside him, the count stopped again. The footman was sobbing and groaning. He rubbed a check against the satin lapel, wetting it with his tears. The count released the buttocks and glided his satin-gloved hands upon and around the footman's body, calming him down for the so much more that was to come.

Satin-gloved hands clutching and spreading the buttocks once more, the count lifted the footman's channel off the cock one inch and then pulled it down an inch and a half. Another inch up and two inches in. Then the interval between the rising and the falling was reduced to almost nothing, as the count lifted and pushed down, farther each time. The footman was trembling in his arms, but his virginal channel was opening to the steady, deliberate mining of the count's patient cock, and the count was deep inside.

Holding his waist with satin-gloved hands, the count pushed the footman's torso away from him, cantilevered from the count's chest. The young man was folded back on knees planted on each side of the count's hips. He could feel that satin strip on the side of the trousers on each side against the side of his knee. So much satin. He moaned his arousal, his channel now pulsating on the impaling shaft. The mink coat billowed out in front but still covered the bodies of the two against the swirling snow and freezing cold. The footman's face was smothered in the satin lining of the fur coat. The young man sucked the satin material into his mouth to keep himself from crying out, as the count began to pull his channel on and off the buried cock. Slowly, deliberately. Nearly all the way off and then with a long pull, all the way down again. The young, until-now virginal footman groaned and flinched with each deep thrust. He ejaculated onto the satin cummerbund, and the count pulled the limp body of the footman back up to his chest and changed the rhythm of the fuck.

The thrusting increased in speed and intensity, and the count was breathing hard now and had his lips planted in the hollow of the footman's neck. The footman was writhing against him, encased in satin, satin gloved hands working his buttocks.

The howling of the wind increased; the shushing of the sleigh rails became more intense and insistent, screaming to be at journey's end. The count fucked faster and harder, and over and above these familiar sounds floated the hair-raising sounds of the baying of . . . wolves. They were closing in on the sleigh in an organized pack, running alongside it now, snapping at the runners and at the horse's fetlocks when the sleigh driver couldn't deflect them from those with his whip. Trying, unsuccessfully as yet, to leap into the sleigh. Howling their frustration and hunger and need at the sleigh. Trembling, the young man rubbed his cheeks against the comforting satin lapels of the formal attire to soak up his tears from the deep taking and from his fear of the snapping wolves.

The sleigh's speed increased, the driver yelled at the horses and lashed out with his whip at wolves and horses alike.

Inside the sleigh, the count fed his ravenous need and hunger as well, as he fucked the small footman faster and harder, lifting him high and slamming him down hard. The footman was writhing on his lap and sobbing, as much in fear of the attacking wolves as of the taking by the count.

A wolf slung his torso into the sleigh and snapped at the hem of the mink coat, getting it in his fangs, but the count kicked at him and the beast fell away. The count didn't lose a stroke inside the footman's channel. He was sucking hard on the footman's neck, feeling the throbbing of the carotid artery. The footman's head was lolled off to the side, his white-knuckled hands gripping at the satin coat lapel.

At the first spurt of the count's ejaculation deep inside the footman, he sank his fangs into the young man's carotid artery. The footman flinched and his eyes rolled back in his head. Another spurt and a deep suck. The wolves howled and whined, and they could be heard falling behind the sleigh, giving up, having lost to a far more powerful force than themselves. Spurt and deep suck. The footman's body relaxed, although he still was rubbing his fingers on the satin lapel. Spurt and deep suck. The footman was sighing, his body completely relaxed in the count's arms. He had a small, distant smile on his face. Spurt and deep suck.

The sleigh had come to a stop—at the entrance door to the count's winter dacha.

The count was in the foyer of his own dacha. One young, alabaster-skinned serving man was pushing the door shut against the offending wind and swirling snow. Another beautiful, young man with alabaster skin was taking the mink coat, and yet another one was brushing at the elegant material of the count's evening dress. All of the men were moving somewhat lethargically, but they all were dark-haired beauties and all responded to the world with silence; slight, distant smiles; and worshipful glances at the Master, the count.

The count slowly ascended the broad, blood-red marble staircase to the bedroom level and went straight to his bath, where another young, alabaster-skinned serving man helped him to disrobe and slip into a steaming bath. While the count soaked, he smoked a cigar and occasionally turned and gave suck to the cock of the young serving man standing close to the side of the tub.

A red satin robe was draped on a chair beside the tub as well, and the young serving man ran his hand over that lovingly as the count played with his cock.

When the count came into his bed chamber, robed in the red satin drape, which was sashed, but open in the front to reveal his bulging pecs and a peek now and then as he walked of his huge, half-erect cock, his chamber was prepared for the night's feeding.

The footman from the sleigh, also bathed and naked, was laying on his belly on a white stain bedspread on the count's bed. His eyes were open and he was watching the approach of the count both with some interest and with more than a bit of awe and worship. He was slowly, rhythmically scrunching the satin material of the bedspread in his fists, seeking grounding and solace in the texture he loved to stroke. The fear and indecision were gone. It was as if he was half drunk, though. He was nearly dozing and was slow to absorb what he observed. He was breathing lightly and sighing, and at first view of the count in the satin robe, he raised his hips slightly and was rubbing his cock head against the satin bedspread, reveling in the sensual sensation of it.

The count sat in a chair facing the bed. He was still smoking his cigar when he entered and held a snifter of cognac in the other hand. He took a puff of the cigar and a sip of the liquor, and put them down next to a set of red satin gloves that had been laying on the table. He took up the gloves and slid them onto his hands; then he took his cock in his hand and slowly ran the red satin over the shaft. He sat there for several minutes, alternating between the cigar and the liquor with one hand, while stroking himself with the satin glove with the other. As he made satin love to his cock, his eyes were on the alabaster body of the footman. In turn, the footman's eyes were riveted on the satin-gloved hand stroking the count's cock. The young man's hips continued moving ever so slightly on the bed.

The count waited until he heard the young man whimper and whisper, "Please."

"I own you now," the count said.

"You have always owned me," his conquered peasant answered in a small, almost distant, voice.

"Not like I own you now. We have only begun. You will endure a level of ecstasy from me now beyond anything you ever have dreamed of. What do you want from me now? Your eyes tell me you want something from me."

"I want your cock. I want you to fuck me. To possess me. Like in the sleigh. Again and again."

The count gave a deep-throated, low laugh and stood up from the chair. He moved over to the bed and sat next to the young man's prone body. The satin robe fanned out around him, and the footman instinctively reached for an edge of it to run through his fingers.

The count let his satin-gloved hands glide over the young man's body, and the footman purred for him. His travels ended at the buttocks, which he gently worked, stroking them and kneading them. Separating them. Spreading the hole wide. Observing it opening to him. Running a satined finger over the hole and listening to the young man moan. Penetrating, a satined invasion. Listening to the young man groan. Moving his body to below the footman's, so that when he separated the orbs he could move his face down and push his tongue into the cavity.

The footman groaned and whispered, "Fuck me, please fuck me, Master."

Giving another low laugh, the count sat up on the foot of the bed and lifted and pulled in the small body of the footman. He made the footman stand on the floor in front of and facing away from him, bend over, and grab his ankles. He then gave the young man's buttocks more attention with his satin-gloved hands and pushed his face into the crack.

The young man moaned. "Please, Master, please."

The count palmed the buttocks, spread them, lifted them, and settled the young man's channel on his cock. Recently taken already by the cock, the footman's channel settled down on the shaft with little trouble. Using the leverage of his feet, the count began fucking slowly up into the channel. The footman sighed and ran his fingers through the satin material of the robe the count still was wearing.

The count moved the young man's right arm to behind the count's back and twisted the footman's body slightly so that he could get his lips into the hollow of the young man's neck. The count's left arm was supporting the young man's back, with the fingers of a satin-gloved hand stroking the nipple of the footman's left breast. The count's right satin-gloved hand was stroking the young man's cock.

The count stroked slowly and deliberately, both with his cock and his right hand, while licking and kissing the young's man's neck and encouraging the carotid artery to plump up.

The footman dozed and sighed and rubbed the satin robe with his hand—and, peacefully, came from the satin-handed stroking of his cock.

This was a signal for the count to increase the speed and intensity of the cock stroking and to suck hard on the young man's neck.

At the first spouting of his ejaculation, the count growled and sank his fangs into the carotid artery. The footman gave a little cry and his head lolled to the side, exposing his neck even more conveniently for the count. Spurt and deep suck. The footman's body jerked, and he ejaculated again inside the now-sticky satin grip of the count's right hand. Spurt and deep suck, and the young man's eyes closed and he was purring.

Spurt and deep suck.

Satin Circus

(A requested fetish story, written for James A.)

The music swells and the lights dim under the big tent, as the excitement builds in the audience and the buzzing conversations subside with the rising expectation that something—something special—is about to happen. Strobing lights and laser beams come up, gyrating around on the floor below and under the canopy of the tent above, showing a swirl of activity here and there, tantalizingly vying for attention, everything everywhere. The audience gasps in unison at the brief glimpses of the spectacles to be amazed by.

The lights dim again for a second and then one beam ignites, roams the tent, and comes to rest in the center of the floor below. It picks out the ringmaster, tall and solidly and powerfully built, with thick chest and small waist and a ruggedly handsome face. He is lifting his white-satin gloved hands in the pose of the concert master about to mark the first downbeat.

The audience sighs, knowing that he is there to bring order to the chaos the opening of the performance portended.

The music rises as the ringmaster in the center of the rings twirls his gloved hands, directing with a flourish the attention of the audience to where one act is starting, and to another ring, when that one is winding down. He is clothed in gold satin, with the dash of a billowing red satin cape. High above his head, the aerialists are flying from one platform on a pole to another. They are young and lithe, bare-chested and wearing skimpy blue satin shorts. The ringmaster has had his eyes on the youngest, fairest of them for some time.

The young aerialist stands, posed for the audiences gasp of awe, on a platform for a brief moment—the youngest of the dashingly handsome and courageous Flying Flauberts. Small of stature, but perfectly formed. Alabaster skinned, with a dark, sultry look. Hard body, smooth chest, oversized arm and chest and thigh muscles to meet the requirements of his profession, flat belly, and tiny waist. With a wave of his raised hand, he grasps the trapeze his partner has just flown off and sent his way, and flies out over the arena.

As the ringmaster directs the attention from the aerialists to a scantily clad woman standing on a white horse with gilded trappings that's prancing around the periphery of the rings with a flourish of his satin-gloved hands, a grip between aerialists above slips, and the young trapeze artist tumbles to the netting below. The ringmaster instantly directs the audience's attention to the cage with the lion tamer, and moves, as deliberately but quickly as he can, over, to the side of the net. The young man appears to be unharmed, only momentarily dazed.

The ringmaster caresses the young man's cheek with one satin-gloved hand while using the other to check for possible damage. He is cupping the young man's basket through his blue satin shorts with the gloved hand when the young aerial artist opens his eyes and gives the ringmaster a glazed smile.

The ringmaster whispers, "You seem to be sound. And this is the day. I can wait no longer. We can use your brief absence as a cover. Your partner need never know."

"Yes," the young man whispers back. "Oh, yes." He moves a hand to cover the gloved hand clutching his genitals through the blue satin shorts as an affirmation of what he wants.

"Take him to my dressing room and lay him on the studio couch there," the ringmaster commands to the two clowns who have shown up and who proceed to carry the young man out of the tent, covering the event with antics that convince the restless and concerned crowd that the tumble was all an act. As the ringmaster waves for his understudy to come forward and take over the circus maestro duties, the ringmaster assures himself that there is nothing wrong with the young man that a little special attention won't fix—that his limbs are unbruised and still malleable enough for the positions the ringmaster is contemplating putting them in. The two of them have been dancing around an inevitable coupling for weeks now and it is finally time for the master to make his mark.

The ringmaster enters his dressing room. The young man is lying on his belly on the satin-covered studio couch, his eyes half open in a semi sleep, watching the door of the trailer for the arrival of the older man. The ringmaster sits down beside him, unzips his gold satin trousers, pulls out his half-hard cock, moves the young aerialist's mouth to his cock, and caresses his cheek with a gloved hand while the young man sucks on his cock head, helping him to engorge. He turns his hip up slightly, moving deeper inside the mouth, and then he rocks back and forth as the young man feeds greedily on the thick staff.

The ringmaster then moves his gloved hand lower to pull the young aerialist's shorts down on his thighs, and he starts caressing and squeezing and kneading the young man's plump buttocks with the gloved hand. The young man moans for him and slides his mouth further down the cock.

The ringmaster moves his gloved hands to the root of his cock and slowly pushes the aerialist artist's mouth down it, holding his head between the satin-gloved hands momentarily and stroking the young man's cheeks with a satin thumb before he lowers his head and takes the young man's mouth in his in a deep kiss.

Then, moving to where he is kneeling between the young man's spread calves, the ringmaster works the aerial artist's, plump, firm buttocks cheeks with both hands. Caressing and kneading and separating them. He spreads the cheeks and leans over and blows on the young man's entrance, being rewarded with a groan and a "Please, master." He runs a satin-gloved finger over the hole again and again, making it pucker and open to him.

The young man gasps as, first, one satin thumb moves into the opening and then another, and the two gently pull, teasing the hole open. The young man isn't a virgin. His hole will open to a man, but the ringmaster knows that it will need to open much wider to take him.

"Please," the young man whispers. "Fuck me. Please."

The ringmaster's tongue goes to the hole and his gloved hands separate and stroke the buttocks.

The young man moans more deeply, and he lifts his hips off the surface of the studio coach, searching for the attention. His hands are stroking the satin covering on the couch.

The ringmaster rises on his knees, grasps the young man's waist with the satin-gloved hands, raises his buttocks, and moves his hard cock into the crack and to the hole. The young man breathes hard and gives little yipping sounds as the ringmaster invades him with the cock to the depth of the rim of the bulb. The young man is panting and groaning, learning now why the time was spent teasing the hole open. The cock is a pulsating monster. The young man writhes and lets out a cry as it sinks in another inch.

The ringmaster holds, clucking words of encouragement, imploring the young man to relax, revolving the portion of the cock that has gained purchase, waiting for the channel to give up its resistance.

"You want it, don't you?" he murmurs.

"Yes, oh yes," comes back the answer.

"Then relax, stop gripping your channel muscles."

The young man whimpers, but he does as commanded, and when the ringmaster feels the channel giving into the cock's authority, he slides in to the full depth of him while the young man howls the possession. The ringmaster immediately starts a slow stroke, which quickly builds up speed.

The young man is writhing under the ringmaster, his own cock dragging back and forth on the satin couch covering, his fists bunching up satin material, his mouth ingesting the satin of the couch and sucking on it, as the ringmaster's gold-satin shirt front comes down on the young aerialist's bare back, pushing his chest into the satin couch, and moving his nipples against the cool, slick material. The ringmaster's cock thrust, thrust, thrust, the only sound in the trailer being the heavy breathing of the younger and older men, the mewings of the young man on how well he's being fucked, and the slapping of the ringmaster's balls against the alabaster thighs of the young aerialist.

As the spotlight in his mind already starts to move again, the ringmaster's thoughts go to the creamy, satin thighs of the virginal juggler's assistant who he has only begun to cultivate.

Only a Custodian

"And a ten-inch cock."

"You're shitting us now," Oliver said.

"Yes, I'm shitting you," Porter answered. "But, really, I would want him to have a nice cock on him."

"Well, high on my list is that he has to be willing to take out the trash without being asked to," Adrian interjected.

"And put the toilet seat down too?" someone asked. They all laughed.

"No, thank god," Adrian answered when he'd finished laughing. "We'd have no problem with that."

Blake pulled his attention away from the discussion. It was probably a mistake for him to come this evening. Adrian had been a friend, like forever. But Adrian was a bit limp wristed, and the guys he ran with—especially this crew tonight—were decidedly so as well.

79

He agreed to meet Adrian at the bar tonight for a drink. He hadn't known that Adrian's gaggle of goofballs would be here too. For nearly an hour they'd been discussing what they wanted in a man. The consensus was moving somewhere between Superman and Donna Reed. The little shit Jeffery seemed to want a combination of the two. Porter only talked about the size of the cock.

They would have laughed, but the closest they'd come to what Blake would have said was that ten-inch cock. It was possibly the first time he'd ever found ground for agreement with Porter.

"You've said you melt to big cocks, haven't you. Blake?" That was said by Porter.

Blake snapped his head around to look at the guy with the orange hair and the ring in his eyebrow. Was he a mind reader? Had he just snatched what Blake was thinking out of the air?

"Yeah, at the party last week when you got a little blotto, Blake. Said you liked big cocks and surprise attacks and playing denial games."

Another head snap around to the effeminate dark-headed one with the big, rouged lips. Oliver.

"You did say all of that a couple of Saturday nights ago at my party," Adrian said, laying a hand on Blake's forearm. "I know it's been a while since you had it, baby, and how important it is to you to be taken care of regularly. Maybe you're just a bit uptight about this crackdown on sexual behavior in the school system. If you weren't so burnt out on the construction worker with the big cock, you wouldn't be shying away from the service workers. You need to accept, I think, that that's the sort of rough sex guy you like."

Blake was opening his mouth to speak, not sure what to say yet, when Oliver saved him by switching the line of discussion, if not the topic.

"Well, as far as I'm concerned, he's got to be a professional: a doctor or lawyer or professor."

"Agreed." That from Adrian and Porter in unison.

"But a professional with a big cock," Porter clarified.

Blake had to agree with that. He'd want the guy to be a professional, and steady and even predictable would be nice. No more adventures for Blake. But why didn't they say teacher? They'd said professor, but what was wrong with high school teacher? That's what Blake was, and he considered himself a professional. He'd be a good catch, wouldn't he?

Not for any of these limp-wristed guys, of course. Blake wanted his man to take charge.

But that thought sent a shiver through him. He shouldn't have come here at all. He should have agreed to meet Adrian somewhere else, not a gay bar. He needed to think more clearly on such things. He was a high school teacher. Being seen in a gay bar could be the end of his career. They were really pressing down on that now. And he'd been here with these screamers for an hour now. Anyone who came in would think he was one of this band. He was careful to cultivate an entirely different look and the way he was perceived, disappearing more into the mainstream. He turned in his chair, preparing to get up and say his apologies for needing to leave.

But as he turned, he saw him, the man that the group had been zeroing in on as the perfect man, at least from what could be seen on the surface.

He was probably in his early thirties, older than the group Blake was talking with. But they'd all agreed on that. They wanted a man older than them, but not really a daddy type, just older. And he was tallish, without being noticeably so, not too muscle-bound but obviously well muscled. He was wearing a close-fitting polo shirt of a light-weight material, and Blake could see every contour of his pecs and six-pack. Even the bumps of his nipples showed. Good biceps. No discernible tattoos. He looked clean cut and professional. More than that, he looked confident, under control—and capable of controlling. Blake liked to be controlled. This guy looked like he could take care of both of them.

The pants fit closely without looking sluttish, and from the look of the creases as the man leaned back on his bar stool and looked out into the room, the ten-incher they all were talking about couldn't be belied. He was achingly handsome. Auburn hair with golden highlights, a five o'clock shadow that looked groomed, sparking eyes. Blue or hazel. A great mouth and smile.

And right now he was looking at Blake, and Blake could attest to the nice smile, because that was what he was doing. At Blake. Was there a challenge in that look?

Blake did a double take. How long had he been staring at the guy without realizing that the guy was looking at him too?

The guy lifted his glass to Blake and smiled. Blake involuntarily smiled back, but he immediately dipped his head and averted his eyes. He'd lowered his head without thought, but he was thinking about it now. Would the hunk see that as a classic form of submission? And was it? And, more significant, was it what the man was looking for? Embarrassed and well aware that the man was still looking at him, Blake turned in his chair, burying his attention back in Adrian's group.

They were discussing muscle tone now. How much was too much? All Blake could think was that the guy at the bar was just right.

"But I don't think we settled on the job thing," the usually silent and not almost "up with the discussion" Jeffrey said. "He needs to be a professional, right?"

"Yeah, we already settled that," Porter said. "A doctor or lawyer. Something like that. And with a great cock."

Right on, Blake thought. The last man he'd had in his life was a construction worker. A great bod, but unreliable as hell. And he usually drank his paycheck before he got home with it. But once he'd gotten home and pushed Blake down on the bed and pinned him to the mattress with that big cock of his, Blake didn't care. Other than that, the guy was a deadbeat. They'd had to live on a teacher's salary.

A teacher's salary, Blake thought. He had to get out of here. He couldn't stay in a gay bar this long. It was risky. He shot a look at the bar. The guy was leaning across the bar, talking with the bar man. Stretched out like that, he looked like a million dollars. And that crease showing in his pants. Yeah that could be a big one.

The guy appeared to be rustling up two beers. He must have seen someone he knew, Blake thought. Or he must be here with someone.

Blake had been here too long. He had a compelling need to leave. He said his quick good-byes and headed for the door. At the door, he turned around. The guy was turned away from the bar now, a beer in each hand, scanning the room. His gaze kept going back to Adrian's table.

Could it be? Blake thought. Could he have been looking for me? But Blake had been in the bar too long. It would be best if he just didn't get into this now. Still, Blake lingered at the door until the hunk's eyes finally scanned around to him. The man gave Blake a level stare and Blake shuddered. Was there a possessiveness in that stare? A challenge, an offer, a command? If he had been sure it was a command . . .

Blake turned and left the bar. Perhaps the man would follow him. If he did, he did. And if he didn't . . .

He didn't. Blake went straight to his car, which was just across the street from the entrance into the bar. He leaned against the car's fender in what he'd have to admit was a "pose" for a good twenty minutes. But the hunk didn't leave the bar. No one did in that time. Deciding he just didn't care, Blake got in his car, drove back to his apartment, took a long shower, and, plopping down on his bed—alone—masturbated to a DVD on his computer.

* * * *

Friday evening and Blake was working late at school. He just had too much to grade before Monday. The place was deserted. The game was at another school at the other end of the county, and everyone else obviously was headed out there.

Blake was concentrating on the grading. It had been an essay test, so he actually had to read them all and try to make sense out of them—which wasn't always easy with high school juniors, most of whom seemed to be majoring in hieroglyphics.

It was a while before he realized he was hearing noises in the building. He thought he was supposed to be the only one in the school at this time. He got up and went into the hall and stood still and listened. Just when he was about to decide he'd heard nothing, he heard it again. It sounded like whistling. A low whistle. He quietly went down to the end of the hall. When there, he looked around the corner and almost swallowed something internal when he saw that there was a man near the end of this other hall. He had a mop and bucket out and was mopping the floor.

Blake took one look and then turned and started back to his classroom. He stopped then, his mind having had time to process what he'd seen. It wasn't just a man. It was a hunk. And he had been shirtless. He was dressed in the brown that custodians wear, but his shirt was tied around his waist rather than on his back. And he was a real hunk. Tanned like Blake wouldn't have thought anyone was tanned.

He turned and went back to the corner and peeked around again. The guy was turned toward him. Great bod and auburn hair with gold streaks in it. Hazel eyes and he was smiling. And he was looking right at Blake.

Good god, Blake thought. The guy in the bar. The guy in the bar is a janitor, a custodian.

"Peekabo," the guy said. And then he laughed. "You left the bar last night before I could come over. Your friends say you're between boyfriends and that you love to fuck. Sorry, I'm not much for foreplay. As soon as I saw you in the bar I wanted to fuck you."

The guy was unzipping himself and out flopped a long snake.

"Your friends said you liked big cock."

Blake turned and fled back to his classroom.

"Your friends also said you liked to play hide and seek and find and fuck games," the hunk called after him. Then he laughed.

Where could he go? What could he do? He was breathing hard. He involuntarily moved his hand down to his basket. He was getting hard. Those fucking friends of Adrian's. He'd obviously said a lot of things about what he liked when he'd been drunk. Most of it was true, of course. But he didn't think they'd parrot it to just anyone who asked them.

Where could he go? What could he do? He looked around the room wildly. His desk. He dropped behind the desk and went into the fetal position. God, the guy was hung. And he was a real hunk. There would have been a time. But Blake was a professional, a high school teacher now. And they were in the high school building, for god's sake. The guy was just a custodian. That wasn't what Blake wanted now. That wasn't . .
.

"Hi there. Your friends said you liked playing games of struggling before giving it up too."

He was standing over Blake, still looking like a hunk. His dong still hanging low out of his fly.

Blake moaned.

The guy reached down with both arms and lifted Blake and set him down belly to desktop and toes on the floor. He covered Blake's body close from behind and held him there immobile while Blake worked through hyperventilating. But his friends hadn't lied, he had to admit it. This was all arousing to him. But, dammit, the man was just a custodian.

"We can have a good time here. I know you want it. I feel you hard for it."

It was only then that Blake realized that the man had a hand between his thighs and was holding his cock through the material of his trousers. He then was holding Blake's wrists to the top of the table, on top of the stacks of papers Blake had been grading, and he was kissing him on the neck and nibbling at his ear. Blake could feel the guy's engorging cock between his thighs, pushing at his basket.

"Now this is what I'm going to do. I'm going to unbuckle you and drop your trousers and your briefs and . . ."

Blake moaned.

"And then I've got some lube and I'm going to do a little work to open you up. And then . . . I've got rubbers . . . I'm going to fuck you deep."

"Please," Blake burbled.

"After I've got you open, I'll ask you if you want it or not. Then it will be your choice. But think about it. I heard you like it deep and you haven't had any in a while. I can handle that for you."

By the time the man had opened Blake up and slapped that big cock of his on Blake's buttocks, Blake was ready for it. Adrian's friends hadn't lied. He did like big cocks and he hadn't had it in so long. But he'd also told them he wanted a professional. They all did. They were all tired of giving out to service and construction guys and then having to take care of them.

"You're tense. You're clinching your buttocks. Relax your cheeks. Unclinch that hole. You haven't said no. I'm going to fuck you."

With a moan, Blake responded to the command in the man's voice. He relaxed and let his body go limp.

Blake cried out and his torso came up off the desk as the cock entered him and sank and sank and sank. And then the guy started to pump him, and Blake flopped back down on top of the desk and moaned and groaned.

"You're sweet," the guy said as he stroked. "Do you like special positions? I do. There are positions that I can get in real deep with."

Next thing Blake knew the guy had turned him to his back and was kneeling on the desktop between Blake's legs, pulling Blake's pelvis up to his, his arms under Blake's waist. Blake's weight was all on his shoulders and his arms were just open out wide as he looked up at the guy.

"Ah, yes, can get deep," the guy murmured as he slowly stroked deep.

"Umm, umm," was about all Blake could manage. He'd never been fucked this deep before. He was loving it. He wanted this again and again.

But the guy was only a custodian. Just another service guy to support.

The guy also was as strong as an ox, he lifted Blake's body off the desktop, Blake locked his ankles at the small of the guy's back and his fists behind the guy's neck, and the hunk proved he could support Blake's entire weight while he pulled Blake's channel back and forth on his cock. Having demonstrated this, Blake was lowered back onto the desktop.

Blake's weight was on his shoulders again, but his arms were stretched right down the line of his torso, scrabbling at the desk top. The guy had grabbed his ankles, lifted his legs, and curled him up on his back. Blake's knees were touching his forehead. The man was stretched out on top of Blake, his head between Blake's ankles and his hands on the desktop on either side of Blake's head. His pelvis was plastered to Blake's groin, penetrating him deeply, and he was rocking back and forth.

Blake had come in the second position. The guy finally came in this one.

He left Blake stretched out on top of the papers he was grading and panting heavily. The teacher had the presence of mind to hope that no cum had gotten on any of the papers.

When Blake dragged out of his classroom, he went looking for the custodian, but he was gone. He wasn't anywhere in the building.

All weekend long Blake struggled with himself. That was the fucking of a lifetime. And Adrian's friends had told the guy exactly right. That was how Blake liked to have it. All of it. All of it except for the guy being a custodian. Blake had had too many men of the custodian type.

Still, on Monday morning, Blake was roaming the now-chaotic halls of the school, looking for the custodian. The only one he found was a guy of wiry but thin build and probably in his late fifties.

"No, sir, tain't no custodian here but me. Wish there was. There's nuff work for more than one."

Blake went to the office.

"That's right, just the one custodian on the payroll here. Thirties, you say? No, there isn't anyone even on the substitute custodian list that young."

Blake moped all day. Maybe if he went back to the bar. But maybe the guy didn't want to be found. Maybe he was one of those one-time guys. Blake had had quite enough of that. Blake had never had anyone that forceful and take charge, though. To have guessed that that was what Blake really liked . . . And to be that smart and only a custodian. Maybe Blake could help him get further ahead. If Blake had been able to find him, of course.

Only a custodian. Shit. Just my luck.

Blake was walking out of the school and toward the parking lot.

"Hi, there."

He looked up. It was the hunk, the custodian hunk. And he was in a Corvette.

"I never introduced myself. My name is Jerry. And, oh, yes, your friends told me I probably should mention that I'm a lawyer."

Blake was at a loss for words. Which wasn't just a phrase. He wasn't able to say anything.

"You want more of it? Want to come with me—for me? If so, climb in."

Blake walked around the car, opened the car door, and climbed in. Jerry wasn't wearing any pants. His hard cock almost reached up to the bottom of the window.

"I thought we'd go some place and you could sit on it. Your friends said you liked surprises."

Maybe Adrian's friends weren't so bad after all, Blake thought.

Sailors and Flyboys

Flyboys

Pete swung into the gym with a big grin on his face. "Fleet's in and I've already talked with Javier. His ship will be in early, on Thursday. Says he can get a three-day shore pass. Time for a special weekend."

"I'm game," Todd answered, but he was looking up at the man spotting him on the bench press and asked, "How about you, Dan?"

"Every weekend's special with you, babe," Dan answered. His idea of spotting was to have his hands on the inside of Todd's bare thighs and stroking them.

Pete was standing in the middle of the gym room at the Air Force base near San Diego, one of several workout rooms scattered around the base for airmen's use, this one being one of the most remotely located ones. He was toweling himself off after his run to the gym. He, like the other three men, Todd, Dan, and Bill, was wearing only a jockstrap, gym shorts, and athletic shoes. All four men, all Air Force officer pilots, were cut superbly. Pete was black; the others were white.

"I'll arrange the BOQ room at the officers' club," Pete said. "But I guess Bill better be the one to go down to the harbor to meet up with Javier and do the hunt. He's the prettiest of the bunch."

Bill grunted his assent at the assignment without losing count in the leg lifts he was doing on another apparatus. Bill indeed was the best looking of the four, although all of them looked great, especially the way they'd developed their bodies. Bill was tall and sultry dark, with some intriguing curling body hair on his forearms, pecs, and in a trail down his sternum, across his belly, and into the waistband of his gym shorts. Broad shoulders and slim waist. Big biceps, washboard abs. The face of a movie star, with a perpetual five o'clock shadow. Bedroom eyes.

"Money for the meals, liquor, and condoms and for Javier's tip go to Todd as usual," Pete said. "Five hundred each should do it, but if it's not enough we all agree to kick in more, right?"

Grunts of agreement were heard all around.

"Make sure you have a good supply of the rubbers," Bill said, turning to Todd. "We almost ran out last time."

Todd was doing his own count of his bar lifts, but he stopped in mid cadence. "Dan! You'll make me lose count."

All he heard in answer was a slurping sound, as Dan had pulled Todd's gym shorts off his legs, pulled his cock out from the jock pouch, and was giving him head.

Todd and Dan could almost be twins—Siamese twins—hooked at the crotch. Both reddish blonds of medium height, and, though well muscled, both on the wiry side. Not an ounce of fat on either one. Both with buzz cuts. Todd was the younger and more handsome of face of the two. Dan, who usually took the lead, as he was doing here, was distinguished by the veins that stood out between his muscles and the skin on his arms and legs, the veins having no fat at all to sheath them. His facial features were more rugged than Todd's. He didn't smile much, and he was more demanding and a bit cruel and rough. He'd had his dick inside Todd most of the time since Todd had come on duty at the air base. Todd, preferably a top, accepted this from Dan but from no one else. What mostly the two had in common, though, was that they liked to share another guy between them—at the same time.

"Could you spot the door for us, Pete?" Dan growled.

Pete picked up two twenty-pound hand weights and moved to where he was standing in front of the door to the corridor, staring through the small window in the door.

"Oh shit, oh fuck," Todd exclaimed as, hunched over him, Dan worked his cock into Todd's hole. Todd's ankles were on Dan's shoulders and Dan was lifting Todd's buttocks with palms that spread the butt cheeks, opening the hole that now hungered for and fit his cock like a glove, and fingers that moved the jock straps out of the way. He revolved the cock head to remind Todd's channel who was boss and then dove deep and began immediately to pump as Todd, gripping the pillars of the weight rack with white-knuckled fists, began to groan and move his hips to the rhythm of the fuck. Dan was thick; Todd was long. Bill, the hunkiest of the four, stopping his leg lifts to pull out his cock, start stroking, and to watch, was both thick and long. The black Pete, the bulkiest and most muscle bound of the four, standing spot at the door and feeling himself going hard at the sound of the fucking, was thickest and longest of the four.

Although not watching, except by way of a faint reflection in the window in the door, Pete could hear the stroking as marked by Todd's groan and Dan's grunt with each thrust and by the sound of the slapping of Dan's big balls on Todd's inner thighs. Pete raised the hand weights to his shoulders. Thrust and groan, up with the right weight; thrust and grunt, lowering the right weight; thrust and groan, up with left weight; thrust and grunt, lowering the left weight. Thrust and . . .

The four Air Force officers were a close-knit group, having discovered their mutual interests in jockeying jets, keeping their bodies hard, and fucking young sailors.

Sailor Tim

Tim stroked down the front of his Navy whites and turned this way and that, looking at himself in the mirror on the back of the cabin door of the dorm-like space he shared with nine other sailors on his destroyer. The clothes were tight on his small frame, with a trim, but well-muscled, torso and legs, but they really looked good on him. The jerkin was tight, showing his definition and his small waist, and the white trousers were tight at the thighs and across the crotch and flared at the hem. It was the first time he'd worn them. His first shore leave on his first naval cruise. He was barely nineteen and fresh out of the Iowa cornfields, getting his first taste of the greater world.

His brother was a sailor too, but he'd done everything he could to deter Tim from joining up, saying that with his blond, pretty-boy looks and small stature, he'd be eaten alive on board a naval ship. That had titillated Tim more than scared him, although now that he actually was in the Navy and had just been on the sea on a tin can with mostly randy men, he better understood what his brother had talked about.

The hedge on the men who had initially circled around him like sharks on the prowl, however, was sitting on a bunk beside him, watching him dress and admire himself in the mirror.

Big Ralph, named that for many reasons, including his bulk, his scare factor on board, and his seniority in the naval enlisted ranks, had become both Tim's oppressor and his protection. He was oppressing enough, though, that Tim was elated that he'd gotten a two-day shore pass in San Diego—and that Big Ralph hadn't.

It had been four weeks since Big Ralph had made good on his pledge to protect Tim from the sailors, including a senior ship's officer, who had been chumming ever closer around Tim as he moved around performing the deck duties of a bottom-of-the chain swabbie.

He just hadn't set up the protection the way that Tim had imagined he would. He'd done it by staking his own claim and staring down the competition. Big Ralph had managed to get Tim reassigned to a top bunk in his own cabin and in the darkest hour of one night, had climbed up into Tim's bunk, naked and already crowned and with a bottle of lube.

Tim woke up on his belly, with a heavy body on top of him, a hand smothering his mouth and nose, and thick, greased fingers inside his channel entrance. He had struggled, but to no avail, with the big man. He managed to bite the hand of his assailant in reaction to the surprise and pain of a hard cock entering him, and, when the hand was taken away, he screamed for help against the attack. But he writhed ineffectually, while Big Ralph laughed and pumped his ass with increasing speed and depth. There was no indication that anyone heard him struggling or, if they did, that they cared.

Tim, who had been curious about what it was all about before coming into the Navy, now knew exactly what it was about. No one came to his aid that night, because every other man in the cabin was under Big Ralph's protection as well. They had all had their first night with Big Ralph.

And Big Ralph, indeed, did protect them from others, as long as they were willing to put out for him.

After spending the night on top of Tim and fucking him again in the morning, with Tim realizing that resistance was both futile and a little late, Big Ralph whispered the rules of their relationship to him. Since then Big Ralph had fucked him as many as three times a week, and, as promised, kept all other takers at bay.

Tim came to accept this as just another aspect of the routine of life aboard the destroyer. But he was looking forward to this two-day shore leave in San Diego for a change of pace.

"The USS *Halsey*. My second year aboard. And you?"

"I'm on the *Shoup*," Tim answered. He looked away and nudged in closer to the table as another older sailor drifted by close to him in the bar and smacked his lips suggestively. "Just four months, though."

"Ah, four months." The guys would be pleased, Javier knew, if he landed this one. The guy was perfect. Probably only eighteen by the looks of him and just the right bod. Javier was judging this on his own body; he'd obviously been just right for the four of them last year. And this guy and he were almost identical in style and body style. This one was a lot prettier than Javier had been, though, he had to acknowledge. The major differences between them were that this guy was a blond and Javier was Hispanic—and this guy seemed so shy and a little skittish of the attention he was getting in this bar loaded with sailors off the ships. Javier wondered if he'd been this shy last year at this time and decided that he'd never been that shy. He'd known the score for as long as he could remember. And the almost palpable fear of the sailors swimming about the guy—he said his name was Tim—could, Javier thought, be put to his advantage.

"That means you've gone through all the hazing on ship then, I guess."

"Yeah, I suppose so." Tim wasn't acting like he wanted to talk about it. Bingo, Javier thought. That means you've been nailed already, little buddy. That's helpful.

"As bad as mine, I guess. Mine included being turned. Which is OK now, I guess, but it was really something at the time. But I got myself a protector and then it was mostly OK. Guy with a face like yours, and your size and conditioning, I bet you've had a really rough time."

"Well . . . it's OK now."

"So, you got yourself a protector too."

"Yeah . . . I guess."

"Makes a lot of demands, does he? Cock too big to handle?"

"No, not really." This given with hesitation. "He's got several sailors he's protecting, and he isn't too big."

Well, baby, you're in for a real surprise then, Javier thought. But with an ass that's still tight, you'll be a hit with the guys.

Tim was looking like he really wanted to change the subject—like he might even jump up from the table and bolt, so Javier changed the subject. He didn't want to lose this one. This pigeon looked like the mother lode as soon as he'd walked into the bar, all glassy eyed and looking like he was lost and might just back out again. The older sailors had seen him immediately and started jockeying for position. It had been Javier's luck that, to Tim, he looked like the most similar, familiar kind of guy and all Javier had to do was motion to him and pull out the chair next to him to get the pigeon roosting in his cage. He'd just come straight to him. Javier wouldn't tell the guys it had been this easy.

"So, this being your first shore leave, you bring enough cash for two days?"

"I've got $200." Tim said it as if he was rolling in cash.

"Well, shit, that ain't enough to get you through supper in a town like this."

"It isn't?"

"No. Did you ask anyone on the ship how much you needed? The prices get jacked up when the fleet's in. Two bills ain't even enough for an hour of pussy. And forget getting a room. You'll have to go back to the ship for the night."

"I will?" The prospect was crushing. Two days shore leave but he'd still be going back under Big Ralph's control for the night.

"'Course there's a way you can avoid that."

"There is? How?"

"I got a friend that would really go for someone like you. And he's an officer. I bet I could get him to feed you and take care of your room for the night. You could go back to the ship at the end of your leave with the two bills still in your pocket."

"For what?"

"He'd want to lay you, of course. But I'm telling you that he's a real hunk. You'd enjoy him. You've said you get fucked regularly on the ship."

"Not all that much," Tim answered. "And I don't know. I—"

"You go back to the ship tonight and your protector is going to fuck you, ain't he?"

"Well . . ."

"And is he a looker? I'm telling you that my friend is a real hunk. And he's an officer. An Air Force officer. He'd treat you right."

"I didn't really come on shore—"

"The hell you didn't. You sayin' you got all outfitted in those tight Navy whites and came into a sailors' bar at 11:00 in the morning just to have a couple of meals on shore and spend a night in a dirty hotel room all alone? You come out to get a little pussy from a dirty whore? You ever even had any pussy?"

He'd lost Tim half way through that. What *had* Tim come on shore looking for? It wasn't a woman. Javier had struck home there; Tim had never been attracted to women. It had always been men who had turned him on, although he hadn't done anything about it until it was forced on him. But why did he make such a fuss with his dress? And how *did* he plan to use his shore leave? Wasn't it more not to have to be on the ship and at Big Ralph's beck and call?

"Tell you what. Let me make the call. Maybe the guy's busy and won't even come. And if he does, you can scope him out for yourself. Think about it. A hunk who will pay for everything and all you gotta do is let him fuck you once. If you go back to the ship, you'll have the same old guy layin' you. At least you'd be tryin' out someone new. Have a little adventure on your shore leave; somethin' to remember it by. I've been laid by this guy. It was heaven."

Javier didn't wait for Tim to reply and Tim wasn't moving real fast in providing a reply. Javier was already pressing the buttons on his cell phone. He winked at one of the sailors hovering around when Tim wasn't looking and the guy came in closer. Tim shuddered, which is exactly what Javier wanted him to do. Bill, who had been waiting for a call, picked it up on the first ring. Javier managed to convey through prearranged signaling that he had a hot prospect and that it would help if Bill came in like a knight on a white horse.

Javier pointed Bill out as he hit the door and let Tim see for himself that the man really was a hunk, and that he looked spiffy and commanding in his closely tailored Air Force officer khakis. Tim also saw that as Bill entered and strode straight to the table, all smiles and in-charge authority, that he gave side looks of staking his territory that had the sailors who had been hovering around Javier and Tim—and had been egged on a bit by Javier when Tim wasn't looking—backing off.

The overall impression was of protection arriving, which placed Bill in a niche with Tim that was just what Javier wanted. Protector/fuck master. It was what Tim understood.

Bill, who liked the looks of Tim immediately, was all smiles and sultry sensuous looks, and touching Tim's arms and, once, his cheek, and, later, his thigh, while he guided a discussion about Tim's life up to this point and moved into everything they could be doing in the next two days other than fucking. No, Tim had never been to an officer's club. No, Tim didn't know they had bedrooms an officer could check out for a guest's use right in the club, something called a bachelor officer's quarters, a BOQ. And that Tim could sleep there in a real nice room if Bill reserved it. Yes, Tim was hungry enough for lunch. Yes, Tim had thought of touring the USS *Midway* Museum, a decommissioned aircraft carrier open to the public, while he was on shore leave. No, he didn't know that they had one of the world's best zoos right here in San Diego.

Tim was completely disarmed. Bill, indeed, was a hunk. Dark looks; black curly hair; an open, friendly smile; a magnificent physique in that Air Force shirt, with curly black hair peeking out of his neckline and on his forearms. Biceps that pushed his shirt sleeve up to his shoulders. A commanding demeanor that held back the sailors who had been zeroing in on the table. His conversation put Tim at ease. The occasional touch of his fingers on Tim's arms and hands sent chills right up the young sailor's spine. And he didn't once mention that going with him would require that Tim let him fuck him. Before long Tim was catching glimpses under the table of Bill's basket—and wondering.

Let the Games Begin

The air base was on a plateau above the city, and as they drove there, Bill told Tim how convenient the officers' club was. Everything was right there together. A dining room that served good, hearty food—all to be put on Bill's club tab, of course—a well-stocked bar, and the wing of bachelor officers' quarter rooms that were well used during the week but more or less deserted on the weekend. It would be no trouble putting Tim up in one of these. It wouldn't cost him a dime. Bill, who indeed loved using the officers' club for the purpose he had for Tim, didn't mention that the club officer was a good friend to Bill and his friend and that he ran a back bar as well as a front one—that the back bar was more for Bill's kind. Nor did he say that because of the nearness of the airstrip and the concern that visiting pilots get good sleep, all of the BOQ rooms were soundproof.

They had steak sandwiches and piles of French Fries and a couple of beers—to add to the two Tim had already had at the bar with Javier—for lunch in the club dining room.

Afterward, Bill suggested that he show Tim the BOQ room he'd booked.

Bill stood and so did Tim, but Javier remained sitting.

"You coming too?" Tim asked.

"No. I'll sit out here a while," Javier answered. And then in a lower voice that at least pretended that Bill couldn't hear, he said, "I think this is where you pay the rent."

Tim shuddered, but he turned and followed Bill back down the corridor leading into the BOQ wing.

He was sitting in Bill's lap on the end of the bed, feeling the hard cock under him through the material of the trousers they both still were wearing. They both were shirtless, though. They were kissing and Bill was working Tim's torso with a hand, while holding him in an embrace with the other arm. He was working slow. All of this was new to Tim. Big Ralph always just went for the fuck and he always did it in the dark. Bill was preparing him, making him moan and sigh. His kisses were making Tim breathless. What he was doing with his hands was driving Tim crazy. Tim felt the bulging of the biceps and also of the man's pecs. He ran his fingers through the man's chest hair. It was silky soft.

Bill unbuttoned Tim's fly, flared the opening, pulled Tim's cock out, and started to slow stroke it. This was attention Big Ralph had never given him. He quivered and felt his hips start to go into a motion that pushed his cock up through the encircling hand and then down again. Up and down. He was fucking himself in the cupped hands. Bill refused to let his lips go and pushed his tongue inside Tim's mouth and flicked it in and out. Tim began to writhe in ecstasy. Bill, much larger and meatier than Tim, just held him fast and continued kissing and stroking until Tim came with a shudder and a long sigh.

"Now me," Bill whispered, coming out of the kiss, and turning Tim and pushing him down on his knees on the carpet between his thighs. Tim moaned as Bill unbuckled himself, pulled down his zipper, and pulled out a half-erect cock.

It was bigger—both longer and thicker—than Big Ralph's was. Tim gasped and groaned at the sight of it—and then at the feel of it as Bill stroked his cheeks with it, always returning to pressing it at Tim's lips. Although he'd never done this before, it had been going on around him on board ship for weeks and Tim had seen several examples of it, so he opened his lips to the cock and did what came naturally in sucking and engorging.

Everything was new to him. He had no idea that sex with a man could be like this. Later he would go over all of it in his mind again—to consider what he liked and what he didn't like. For now he'd do whatever was demanded of him. He'd pay the rent and it would be over.

He was laying at the foot of the bed, with his butt on the edge. He was staring straight up at the ceiling and was arching his back and then releasing, arching and releasing, bunching up wads of the bed spread and releasing. Bunching and releasing. Gasping and groaning, every neuron of him concentrating on his cock and balls being sucked, on the tongue going to his channel entrance, on the lubricated fingers invading his ass.

Bill then was standing over him, between his thighs. Naked. A magnificent, slightly hairy body. Long, thick cock standing out and curved up from his black, curly bush. A smile on his face. Rolling a condom on his cock.

Tim trembled and began hiccupping deep in his throat, as Bill gripped and lifted and spread his thighs, rolled his pelvis up, and placed the bulb of his cock at the entrance.

"Oh, shit, oh fuck!" Tim cried out as the bulb pressed in a bit and revolved, seeking entrance.

"You've never had one this big, have you?" Bill asked.

Tim shook his head.

"But you have been fucked before?"

Tim nodded and covered his face with his arm.

"No don't do that," Bill said. "I want to watch your eyes while you take it. I'll go slow and be gentle, but don't deny me the view of you taking it."

Bill was slow and gentle—at least until he was in and Tim had opened to him and was moaning how good it felt, how filling it was, how he'd never had it this good before. And then Bill started pumping and Tim started writhing and crying out a commentary on where the cock was—everywhere—and what it was doing to him—sending him over the moon.

"That was great. You're so sexy. A natural," Bill said after he'd withdrawn and rolled the condom off his cock. "Now, why don't you go get a shower and then I'll take you out and show you some of the sights of San Diego. We'll do something with your shore leave other than spend it here, fucking." He pulled Tim off the bed, turned him toward the connecting bathroom, and gave him a slap on the rump to get him going.

Tim spent the shower trying to decide whether he really wanted to see the sights of San Diego or just stay here and be fucked by Bill again. All thoughts of doing it once to pay the rent and that was it had floated out of his mind and desires. Javier had said he'd only need to do it once—or at least had strongly hinted that. Tim wasn't sure that he didn't want to do it constantly over his two-day pass. Where would Bill spend the night, he wondered. He lived here and had his own place, of course. But was this room for just Tim or for both of them? He now wanted it to be for both of them.

He walked out of the bathroom with just a towel around him and stopped dead in his tracks. Bill was sitting on the side of the bed, still naked, but, most tellingly, with another condom rolled on his erect cock.

"I decided there is plenty of time for sightseeing. Come here." He reached over and pulled the towel off Tim. "Unless you don't want to."

Tim quickly showed that he wanted to. Bill marked this as a done deal for his friends' plans for the weekend.

This time Bill fucked Tim on his lap. Tim was sitting in his lap, facing Bill. His torso was laying back, supported by Bill's long, strong arms, with Bill's hands hooked over Tim's shoulders. Tim's legs were stretched out on the bed behind Bill. Bill's long torso was hunched over Tim's chest. Bill pulled Tim's channel back and forth on his cock. Bill was looking down intently into Tim's eyes, watching them come alive and flash and burn as Bill increased the pushing and pulling. Faster and deeper, ever fast and deeper, until both men cried out, coming nearly together.

Two hours. Paying the rent had taken two hours. Or so Tim thought. They showered together then, Bill making a joke about conserving water in drought-ridden southern California, and Tim almost wanting to be taken again from the arousal of Bill soaping up and rinsing off his body.

Javier wasn't there when they came back to the main part of the club, so the two of them drove off in Bill's Mustang convertible. Bill drove Tim down from the plateau and through the old, historic part of the city to the docks, where they toured the USS *Midway* Museum. Tim was like a little kid in his need to explore everything, and the actual little kids present all wanted to ask Tim, dressed in his Navy whites, about ships and sailing—and he stood with many of them for the photos they wanted. More than one of them asked Tim if he was a museum guide, and Tim almost wished that he was. Standing by, Bill nearly laughed, at what the parents of these kids would think if they'd known that Tim had been riding his cock just an hour earlier.

From the ship, they checked out Balboa Park, and then Bill took Tim to the San Diego zoo and watched him revert to a young child again. Bill had to keep telling himself that Tim wasn't a child, that he was a delicious young man with a sweet ass that was going to be reamed beyond his wildest imagination over the next two days. The thought didn't make him apprehensive, though; it made him go hard. He wanted nothing more than to pull Tim behind the monkey house and bang him again right there. He settled with buying Tim a stuffed monkey toy, which Tim accepted with a big smile and held close to his chest as, in the gathering twilight, they drove back up onto the plateau and to the welcoming arms of the officers' club.

Dinner and Dance

Javier was at the dinner table when Bill and Tim entered the dining room. But he wasn't alone. Pete and Todd and Dan were there too. They were drinking, waiting for Bill and Tim to arrive. They were all smiles for Tim when he was introduced to them. He was everything they had hoped for. Their smiles broadened as Bill went around to his friends to whisper how much greater than they anticipated Tim's ass was and how much the innocent he played while he was being played. While Bill was making the rounds, Tim was telling Javier what he'd seen that day and, with a blush now that he thought about how immature having the stuffed monkey was, still couldn't resist showing Javier the prize Bill had given him at the zoo. Javier beamed at the news, contemplating a bonus on his finder's tip.

Tim contemplated Bill's new friends while they were eating dinner. Dan and Todd didn't bother him. They obviously were into each other. Pete worried him. He was a hulk, and a black hulk at that. Tim didn't think of himself as prejudice, but there weren't all that many blacks in the Iowa town he came from, and he had learned to be wary of them since he'd entered the Navy. On ship they seemed to move in packs, and they'd give him the most worrying looks. He'd been warned about their interest in gangbanging sailors they could isolate in hidden compartments. And in the shower room, he'd seen that, to a man, they were lower hung than the whites and Hispanics he saw. They both made him shudder and fascinated him. And this Pete was no different. He seemed to be the Alpha Dog of this gathering of friends. All of the other men deferred to him, and, although he didn't say much—just sat there with an inscrutable half smile on his face most of the time—when he did speak, everyone stopped what they were doing and listened. And when it came to developed bodies, although all four of these guys were built like tanks, he was the awesome one.

After dinner, Pete led the way toward the back of the club. There was activity in the front bar, but they found that there was even more going on in the back bar. One wouldn't have known it before opening the doors into the bar. Although they were met with raucous noise from a DJ sound system, they heard practically nothing before opening the doors. The building had really good soundproofing.

The back bar was all guys and most of them were shirtless—which all of Pete's crew, including Tim, were in short order. Guys were out on the floor dancing with each other. The DJ was up on a platform, at one end of it. In the middle of the platform was a pole going up to the ceiling. The guys all bellied up to the bar and Bill took possession of Tim. Bill perched against a stool, facing out into the room, and just pulled Tim's butt into his crotch and embraced him with his arms. He played Tim's bare chest with his hands, letting one glide down occasionally to cup and squeeze Tim's basket. When he did this, Tim would turn his head and they'd kiss deeply. Tim was getting the idea he wouldn't be sleeping in the BOQ room all by himself, and he had warmed up to that idea. Bill's fucking was nothing like Big Ralph's was.

A couple of more loud songs with a strong beat and Javier was on the platform, dancing on the pole, and slowly shedding parts of his Navy whites. Dan and Todd were at the end of the bar, on stools, and kissing and touching each other with their hands. They also, though, were watching Javier dance. Pete was sitting in the stool next to Bill and Tim. He was turned toward those two and was watching him. Again the little half smile. Every once in a while he'd take a swig of his drink, but Tim got the impression that he didn't look at the drink—that he continued watching Bill play Tim's nipples, suck on his ear lobe, and cup his basket with his hand.

Tim could feel how hard Bill was for him—and that aroused him too—and he was beginning to wonder if Bill was going to fuck him again right there on the bar stool—with the black bruiser, Pete, watching. It seemed possible. Some of the other guys in the room were fucking. The party was getting pretty wild.

Tim didn't know if he cared or not. This wasn't costing him anything. This certainly was different from life on the ship. And this certainly was some shore leave. Bill was such a hunk. Tim couldn't wait to be alone with him again.

They went into a long kiss, with Bill stuffing his hand under the waistband of Tim's Navy whites, which wasn't an easy thing to do as tight as the trousers were. Tim's balls were now being cupped flesh on flesh, and he'd gone hard. He was panting. If Bill stripped his trousers off and put him on the cock right here, right now, Tim would have been happy.

When they came out of the kiss, Tim looked at the platform. Javier had been down to his briefs when they had started the kiss. Now he was gone. Gone too were Dan and Todd, and Tim assumed they had gone off to some corner to hump. They practically had been doing it there at the bar. He didn't know where Javier had gone off to, though.

Bill pressed another beer on Tim. This was, what? his eighth or tenth beer of the day? He'd lost count. Bill made him chug it, though. Then Bill moved his lips to Tim's ear so that Tim could hear what he said over the noise of the crowd and music, and growled. "It's time to go to the room."

As they were walking down the silent, dark corridor of the BOQ, seeming like a cemetery in contrast to the noise of the party room, with Bill guiding a somewhat dazed Tim with a hand on his buttocks, Tim was not unaware that Pete was following behind them.

* * * *

Fifteen minutes later, Tim was lying on one of the queen-sized beds in the room on his side, cupped into Bill's chest. Bill was holding Tim to him with an arm around his chest. He was lifting Tim's upper leg with a hand under his knee. And his cock was slow-pumping Tim's ass. Tim was moaning through a slack jawed mouth. His attention, through glassy eyes, was riveted on the other queen-sized bed.

Todd was lying on his back, his arms embracing Javier's chest. Javier was lying on top of him. Todd's thick cock was stuffed up Javier's ass. Todd's legs were laced through Javier's, holding them imprisoned and spread. Dan was kneeling between the spread legs, crouched over Javier's chest, his arms stiff-armed on either side of the chests of the men below him. His hips were cruelly punching at Javier's hole, pistoning his long cock inside Javier and on top of Todd's stretching and hard, but dormant, cock. Javier was squirming and breathing hard at the double invasion.

As Tim watched, Dan slowed down his thrusts, but Todd's movement came to life. Javier was crying out. Some of it was expressing unbounded pleasure. Some of it wasn't. But Javier was a trooper and knew what he was being paid by these men to take.

As if the atmosphere was turning up the lust dial, Bill started pistoning his cock inside Tim as well and Tim buried his face in the bedspread, groaned . . . and ejaculated.

Pete, naked, was sitting in a chair, watching, and pulling on his cock.

Twenty minutes later, Tim was lying back, cantilevered over the surface of the bed. Pete was kneeling, his knees pushed under Tim's buttocks and gripping his sides to hold his torso off the bed. Tim's legs were stretched out beyond Pete's hips. Tim's torso revealed that he already was spent—and, now, was overpowered, nearly overstretched. He was just lying back, his arms dangling at his side, his head flopped back, staring at the headboard, jerking just a bit at every long push of the channel off the monster cock and then a tired gasp at the long pull of his channel back onto the shaft. All of Tim's fears and anticipations were being realized. A black man's cock that was thicker and longer than anything Tim had ever seen hanging between any man's thighs, white or black. A fuck that was both horrendous and glorious. A filling that surely would split him, but somehow didn't.

Tim hadn't been asked if Pete could fuck him too. But Tim was no dummy. Six men in this room with two beds, two of them small, young sailors and four of them big, hulky Air Force officers. Tim knew that he'd found the gang bang that he'd been avoiding on board the ship.

On one side of the bed beside him, Javier was on all fours and Bill was crouching over his hips pistoning him hard. Next to them, pointed in the opposite direction, Dan was in the same position on top of Todd.

Alone but still moaning at Pete's taking, Tim was dozing. Bill was sitting next to him, stroking his cheek with his fingers. He lowered his mouth to Tim's ear. "You were really hot with Pete. If you can take Pete's cock, you can take any man's. It's good preparation."

Preparation for what? Tim wondered. He heard growling and grunting in the room, beyond the beds. The room reeked of musk and the smell of sweat and cum. Pete was stalking Javier on the other side of the room. Both were in a crouch and Javier was feinting this way and that, testing Pete's reactions, while Pete was moving from one side to the other, trying to figure out the smaller man's pattern. Pete's gigantic cock was waving out in front of him. Freshly crowned. Tim knew it was a new condom, because he had felt Pete fill the one he was fucking Tim with. When he had pulled it off his cock, it was thick as a sea slug, filled with cum. It was a slight thrill to Tim that he had caused Pete to cum that much for him.

Bill moved Tim to his back and was sucking on his nipples and lacing fingers in his balls and tugging on them. Dan and Todd were lying on their backs next to each other on the other bed, resting. Tim dozed off.

He woke again to the feel of hands on his ankles, pulling him toward the foot of the bed. It was Todd's turn to fuck him. Tim groaned. Dan was still on his back on the other bed. Pete had caught Javier. Javier was suspended, horizontally in the air over the floor. He was gripping the arms of a chair in both hands. Pete was behind him, between Javier's legs with them spread out from his hips like Javier was a wheel barrow, and he was slow-fucking Javier's ass. Javier was sweating like a pig and groaning deeply.

The shower was going. Bill was missing, so Tim assumed he was the one in the shower. For some reason, Tim felt a loss of his protection, although he had a flash of anger in the realization that Bill hadn't protected him from anything and was unlikely to.

"No, please, enough," Tim murmured, but Todd wasn't listening to him. He gathered Tim up in his arms and turned him as Todd sat on the end of the bed. Tim heard a roar from the other side of the room. Pete had come again. Dan stirred and sat up in the other bed. Todd lowered Tim's channel on this thick cock, with Tim sitting in his lap, facing the room. Javier was on the floor in front of the chair, curled up, and Pete was standing over him, rolling the condom off his still-hard cock. Once again, the spent condom reminded Tim of a sea slug. Todd was raising and lowering Tim on his cock and murmuring in his ear how tight and sweet he was. Pete walked by the bed and dropped the spent condom in a waste basket and peeled another packet off a string of them on the bedside table. A tired Tim, eyes slitted and seeing everything as a blur, leaned his head back into Todd's shoulder as Todd, his arms crossed under Tim's diaphragm continued to lift and lower his channel on the thick cock.

Tim opened his eyes to the feel of a hand on his shoulder. Dan was standing in front of him, holding his cock up in his other hand. Tim took the cock in his mouth and started sucking it hard.

"Lower and stretch him," Dan said, and Tim felt himself being lowered on the surface of the bed on top of Todd's chest. Todd's legs were pushing on Tim's, raising and spreading them. Dan was crouching between the spread legs and Tim felt the bulb of the long, now-rehardened cock at his rim above the root of Todd's buried cock.

"Noooo," he moaned weakly. They were moving in to trap him in a double penetration.

Pete voiced some sort of command, though, and was brushing Dan aside and reaching down and pulling Tim off Todd. He pulled Tim out into the center of the room. Tim was just about to voice some form of thanks when Pete bent him over at the waist and started entering him from the rear. Tim groaned weakly. When Pete started pumping him, Tim's legs went to jelly, and Pete put an arm around his waist, pulling his feet off the floor, and went into a balancing crouch. He continued pumping, faster and deeper. Tim ejaculated weakly, shortly before Pete did so more strongly. Then Pete just let Tim sink to the floor in a heap. Javier wasn't far from him, also still curled up on the floor.

Bill had come out of the bathroom and stretched out on the bed. Dan and Todd took their turn in the shower. Pete went and sat in the chair. When Dan and Todd had showered, he nudged Javier and told him to go clean himself. With a groan and a grunt, Javier slowly raised himself and went off to the shower. When he was done, Pete rose from the chair, picked Tim up, slung him over his shoulder, and took him into the bathroom. Tim just stood, weakly in the shower as Pete soaped both of them up roughly and let the shower rinse them off. He tossed a towel to Tim, who was on more sure legs now, and went into the bedroom with a towel to dry himself.

When Tim came out of the bathroom, the lights were off in the bedroom. In the light from the bathroom, Tim could see that Dan and Todd were in the far bed, with Javier between them. Pete was in a chair with his heels on the bed where Bill was stretched out. The level of snoring indicated that maybe they all were asleep.

His ordeal was over, he decided. Was this worth free room and board during his shore leave? Whatever it was, it was something he'd never forget. And it wasn't necessarily bad. Now that it was over, he could concentrate on the pleasure of it. What Big Ralph gave him wasn't fucking. This had been fucking. Lying under Big Ralph from now on would be no big deal.

He switched off the bathroom light and went and collapsed onto the edge of the bed Bill was on, seeking whatever privacy he could get. Bill's arm came over and pulled Tim into the curve of his body as he turned toward Tim.

In the middle of the night, Tim woke. Bill also was awake and saw that Tim's eyes were open. "Have you ever been fucked like that before?" he whispered.

"No," Tim answered honestly.

"We enjoyed you. Like Javier, we'd enjoy doing you any time you come in on shore leave. You won't find a cock like Pete's anywhere else. You're spoiled for it now."

"We'll see." Tim was suddenly mortified. He'd meant the "we'll see" to be finding any better fucking than Pete did. Bill probably took it as an answer that he wanted it again the next time he had shore leave. He was right in that.

"Good," Bill murmured. "When I take you back to the ship, I'll give you contact numbers. Next time, we'll pay you the same we pay Javier—$500 for the weekend for unlimited access."

Unlimited access, Tim thought. What a strange way to express it. He was on the verge of laughing about that, but his attention was arrested. Bill was moving him.

"It's late," Tim whispered. "We should be—"

Bill laughed. "We got you for the weekend, little buddy. You're going to be fucked all through the night."

Tim moaned. Bill was on his back, pulling Tim over on top of him on his back. Bill was getting his legs between Tim's and lifting and spreading Tim's legs. His cock was sliding into Tim's channel and his arms were lacing through Tim's and stretching and trapping the young sailor's arms over his head.

Tim woke up laying on his belly diagonally in the bed. Dan was saddled over his hip and fucking down in him. Pete was doggy fucking Javier in the other bed. Tim's head was hanging over the side of the bed and he was staring down into a waste basket half full of spent condoms.

Todd and Bill were nowhere to be seen or heard.

Dan filled his condom and got off Tim and went to the shower. Tim was moving to get off the bed when strong, brown hands gripped his waist and pulled him down to the side of the bed, moving his feet to the floor. Tim was bent over on the bed on his belly. Pete entered him and began a strong stroke.

Javier got off the other bed and went into the bathroom, and, presumably into the shower. When both Dan and Javier came out of the bathroom, they stood there, toweling off, and watching Pete stroke on inside Tim.

Tim was moaning and panting and gasping. He had been a bit premature in thinking it was all over the previous night.

Dan and Javier continued watching as they dressed. Pete stroked on.

After the two had left the room, Pete shot his load, pulled out and went to the shower, tossing his sea slug of a spent condom in the waste basket on his way to the bathroom.

He hadn't said anything at all to Tim. Tim was just there for their special weekend.

It was nearly noon when Tim struggled into the dining room, so he ordered a hamburger and shake with fries. Pete and Javier were gone. Bill was there. He'd finished eating, but he said he would wait around and take Tim to see something else of San Diego after he'd eaten and then take him back to his ship.

Dan and Todd weren't there, but they came into the dining room as Tim was finished eating.

"Want you back in the bedroom after you're done here," Dan said. "We got interrupted doin' you together last night. We're not done." Then they walked on toward the corridor to the BOQ rooms.

"No," Tim said to their departing backs. "No," he said, turning to Bill. "Please, no. I've had enough. You guys have had enough of me."

"It's still the weekend," Bill said.

"No," Tim said, starting to rise from the table.

Bill stood, gathered him up, tossed him over his shoulder, and started walking down the corridor.

Dan and Todd took him the way they had started to do the previous evening. Todd was under Tim on his back, Tim's back on him, Todd's cock buried up Tim's channel. He was embracing Tim's chest with his arms and pushing Tim's legs up and out with his. Dan crouched between Tim's legs, forced his cock in over Todd's, and did most of the pumping.

Tim lay there, whimpering and trapped between them. It wasn't as bad as he had imagined it to be. Pete had reamed him well for it.

Back to the Sea

Before taking Tim back to the ship, Bill drove him up the coast in the Mustang to Sunset Cliffs Natural Park. They parked in a lot right next to the cliffs, and Bill pulled Tim over toward him, wrapping an arm around his neck and took him into a deep kiss. He moved the other hand under his jerkin and rubbed his nipples and glided his hand over Tim's chest. They were looking out over the Pacific on a beautiful, rugged section of the Pacific. He unbuttoned Tim's Navy white trousers—not that Navy white anymore—fished out his cock and slowly stroked him.

111

"You were terrific, baby," Bill murmured. "Can't get enough of you."

You and three others, Tim thought. But he was melting to the man. He was such a hunk and he had such a beautiful smile and a soothing voice. Tim could almost believe him.

"I'm sorry if it was a bit taxing . . ."

A bit!? Tim thought.

". . . but it's because your body is so beautiful and yielding. You are a natural. We must have you again."

Tim's hips were moving, thrusting up inside the hand encasing his cock. Was this what he wanted too. Would it be pabulum with Big Ralph from now on? Maybe this was what he wanted after all.

Bill's tongue was inside Tim's mouth, swabbing it. He took Tim's tongue in his mouth and sucked on it. He was pulling on Tim's cock harder. His thumb was pressing into Tim's piss slit, slicking around the precum Tim was producing.

This was more than fucking. This was fully arousing, more attention being paid to Tim's needs than anyone had done the previous day. He could lay under Bill and fully enjoy him. Of them all Bill had done him best. And he was the best looking, the hunkiest, the best talker. The kindest.

Both of them were aware that Tim was tensing. Bill withdrew from the kiss and moved his mouth down to cover Tim's cock and to suck until Tim came.

No one in the previous day had cared when and how Tim had come. Just now, here with Bill. Only Bill cared. He'd been given a telephone number. Was it Bill's. He could call the next shore leave and meet him again if it was only Bill.

Bill came back up and went into another kiss on the mouth. He had been holding Tim's cum in his mouth and it rolled around between their mouths. Tim moaned deeply. This was a new sensation. Not all that unpleasant. The most intimate sharing he'd ever done with a man.

"Come let's walk," Bill said, rebuttoning Tim's fly.

They got out of the car and, arm and arm, walked alongside the cliff. A hundred yards along the cliff the foliage got to be denser, trees and bushes came closer to the pathway.

Suddenly Bill lifted Tim off the ground and dragged him into the bush. He was pawing at Tim like a wild man. Tim was struggling against him, but it was no use. Bill pulled off his trousers and briefs and forced him onto all fours in the scrub, thrust inside him, and pounded, pounded, pounded his ass.

Tim sobbed and writhed under Bill's thrusts, the most brutal that Tim had had all weekend. With a yell, Bill pulled out of him and shot off across the small of his back. Tim rolled over onto his side and Bill stood, crouching over him, panting.

"Get up."

Tim whimpered something neither one of them could understand.

"I said get up."

Tim didn't. Bill kicked him in the ribs. He still couldn't rise.

Bill reached down, pulled him up, slung him over his shoulder, marched back to the car, and dumped him over the side of the convertible into the passenger seat.

As they drove back into the city, with Tim curled up in a ball in the passenger seat as far away from Bill as possible, Bill spoke only once. "$500 for the weekend plus room and board. We don't make love; we fuck. It's good money. Think about it and call us your next shore leave. You're going to find that you don't want vanilla any more after us. So you'll call."

At the dockside, he stopped near the gangplank to the USS *Shoup*, reached over and opened the passenger door, and nudged Tim out onto the blacktop. He reached over and pulled the door closed and then drove off without giving another look.

A couple of sailors passed Tim as he was struggling to stand up. They'd seen drunks coming off of shore leave like this, though, so they just passed him by.

Tim was happy for three weeks. Big Ralph kept the other men off him and fucked him three times a week. Bill had been right, though. After Pete and his friends Big Ralph's fucking was bland. Tim started to let the occasional bruiser fuck him without letting Big Ralph know that he was doing it. He found two guys who wanted to fuck him together, but Tim discovered that what they had in mind was one after another, but at the same time. And it was pretty bland.

One twilight he arranged to be standing near the hatch doorway to a rope locker, apparently unaware of a group of black sailors moving around him, ever closer, but knowing they were there. When they fucked him on coils of rope in the dark, one after the other as several hands held him down, all big dicked and heavy pounders, Tim felt about as close to the thrill he now associated with his Air Force officer weekend as he'd ever gotten.

Three months later, the *Shoup* was pulling into San Diego again to let its sailors go on shore leave—and Tim was looking around in his kit bag for Bill's telephone number.

Solicitous Service

Goran saw the young man standing nervously at the reservations desk and liked what he saw. He was even happy that Serge, the maître d, was pretending not to see the young man, because that meant that Goran, the waiter, could see him to the table—and could make contact of some sort with him on the way there. Goran was one to make an immediate assessment of the playing field and pick out who he would like to play with.

"Table for one?" he asked, as he approached the young man at the entrance of the terrace section of the Great Falls, Virginia, Serbian Crown restaurant. It was an exclusive suburban restaurant on the Potomac Palisades south of Washington, D.C., that was frequented both at lunch and dinner by the rich and powerful of the nation's capital. Goran felt it was perhaps to be his good fortune that the maître d hadn't considered this young man identifiable as rich or powerful.

"No, two, please," the young man said with a shy smile. "I'm meeting someone here. I'm surprised he isn't here already, but I don't see him."

"Certainly, umm, will this? . . . Perhaps if we have a name of your dinner companion so that we know who to bring to the table." Goran suddenly realized that he needed to know whether to seat the young man by the door to the kitchen or in a prime spot. The maître d would have his hide if he guessed wrong.

If it were up to him, though, he would seat the young man in his lap. He couldn't be more than twenty-four and was movie-star handsome. Dark, Mediterranean features, with black curly hair, full lips, and blue-green eyes the color of that same sea. He was dressed presentably enough for the maître d. He just hadn't been recognizable as someone important. And he was beautifully formed. He also looked like what Goran went after—a submissive, who'd just let Goran have his way with him.

"Uh, of course. Senator Julian Jamison."

Goran practically snorted, both from surprise and amusement. Senator Jamison was about as glorious as clientele came in the Washington area. The maître d would swallow his teeth when Goran told him whose luncheon companion he'd stiffed—and rightly so. And Goran couldn't help but get approval for having saved the situation.

"Very good, sir. How about this table here?" Goran had taken a u-turn into the center of the dining area.

"Umm, maybe something a little more out of the way?" the young man asked shyly.

Goran's antennae went up. An almost obviously submissive young gay man—like most gay men Goran could tell these things with a great deal of assurance—meeting a prominent senator and asking for a discreet table. His prospects were looking up. The restaurant had such tables, of course. "How about that one over there, blocked off from the other diners a bit by the trellis and grapevine?"

"Perfect. Thanks." The young man gave Goran a shy smile and looked down.

Bet he knows, Goran thought. The dip of the head; bowing to the Alpha Male. Bet he knows that I'm a dominant. Bet he knows I'll fuck him if I can too. Bet he's already resigned to letting me, if an opportunity opens up.

Goran placed the palm of his hand on the young man's back to guide him over to the table—and to check out his speculation—and was rewarded with a slight shudder. Another good sign. Surrender. Only opportunity lacking.

Goran was just the ticket for a certain type of young man. His was body-builder built and a bit thuggish looking. He was of Serbian descent—as all of the crew at the Serbian Crown were—and he clearly was a dominant and demanding sex partner. He was in his mid thirties, old enough to be well experienced and yet young enough to be vigorous and have stamina. Goran sought out the handsome, submissive types who he could fully master, and, he was happy to say, he couldn't remember ever having had an unhappy customer.

And this young man, Goran gauged, was exactly the type of young man he specialized in.

"May I get you something to drink while you wait?" Goran asked, solicitously.

"What? Oh, yes, a glass of sauvignon blanc, please. The house wine would be fine." Another submissive dip of the head after he had spoken.

"Certainly sir." A smile that was as assured as it was possessive.

Goran had the pleasure to inform the maître d, whose eyes were drilling into him as he approached for giving up a key table, who the young man was waiting for. He stayed around the reservation desk only long enough to see the maître d blanch at hearing the senator's name and for beads of perspiration to dot his brow, before he hurried to the bar to pour a generous glass of better-than-house wine, reasoning that the more wine the young man drank, the more opportunity Goran would have with him. Then he went into the kitchen and, invoking the name of the senator, rustled up a choice appetizer and then returned to the young man's table.

The young man was sitting, looking pensive, and not noticing Goran's approach. His hands were on the table, with one fiddling with his napkin, and Goran managed to brush it with his, making sure to brush the thick blond hair on the back of his hand against the young man's hand, as he set the wine glass down. Another little shudder from the young man rewarded Goran's effort.

"The wine. And the kitchen would be pleased if you would try out this appetizer—on the house—and let me know how you like it." He stood close over the young man and smiled down at him. He made sure his crotch, with its decided bulge, was at the young man's eye level.

"Oh. Thanks." The young man smiled up at him. It was a radiant smile. His eyes were flashing like he was excited about something. Goran hoped that, before he left, he'd be excited about Goran, but he knew that it was too soon for this smile wholly to be for him.

"Your wish is my command," Goran said in a soft voice, although this was the opposite of what he was hoping for down the road—he wanted to command and he planned on being hard if he did. That's what a submissive young beauty like this needed—a pounding deep inside him, rattling his world completely. "If there's anything . . . anything at all . . . that I can do for you, don't hesitate to ask."

They both heard the arrival of the senator at that point and both looked up. He pulled up in a stretch limousine, with both driver and bodyguard, and the maître d was beyond vociferous in greeting Jamison.

Goran backed off, watching the obviously important, trim, for all appearances prematurely gray-haired man move across the restaurant floor toward the table. There was something in the way the man looked, though—a bit embarrassed and uneasy—that told Goran that perhaps this meeting wasn't going to go completely as the young man had planned and hoped. If not, Goran's prospects had just increased tenfold.

* * * *

As the senator walked across the mostly empty terrace dining area, Goran's eyes went to the young man. He's stricken, he thought. There was no doubt that the senator was spiking him. Goran suffered a twinge of regret. It wasn't likely that he could compete with riches and power—unless, of course, he could get his dick in the young man. That would level the playing field real fast. This type of submissive settled right down once you had your dick in him.

The young man rose from the table. "Senator."

"Tyler," the senator answered. His voice was a rich baritone. His smile was one that surely gave comfort to his constituents, but, to Goran, it looked a bit strained, and the senator wasn't making eye contact with the young man. Again Goran sensed that there was something wrong here   and that it probably was something the young man wasn't aware of.

After he had taken the food and drink orders from the senator and the young man—being happy that the young man ordered a second glass of wine—the waiter was drawn away to take the order of another table, and then another.

There was a chill in the air at the table when he returned with the drinks. The two were still engaging in small talk, but the young man was repeating, "What is it Julian? What aren't you saying? There must be a reason we're meeting like this rather than in the office or at the apartment."

Their food was ready when Goran went back to the kitchen. The young man was engaged in animated conversation when he brought the food to them, but he stopped and looked down at the napkin in his lap while Goran served the food. Goran tried the typical "I hope you enjoy" small talk, but the young man didn't respond and the senator was a bit brusque and dismissive.

Goran wasn't liking this pretentious senator and had the urge to tell they young guy just to give him the finger and walk off.

The really nice thing about this table mostly being hidden by a wall at the side and a vine-covered trellis toward the restaurant proper was that there was a place a waiter could stand right where the wall and trellis met where it would appear that the waiter was being attentive to the tables but yet he couldn't be seen from the table behind the trellis and could hear what was being said at that table as clearly as those at the table could. This was one reason why this was Goran's favorite table to attend.

"You can stay in the apartment until the end of the month, of course," the senator was saying. "I doubt that will be a problem if you're going back to Louisiana, though."

"I don't understand, Julian," the young man replied in a snuffly voice. "What have I done? I've always been discreet and I've tried to be careful. And both the job and cutting us off at the same time. I just don't think I can—"

"It's the kindest way for it to end," the senator said. "We both knew there would be an end to this someday."

Yeah, right, Goran thought. But this was getting interesting. He just might be able to make something out of this.

"I don't—"

"It's my fault. I should never have started this in the first place. It's too risky. People will find out. It will ruin your life."

You big shit, Goran thought. I'll bet you seduced him. In fact, I know you did. He doesn't look like he has an aggressive bone in his body. You just pushed him up against a desk one night, and once you'd gotten your dick inside him, he was ready to do anything you wanted. And ruin his life? Please. It's your skin you're worried about. You don't give a shit about him. You used him for as long as you thought it was safe. And now you're throwing him away.

"Please, Julian. There must be some way. And at least . . . at least let me keep the legislative assistant job until I find something—"

"It's already too risky for that. I think some of the staffers are already talking. No, it's best if we make a clean breast of it. Ummm. Have you tried these scallops? They are absolutely delicious. Come, you haven't touched your meal. No, you best go back home to Louisiana and let the whole affair . . . just let it all vanish. A few months and we'll both not even think about it, I'm sure."

"I'm not sure at all," the young man said. "I could go to Idaho. Find a job or something in Boise. Then when you went back home—"

"There's really nothing else to discuss about it, Tyler. It's over. It's finished. This really is the best way—especially for you. I can't really blame you. You were like a disease. But it isn't right. We must move on."

I wonder what other young staffer he's found to fuck, Goran wondered. Will he move him into the same apartment? He couldn't feel any resentment, though. He was a shark himself. And he was smelling the chum in the water.

"If you aren't going to eat those scallops, you might as well send them over here," the senator said right before Goran had to leave his vigil to serve at another table.

* * * *

The next chance Goran had to look at the table behind the trellis, the senator was gone. But the young man—Tyler, Goran now knew—was still sitting there, in shock and crying quietly.

Hot dog, Goran thought. He headed straight for the bar and poured another glass of the better, heady sauvignon blanc.

"Here," drink this, Goran said, putting the glass of wine down in front of Tyler and pulling the chair the senator had vacated around to the side of the table so that he could sit close to the young man. He moved a knee so that it was between Tyler's knees. Tyler didn't seem to notice. There really was no doubt in Goran's mind now. Get something between the thighs of a submissive like this, and he's yours.

"I didn't order this," Tyler said in a small voice.

121

"But you need it, I can tell. It's on the house. The service here is the best."

"Thanks," Tyler said, picking up the glass and taking a deep drink. "Yes, I did need that."

"There's as much of that as you want," Goran said. "And I give the best service. The very best." He had a hand on the suit coat sleeve of Tyler's forearm. Tyler looked up and saw the expression on Goran's face and then looked quickly away.

"I'm sorry. I should be going." Neither one of them believed that.

"Not until you're feeling better. And you must know what would make you feel better."

"I don't—"

"Tyler. Your name is Tyler, isn't it? I overheard. My name's Goran."

"You overheard?"

"Yes. A lot. I know what that jackass has been doing to you."

Tyler let out a little moan and took another big swig of wine. That was fine with Goran. Let him be tipsy.

"I don't want to talk—"

"Yes you do, Tyler. You want to scream to the treetops above us about it. The man has taken fucking advantage of you and has cast you aside." He hadn't used the word "fucking" by accident, and he saw how the use of the word jolted the young man. "What you need is to get right back on that wagon. Show him for the bastard he is. Show him with a younger, more fit man. Someone with a real cock."

No sign of shock. Goran was home free, and he knew it. And his young Tyler knew it. They were going to fuck.

"I don't know. I really should be . . ." But it just trailed right off and Tyler showed no signs of leaving. Goran's beefy thigh was now pushed far in between Tyler's legs. He was rubbing his knee against the young man's crotch.

"Here give me your hand, Tyler." Tyler looked at him blankly. "Give me your hand." The voice was commanding; just the tone the young man needed. Goran took the hand and laid it on his basket. "Is that bastard the man I am?"

Tyler gave an unintelligible squeak. But he didn't try to take his hand away. Goran wouldn't have let him if he had tried. They were over the hump now. Goran would give the direction and Tyler would respond as directed.

"I don't want to rush you," Goran said, clearly wanting to do just that—and knowing his submissive males well enough to know what worked. "But I want to fuck you and show you that that old bastard isn't worth another thought. You're worth ten of him."

Tyler just looked at him dumbly. But he wasn't trying to get away.

Goran stood up. "Come back to the back. You don't want to leave looking like that. I'm going to fuck you and then let's get you cleaned up."

Tyler stood and put his hand in Goran's and let Goran lead him back into the restaurant building; through the empty dining rooms, already set up for the dinner service; down the hall past the guest bathrooms; and into the back of the restaurant and into a bathroom used by the service staff. He shot home the lock on the door and crowded Tyler into the wash basin, pushing his pelvis into Tyler's and grinding his package against Tyler's crotch while he took possession of Tyler's lips with his. Tyler's mouth opened right up and Goran scooped out and sucked suggestively on his tongue. Tyler was making little mewing sounds.

As Goran surmised would be the case, from the moment that he had Tyler pinned to the edge of the double-sinked vanity with his pelvis thrust between Tyler's thighs, Tyler was completely docile and submissive. Goran came out of the kiss, stripped off his own shirt, and placed Tyler's hands on his biceps and then on his pecs.

"I'll bet your senator isn't built like this," Goran said. "Go ahead and feel what a real man feels like."

Tyler moved his hands around on the bulges of the muscles as instructed. He was panting softly.

Goran dropped his pants and briefs and stepped out of them. He took one of Tyler's hands—with Tyler just giving it up docilely and giving Goran a glazed look—and placed it on his genitals.

"Does your senator come equipped like this?" Goran asked.

"No," Tyler answered in a small voice.

"I want to fuck you. I think it's what you need too. Do you want all of this inside you?"

"Yes, please," Tyler answered, and he started to paw tentatively at the buttons on his shirt as if he wanted to help get on with it but wasn't sure how. While pressing into his crotch with a now-free cock and rubbing up and down with it, Goran brushed Tyler's hands away and started pulling off the young man's suit coat and then his shirt and trousers, folding them pretty neatly and stacking them on top of the hand towel hamper next to the basin.

Tyler was breathing heavily and was beginning to move his crotch against Goran's. His hands had reached out and were gripping Goran's side half way between his waist and his pecs. "Hurry, please," Tyler murmured.

"Want it now, don't you?" Goran said, with a laugh. "We can make you forget all about that bastard. We're going to have a good time, you and me."

"Please. Please. Fuck me. Don't make me wait."

Goran lifted a now-naked Tyler and positioned him standing and hunched over the toilet while Goran felt around in his pants pocket for his ever-ready condom packets. Those found, he spread Tyler's butt cheeks with his hands and buried his face in the crack. Tyler began to moan and mutter a progression of "fuck me's" in a low voice. Goran reached through Tyler's legs and milked his cock.

When Goran had moved him back to the basin and perched his butt at the edge and Tyler had sunk his shoulder's back into the mirror over the basin, Goran slowly entered Tyler's channel while Tyler huffed and puffed and moaned and groaned. "Oh, shit, oh, fuck. You're so big. Yes, yes, fuck me."

Tyler lifted his ankles to Goran's shoulders and grabbed the Serbian's heavily muscled upper arms while Goran grabbed Tyler at the waist and pulled his channel on and off his cock in rotation with holding him still and pounding his ass deep.

Tyler came first, in a stream up Goran's belly, and Goran filled the bulb of the condom soon thereafter.

"Again," Tyler begged.

And, as much as Goran wanted to fuck him again, Tyler was just a bit too submissive for him. And Goran wanted to do something else for him.

"I don't think that would be wise, as nice a piece as you are," Goran said. "I just wanted to fuck that bastard who's just ditched you out of you. I think we've managed that. Why don't you shower and clean up now—there's a shower stall right over there. Make yourself presentable again and then I'll come back for you in a few minutes. Another fortifying glass of wine and I think you'll be able to handle life from here. Don't think of that bastard. You are a great lay and highly desirable. Get back out there again. A better man than that one will come by fast enough."

This revealed another aspect of Goran. With him it was mostly the chase and the assertion of dominance. He wasn't one for entanglements. He was more of a notches-on-the-belt man. Tyler had, indeed, had a nice tight channel and was a pretty little thing to fuck. But Goran felt no need or great desire to do him more than once.

While he spoke, Goran was sponging himself off with a wet towel. Then he put his own clothes back on and returned to the terrace. With luck, he thought, just the man Tyler needed would have arrived for his regular Tuesday lunch. And when Goran got out to the terrace, he saw that the man, indeed, was there. He made a beeline for him.

Fifteen minutes later Goran was guiding Tyler through the bar area, stopping there to pour another glass of premium red, and taking Tyler out onto the terrace.

"Tyler," he said, "This fine-looking gentleman, who I can verify has a nice big cock and a superlative sex drive, is Keith Engle. I have told him about you and he's eager to meet you."

A smiling, very presentable man of forty-five or so, smiled happily at Tyler and eagerly invited him to sit down.

"In addition to loving to fuck young men like you, Tyler—and being very good at it," Goran said, "Mr. Engle here works for the *Washington Post*. He says he'd very much like to talk to you about the extracurricular activities of one Senator Julian Jamison."

First and Only

"Yes, hold just like that, please. You pose well."

"As well I should," Philip answered as he put an arm up to lean on the frame of the door out to the balcony. All he was wearing was an opaque dress shirt, unbuttoned and gaping open, which was made even more opaque—luminous even— by the backlighting of the sun beyond the balcony of the eleventh-floor, Darlinghurst, Sydney, apartment. Philip's trim, well-muscled, but not overly so, blond body was gorgeous in its smooth-muscled sculpted lines. His cut cock hung low, nestled in a well-defined nut sack. The only jewelry Philip was wearing—by request—was an elaborate Esculpta cock ring at the base of his cock, made of black rubber, with silver lions' heads on each end, that wound around the base of the cock more than once, showing the lions' heads at the top, facing away from each other.

"How about this?" Philip asked after Steve had taken a couple of photos. He lowered his head, looking at his feet, so that his face didn't show, just the tousled top of his blond, with golden highlights, head of curly hair.

Steve, about ten years older than Philip—thirty-five to Philip's twenty-five—dark-haired, slightly hirsute, rougher looking, more heavily muscled and solidly built than Philip, put the camera down, turned to his easel, and picked up a chunk of black charcoal. "Perfect. Now if you can hold that pose for fifteen or twenty minutes, we're home free." He was dressed only in gym shorts, pulled down in front by a heavy basket, and flip-flops.

"There, done," he said some fifteen minutes later.

"Can I see it?" Philip asked, raising his head. He had remained stock still the entire time.

"Later," Steve answered with a husky voice. "First we fuck. I told you you'd pose and I would sketch, and then we'd fuck." He had lost the gym shorts and was in magnificent, uncut erection.

"Where?" Philip asked, his eyes big in confirming the size of Steve for real for the first time outside the pages of a glossy nudes book. Philip felt himself going hard.

"Sit on the chair on the balcony. I'll be out there in a minute."

The minute was spent gathering up lubricant and condom packets.

Coming out onto the balcony, Steve sank down on his knees in front of Philip. He grasped Philip's legs under the knees and parted and lifted them while he pulled Philip's buttocks forward and rolled them up. He spent several minutes licking down the side of Philip's cock as it engorged, sucking on his balls, and seeking out his hole with a tongue before he returned to Philip's cock, deepthroated it several times, and then gave him the preliminaries of a blow job in earnest, while Philip moaned and bucked under him, talked dirty, and clutched at Steve's curly black head hair with his fingers.

At length, Steve pulled his mouth off the cock, and this was when Philip thought he would be fucked. He was prepared for that. For some time now he had welcomed the thought, even as thick and long as Steve's cock turned out to be.

But Steve surprised him. When he opened a condom packet, he rolled it down on Philip's cock instead of his. Then he dribbled the crowned cock with lubricant, palmed more of it, and rubbed that into his own asshole as he stood and crouched over Philip's lap. He lowered his channel on Philip's cock and started, first, a slow rise and fall rhythm on the cock, pulling Philip's face into his chest, the young man's lips onto a nipple nestled in black, curly chest hair. Philip placed his hands on Steve's waist and groaned at the surprise pleasure of his cock being worked by the older, well-experienced man.

After a few minutes of a gentle rhythm, Steve began picking up speed, fucking himself hard and deep on Philip's cock. Philip raised his head and Steve cupped his ears and brought his lips into a deep kiss. Philip reached down and started stroking Steve's cock in a rhythm matching Philip's ever-faster rise and then slam down on the cock. Philip flopped his head back as he came out of the kiss and cried out "Oh, fuck, oh, fuck, of fuck!" as Steve went after Philip's arm pits with his tongue and teeth.

They came almost simultaneously—the very first time they had sex. It was not the fuck that Philip had expected by a long shot, but it was a good one for him.

* * * *

Earlier in the day, if Philip was being honest with himself, which he always liked to try to be, he was bored and cruising. He was on the second day of a three-day layover in Sydney, and, having nothing else to do—he wanted to go to a beach, but the directions that anyone had given to him on getting to one had been too complicated—he found himself seeking out the gay districts of the city in search of some action. He'd never been to Sydney—or Australia, for that matter—before. He'd been told that there was a gay district in the southern Sydney sector of Darlinghurst, within walking distance from his hotel in the harbor area, and he had found a gay bookstore, The Bookshop Darlinghurst, there and was perusing the book offerings—and the clientele. He hadn't been laid in nearly a week, and he was getting jittery.

There were several young men there. Only one was brawny in the way Philip liked his men, though. Heavily muscled and wearing gym shorts and an athletic T-shirt with deep cuts in the armholes that showed tight, curly black hair peeking out here and there and in more profusion at the armpits. He looked like a footballer and like he could be rough in sex. He also looked several years older than Philip. All of this was enticing to the young man. But the man's attention seemed to be elsewhere.

Philip moved to the table of art books. He saw the 2013 edition of the Dieux du Stade Calendar, featuring artistic nude shots of the rugby players of Paris. He didn't have this edition of the calendar yet and thought this would be as good a place to buy it as anywhere. But as he reached for it, so did another hand. A bigger, rougher hand than his, with tight, curly black hair on the back of it. The hand came down on top of his and held his hand.

"Oh, I'm sorry," Philip said. "We seemed to have been reaching for the same calendar at the same time."

"I would have thought this book over here was more to your interest," the man he'd already scoped out said in a rich baritone voice.

"Uh, which one?"

"The Henning Von Berg photo book. *Alpha Males.*"

"And why did you think I might be interested in that one?"

"All of his models are particularly hung. That's the point of the book. The lower hung a man is, the more he is Alpha material, according to Von Berg."

"Oh, and am I supposed to be impressed by big cocks?"

"I certainly hope so."

God, he's cocky—pun intended—and confident in himself, Philip thought. Then he went on to append, as well he should be, as he looked down the line of the man's torso from

130

his muscular pecs to his solid waist and the way his gym shorts were pulled down in front. Philip could make out the line of a thick cock, and there were two silver lions' heads peeking above the center of the waistband, just above where the man's cock would be rooted. If that was a cock ring, it was something Philip, who had pretty much seen it all, hadn't seen before and, thus, was impressive. It didn't even appear that he was wearing a jock or briefs under the gym shorts.

"There are several copies of the calendars," he said. "We can both have one." But the man still had his hand on Philip's and Philip hadn't tried to take his away. He had come in here on the off chance of picking up a hookup for the afternoon. And this guy fit the bill. Philip didn't want to discourage him.

"You don't sound like you are from around here, and I haven't seen you in here before," the man said.

"No. I'm an American. This is my first time in Sydney. I'm just here for a few days this time, although I'll be back frequently now. I haven't seen much of anything."

Offer to show me something, Philip was thinking. I think you know what I want you to show me. You're cocky enough to assume that's what I want to see. And I'm needy enough for you to be right.

"Ah, an American. So, what part of America and what brings you here?"

"I live in Los Angeles. I'm an air steward. Just signed on for the Los Angeles-to-Sydney route. I'll be here a couple of times a week for a couple of days."

Take me somewhere and fuck me, Philip added in his mind.

"An air steward. Qantas?"

"No, Delta."

"And your interest in this art work is?"

Because I'm gay and cruising, Philip screamed in his brain. Because I'm looking for some hunk to fuck my brains out. I'm bored. And because, like the men in this art book, you fit the bill and know you do. But what he said was, "I'm also a model. On the side."

"Ah, a model . . . on the side And maybe all that entails."

Yes and on my back too. Go ahead and say it. Go ahead and make something out of it. Tell me you want me on my back.

But the man just repeated himself. "A model. I could have guessed. Nudes?"

"Yes, sometimes. But mostly underwear . . . and jeans . . . and swim wear ads."

"So, as good as nude, considering the ads for those these days."

"I guess you could say so."

Ask me to go with you somewhere, Philip's mind was begging.

"And an escort too, I'll bet," the man said. Philip had been looking away from the man and now his gaze snapped back to the man's face. He was giving Philip a level look and had a slight smile on his face. If he was moving in for the hookup—which Philip welcomed—this was the most direct stab at it Philip had heard from anyone who wasn't drunk. Philip shuddered a bit. The man was a strong dominant. Philip would be manhandled. This was like winning the lottery.

"Are you always this forward?" Philip asked. He intended to make it sound insulted, but he didn't think he'd accomplished that. And he wanted to hook up anyway.

"When I see something I'm interested in, yes. So, are you an escort in Los Angeles too?"

"Yes, when it suits."

"Both ways?"

"Excuse me? What do you mean? Both men and women? We're standing here in a gay bookstore, you know. But women hire me to escort them as well as men."

"I mean top or bottom or versatile?"

Philip gave it a few seconds to make the man wonder if he was home free—although, of course he was. He was a real hunk and he was crowding in on Philip just the way that made Philip melt to a man. "Yes to all of it," Philip answered. "Both men and women, both top and bottom. Now is that all you wanted to know? Are you really asking if I'll go with you—let you fuck me? Wanting me to say that I want you to fuck me?"

"Well, what I really wanted to know—what drew me over here—is wondering if you would model for me."

Was that a "gotcha" grin on the hunk's face?

"You're a photographer?"

"No. I'm a sketch artist. Charcoal mostly—because it's faster. I like to capture expressions and poses instantaneously."

"And should I ask what else you do as you did with me?"

"You mean other than fuck my models?"

"Yes," Philip answered, his face turning red. It wasn't this man who was going to be embarrassed by direct talk.

"No problem. No secrets. I'm in construction."

"Oh, a construction worker." Yes, he did look a little like a construction worker, Philip thought. Solid, compact, hunky, and a bit rough. And he was dressed for the part. That didn't make much difference to Philip. He liked them a little rough. And this guy had an attitude that suggested he'd drive real hard. Philip also liked casual sex. This was working out well for him.

"Not a construction worker. I said I was *in* construction. As in an architect. High-rise buildings. I work here and in Brisbane. But I live mainly in Brisbane because there's a lot of construction there. More than here. I keep a place here too, though."

"Your place is nearby?" This was where Philip expected to be asked baldly to go there with him. He would just as baldy say yes.

"Yes, just down the street a bit. So, I wondered if you would sit for a drawing for me."

"In the nude, and then we'd fuck?" It was time to stop dancing around the topic of interest to Philip?

It came right back. "Yes, something like that. If you wanted a big cock, applied well."

"Yes."

The man looked a little surprised. He apparently hadn't expected this so fast after all the work he'd done, all of their playful bantering. He backpedaled a bit. "But you said you were a professional model and a rent boy. No preliminary negotiations? No 'It will be this much'?"

"I said escort, not rent boy. Don't cheapen it. I don't need your money."

"But you want to fuck. You came into a place like this looking for a fuck. I can tell."

"I said yes. And I've also said I don't need your money. Yes, I want to fuck. Yes, I came here looking for a hookup. And I think you'll do fine—if you haven't been hyping what you don't have. But you could pay me in some way for the modeling. There's something I need someone to do for me."

"What's that?"

"I've wanted to go to a beach. I've heard there are good here. But I have no way to get to one or any idea what direction to go in."

"You want me to take you to a beach in exchange for a fuck?"

"As the price of modeling. The fuck would be free. I want it, and I think I'd enjoy having it from you. I won't lie about that."

"You have a suit with you? I only ask because whether or not you do determines which beach I take you to."

"Not with me, but back at my hotel."

"Which is your hotel?"

"The Grace on the corner of King and York."

"The art deco one near the harbors? That's on our way to the beach I have in mind."

"Bondi beach? That's the one I've heard the most about."

"I'm thinking of a more private one. Obelisk beach. On the other side of the entrance into the bay from Bondi beach. It's more private."

"OK. How are we going to get there?"

"I have a ute. We'll take that."

"A ute?"

"The Aussie version of what I think you Yanks call a pickup truck combined with a sport's utility."

"Let's go, then. I'll get the calendar. You might want one too. You look like a rugby player too."

"I've scrummed in my time, yes. But those are French guys. They wouldn't measure up to us Aussies."

Still boasting? "Maybe you should buy the *Alpha Males* book, then. You said it covers champion hung guys. You could compare."

"I don't need the book. I'm in it. Page 32."

With trembling hands Philip flipped the pages of the glossy photographs of nudes. "Holy shit. That *is* you. Holy shit."

"Shall we go?" the man said, with a smile, as he put the palm of his hand on the small of Philip's back and started guiding the nearly hyperventilating young man toward the bookstore's door.

Already taking charge. Philip trembled with anticipation.

The man's ride turned out to be a sleek and sporty lime green Ford XR8, which he extracted from an underground garage nearby underneath a high-rise apartment house that Philip thought might be where the man had his Sydney digs.

* * * *

The man, who introduced himself as Steve on the ride to the hotel, sat in a chair and watched Philip undress in his hotel room and then pull on a skimpy Speedo. Philip kept looking at the bed. He did want to go to the beach, but what he really would have liked would have been for Steve to fuck him with that monster cock before they went—if, of course, the photograph in the art book hadn't been photoshopped. Philip was real interested in checking that out.

But Steve didn't take the hint. He just sat and watched. And Philip wasn't going to beg for it. At least not yet.

"Don't you have a suit?"

"In the ute, yes. But I'll wear what I have on," Steve answered. Philip hoped that Steve would be going into the water. He couldn't wait to see a pair of wet gym shorts hanging

135

off the guy. He was still wondering if those silver lions' heads were attached to what he thought they were. There wasn't much they could be attached to if not that.

Obelisk beach was out Middle Head Road, toward the harborside town of Manly, on the north shore of the long bay stretching inland to Sydney.

The section they went to was a gay beach permitting nude sunbathing, and although there weren't many guys on the beach, they tended to be paired off and were making out most of the time. Not actual humping, as that wasn't allowed on the beach, but everything up to penetration, and there were many pathways leading in from the road to the beach covered in heavy foliage. Pairs of men could go off into the bush for their fucking and then come back and perhaps pair off with others for another round. Several eyed Philip and Steve closely in passing, but a good look at Steve told them it was best to move on and perhaps take their chances with Philip later if he was alone then.

Philip and Steve mainly made out—heavily so, and in fact probably a bit beyond the beach's "no penetration" rules. They didn't go off into the paths, and they didn't stay long on the beach. Steve obviously had an agenda. He was the aggressor. That was the way Philip wanted it.

After they had lain on a beach blanket, side by side, on their backs for a while, Steve rolled over on top of Philip. He didn't let his weight rest on Philip except at their crotches, propping himself up on his elbows and his knees, but what he did to Philip couldn't be called much less than a dry fuck—with enough penetration, despite the two layers of material, to make Philip moan for more. His knees were between Philip's thighs, his arms were cradling Philip's back, and his hands were cupping Philip's head, holding him captive, while Steve ground against Philip's basket with his own and trapped Philip's lips in deep, tongue in mouth kisses when he wasn't ravishing Philip's nipples with his lips and teeth.

Rolling Philip's pelvis up by forcing his thighs under Philip's, and after rubbing the underside of his nearly unclothed cock over Philip's hole at length while Philip shuddered and writhed under him, Steve pressed his cock head, fettered only by the thin material of his gym shorts and the not-much-thicker material of Philip's Speedo, against Philip's hole and actually managed a bit of penetration of the bulb in short jabs that had Philip gasping and counterpressing, bringing the gigantic bulb a bit further inside his opening, sighing for him, and whispering of moving into the foliage and completing the fuck. Philip, panting hard and groaning and moaning, begged and whined for the fuck, but Steve just laughed. At length Philip came in his Speedo and collapsed under Steve.

"Fuck me for real now, please," he whined.

"Drawing first. Then we fuck for real. Had enough of visiting a beach? Are you ready to go back to my place now? Now that I have shown that I can make you come even without taking our clothes off?"

"Oh, god, yes."

* * * *

After Steve had surprisingly (to Philip) fucked himself on Philip's cock on the balcony, he rose from Philip's lap.

"You have no end of surprises in you, do you?" Philip asked.

"It's all a progression, a conditioning—all by my schedule, my personal rules. And, trust me, you will not leave here before you've been royally fucked. It's late. I'll go fix us an omelet for dinner. You want a glass of red wine? You'll be staying here the night."

It wasn't a question.

"Yes . . . thanks," Philip answered, still confused that it was Steve who had his channel spiked—and aroused at what the man was promising was to come. And not just by what he said—also by the confident way he strutted around in the nude in his apartment, and with what was swinging between his legs. Philip would have to think about all of this. Perhaps he was more aroused by this strange approach Steve was taking than if he had just fucked him in the hotel room. Above all because now he'd seen—and handled—the man's hard cock, and now he knew, with a shudder, that he would be taxed to his limits when he had to sheath it. Sometime. Unless the man was just toying with him. He certainly had been toying with him.

Philip got up from the chair on the balcony after a few minutes and entered the living room, which, in one longer-than-wide space, ran into where the dining table was and then to the open kitchen beside the entry door. The eleventh-floor residence at Park Apartments on Oxford Street did have a bedroom and bath off this room. The apartment was small, but Steve had said he lived most of the time elsewhere, and Philip thought this place still was probably expensive. It was more than a hotel room; it was high in the building, and it had a spectacular view toward the city center and Circular Quay where the Sydney Opera House reigned.

Retrieving his glass of wine from the counter between the kitchen and the dining area, Philip started to make a survey of the room. He was still wearing just the open dress shirt Steve had sketched him in. His first stop was at the easel where Steve had been working. He had to admit that Steve had a great deal of artistic talent and had captured him—flattered him even—with a minimum of strokes of the charcoal. If anything, the artist had been generous with the hang of his cock. The sketch was sexy and arousing in its own right. The artist had a talent for focusing on the physical aspects of sex without losing the features that made the individual recognizable.

That led Philip to pay more attention to the rest of the room. He had been so focused on being fucked when he'd come into the apartment that he hadn't paid much attention to the furnishings and decor.

The furniture was spare but obviously of high quality. And the walls were covered with other charcoal sketches—all of other young men, like him. But there many different men were depicted. Gorgeous young men. And the sketches seemed to come in pairs for each of the young men, one an artistic pose like Steve just had done of him, and a second one of the young man in dishabille, sometimes entwined in sheets and other times just a heap on the floor. These, though, were just as sexy looking as the formally posed ones, maybe more so because of the sense—almost a smell—that came off of them of musky sex. And there was a quality about them that made Philip feel exhausted, spent and just a bit apprehensive. They made him conscious of a catch in his breath.

These young men had been sketched after being fucked totally. Fucked by Steve, Phil was sure. Maybe fucked again after a quick sketch was done.

At one point, while standing and looking at one of these sketches, Philip had to put his wine glass down on a table, he was trembling so much. The young man looked like he had been fucked to within an inch of his life—and yet there was a sublime, if exhausted, smile on his face as if he would volunteer to die that way given another chance. What, Philip wondered, about the sketch led him to think of the fuck as having been cruel and totally taxing? Then he thought he saw it. The sketch of the young man was from his feet looking up his torso to a face of blissful exhaustion. The view was between spread and bent legs. His hole was gaping, not yet closed, sketched immediately after the cock's withdrawal. And he had been reamed extraordinarily wide. Big splotches of cum still glistened on his belly. Philip looked up and down the walls, suddenly concerned whether there had been another chance at this heaven for that young man. But he saw no more sketches of him.

He moved into the bedroom. There he found a large-sized platform bed and more sketches on the walls. Look as he might, though, Philip couldn't find any more than just those two sketches of each of the subjects. It was almost scary. In each instance the second sketch gave off the vibe that the young man had just been taxed to the limit—but would beg for more, given the opportunity. More gaping holes, more prodigious globs of cum. And yet there was no evidence there had been further sketches of any of them. It was disturbing to Philip. When—no, if—Steve got around to fucking him, would it be satisfying and a memorable experience encouraging more encounters with more men, or would he become a sex slave to a single man who showed him what sexual divinity was but who left him incapable of being satisfied by any other man? His mind kept going back to the length and thickness of that cock and to the evidence that Steve would be a cruel and expert lover.

And to those gaping bung holes after Steve had reamed them.

He shivered at the realization that he loved the idea of such an encounter, and scaring him at the prospect that it would ruin him for full pleasure from other men.

He obliquely broached his concern with Steve while they were perched at the kitchen counter and eating their omelets.

"What's in this omelet?" Philip asked.

"Left to right."

"Meaning?"

"Meaning I stood at the refrigerator and took what seemed to fit from left to right. Luckily I found eggs."

"Ah. Well, it isn't bad."

"Most any food isn't bad after sex," Steve said. "And before more sex."

"Speaking of sex. All those sketches on the walls. Those all guys you've brought here and fucked?"

"Yes. You should see the walls on my house in Brisbane."

"But *you* fucked them, right? It was *you* who put them in the condition of those second sketches?" These were questions Philip really wanted to ask. Not just had Steve been the one to ream them that way but also was he really a top? It was disturbing that he hadn't fucked Philip yet. Why had it been Steve on his cock? Everything else but the reality so far pointed to Steve being a piledriver. Was this just a mad game? Was some mad rapist confederate lurking around in the shadows somewhere? Someone physically repulsive?

"The evening is young. Eat your omelet. It will give you strength."

"There are only two sketches of each. Were they drawn on the same day?"

140

"Yes."

"But only the two?"

"I should have warned you. I'm a first and only sort of guy," Steve said. "It seemed from how much you were on the make for casual sex at the bookstore that you'd be cool with that. I just do a guy the one day. But I totally do the guy."

"Was I that obvious at the bookstore?"

"Sure were. And you're that obvious now. You want me to fuck you right now, don't you? You want me to prove that I can fuck your brains out. Even though what we just did was great at the time, you won't be satisfied until it's me plowing you. Until I ream you a wider one."

"Yes," Philip admitted.

"Sorry. It's on my schedule. At my whim. If you weren't showing you wanted it so bad at the bookstore, I probably would have just moved on."

"Really?" Philip asked, surprised.

Steve took a minute. "OK, not really. I really did want to sketch you. And not just the first one. I want to sketch the second one. And I think you're going to be a real nice lay when we get there. But more than just this once? I don't think so. When you fly away to L.A. in that Delta jet of yours, this will just have been an interesting encounter—one from which you will be humming and can't close your legs when you walk down that airplane aisle. It will be interesting for me; I hope it will be interesting for you too."

"That's it? I don't even get my own version of the sketch?"

"No. I got my rules. I sorta broke them for you, but you have such a great look. And your cock did me good too. I don't really know yet if you're a good lay."

"You broke the rules for me?"

"I don't knowingly do rent boys. I like them fresh or gently used."

"And do they stay gently used?"

"No. I fuck them silly and ream them a wider rectum and colon. I like to stretch their canals myself."

"You do any virgins?"

"You've seen some of these sketches. You can figure that out yourself."

"I'm not sure. I think you were generous with my cock in the sketch you just did of me. I think some of this is to serve fantasy."

"You measure yourself short, then. Pun intended. I sketch with integrity. Even in the 'second' sketches. I sketch what's there to see. I saw you looking real close at some of them. Does that scare you?"

"Yes, a little." Which was a lie. It scared Philip more than a little. But it aroused him even more. He was already hard. He felt his juices stirring.

"Good. It's supposed to."

"Do you always talk to your men so openly about this on that one day—the day you sketch and do them? They can't all want to hear you are going to ream them wider. Although when they see you naked, they must realize that's going to be the case."

"No. You're the first one I've gone this far with in what I say. I stop when I sense they can't take any more of the truth. But I do them just the same. You are different from the others. Maybe it's because you are a rent boy. I have sensed from the beginning that you want this—all of this. But it isn't all I want. There is fear in their eyes before I stop telling them what is happening and why. I need that and look for that. I haven't seen that in your eyes yet."

"And you think you can't do that with me—ream me a wider one? Master me totally in that way? I'm an escort, not a rent boy, I'll repeat. I think there's a significant difference in fee structure and services. I make entirely too much from it to be called a rent boy."

"I'm gonna make you cry, Mate. It's in the rules. I don't know about stretching your rectum and colon, though. And that's why I should really be doing this by my rules. Reaming fresh channels is the thrill for me. Yes, I do virgins. Most of them are virgins. But they all want it, and I dare say they all leaving wanting more of it. I want them tight and to leave them big enough to drive a ute into. But I'll plumb you deeper than a fresher guy. We'll see how much you can take. No one has taken it all yet. Because you're a rent boy, I'm going to give it all to you whether or not you beg me to stop. Does this make you want to head for the door?"

Philip looked away and took a long drag on his wine. But he showed no inclination to head for the door.

"Ah, two hands on the wine glass, you're trembling so bad. I've reached you at last. And I bet you're ready to come right here and now. I bet you could come with me just telling you what I'm going to do to you."

"Yes," Philip whispered.

"Look at me."

Philip turned his head back toward Steve.

"I see it now. A trace of fear."

"Yes."

"Come to my bed now."

"Yes."

* * * *

Twenty minutes later they were on the bed. Philip was on his back, and once again Steve was using Philip's cock. Steve was suspended over Philip's prone body like an upward-facing crab. His knees and elbows were bent and his head flopped back between Philip's feet. His buttocks were in motion, rising and falling on Philip's cock. Philip was groaning from an experience he didn't often have unless the man he was escorting was a lot older than Steve and with a lot less muscular body than Steve's. Steve had told him just to lay there and stay hard, which he was doing with the help of the Esculpta cock ring, and that Steve would do all of the work. Steve was showing that he could work Philip's cock expertly even in this position.

After ten or fifteen minutes in this position, Steve flattened his legs with them running beside Philip's torso and his feet beside Philip's legs. Steve's torso was still suspended over Philip's thighs and his fists were gripping Philip's ankles. He pistoned his ass back and forward on Philip's cock, and

Philip gripped Steve's cock in two hands and stroked him, until, with a cry Philip filled the bulb of his condom.

Steve rose off him then and went across the room to his bureau where he'd put his glass of wine. He watched as Philip cooled down and regained his regular breathing. But when Philip rolled off the bed, stood, and started to walk toward his own wine glass, Steve set his down, walked swiftly toward Philip, picked him up and slammed him down on his back on the edge of the bed, stuffing a pillow under the small of Philip's back to raise his pelvis. Kneeling between Philip's spread legs, Steve's mouth went to Philip's balls and hole, which he attacked with slurping sounds, as Philip arched his back, began to breathe heavily again, and moaned to the ceiling.

It was coming, surely. Surely Steve would fuck him now. Philip was panting with short, ragged breaths, already filling out again. That cock would be inside him soon. He spread his legs as widely as he could in anticipation of what he'd have to take. He was frightened and exhilarated all at once.

Rolling the spent condom off Philip's cock, Steve deepthroated him while he started working lubricated fingers into Philip's hole. Then, standing and crowning his own cock, Steve muttered, "Here's the part where you cry." He reached down to Philip's cock and wound the Esculpta cock ring off its root and transferred it to his own staff. The lions' heads that had overlapped around the root of Philip's quite presentable cock didn't even meet when the cock ring was wrapped around Steve's root.

Philip groaned as the thick cock head pushed in beyond his rim. Steve pushed a little farther, while his hands held Philip's legs and extended them as wide and high as possible. And then he held. But only momentarily. Philip arched his back and did cry out, again and again, and was sobbing within minutes, as Steve thrust his thick cock deep in one long, wrenching motion and then started stroking hard and deep in long, thrusting strokes.

"Holy sweet jezuss," Steve muttered as Philip's channel sucked his cock in deep and Philip started causing his channel muscles to undulate over the thick cock. "You can take me deep, all the way. I don't think I've ever . . ."

Philip didn't have to be told he'd taken all of the cock. He could feel the lions' heads of the Esculpta cock ring rubbing against the rim of his hole. "Oh, daddy, oh, daddy, oh daddy, fuck me deep," he cried out in a monotonous litany as Steve, panting heavily himself, did just that. Philip writhed and bounced around under Steve, as Steve fucked him hard and fast.

"I've never. Oh damn, oh shit, you're good," Steve mumbled with a deep moan of his own. "What you do with those canal muscles . . ."

Steve drove Philip's body up onto the center of the bed with the pile-driving thrusts of his cock, ending up with his knees under Philip's buttocks, and Philip just laying there, spent, his arms akimbo and his head turned to the side, with his mouth yawning in a sloppy grin and creating bubbles and his body jerking slightly with each deep thrust of Steve's cock.

"Shit, you're beautiful like that," Steve muttered. And then he had pulled out of Philip and was gone for a few minutes. But he returned to exactly the same position inside Philip and raised a camera to his face and snapped off some shots of Philip's head and torso in well-fucked dishabille. All the time he continued stroking inside Philip's channel. Then he moved the focus of the camera down to where the lions' heads of the cock ring were rubbing against the rim of Philip's entrance as Steve stroked deep and fired off a few photos. "Still can't believe you're taking all of it," he muttered.

Philip dozed off momentarily soon after Steve had finished him, pulling his cock out, ripping off the Golden Ticket Magnum, and shooting off on Steve's belly in four prodigious ejaculations. His eyes opened to find Steve sitting on a kitchen stool, hovered over the foot of the bed, and his easel in front of him.

He was sketching the after being fucked silly visage of Philip, just like he'd done with all of the young conquests before Philip. Moaning, Philip flopped an arm over his face and tried to shut out the world. It had been a glorious fuck—all that he had hoped for. But it had worn him out.

"Yes, I like that better," Steve muttered, tearing off the sheet of art paper he had been sketching on and then starting all over with a new one. "Keep the arm over the face until I tell you you can move it. And spread your legs more, stuff the pillow back under the small of your back, and bend your legs, putting your feet flat on the mattress. Yes, like that. The widest hole yet, I think. All of it. You took it all."

Philip was asleep before he received permission to move.

In the dark of the night, awakening to discover that he had been stretched out beside Steve on the bed, he only had the briefest moment to think of that because Steve was pulling him up on all fours and mounting his hips and fucking him hard and deep again. He crouched over Philip close and murmured in his ear, "So tight and yet taking it so deep and expertly. Baby, I could fuck you forever."

"It's hard not being tight for a cock like yours," Philip murmured dreamily back. "Yes, there, just like that. Again and again. Oh shit. Oh FUCK! Oh god, you are the best. The very BEST!"

But when he woke in the morning, it was to find he was alone in the bed. Upon inspection, he realized that he was alone in the apartment as well.

This must be what first and only meant to Steve, he thought. So much for "I could fuck you forever." Use them and leave them—without a word of thanks or an assessment of how the other guy had done in the sack. Philip realized, though, that this was what was bothering him the most. Steve had leveled with him on what this was, and, as far as using, Philip had come out cruising looking to use another guy's cock. He hadn't been looking for anything more than a casual fuck. As ferocious as the fucking had been and as taxing as Steve's huge cock was, Philip had to admit that he had loved it. He had never taken a cock that long and thick before, and he felt a sense of accomplishment that he had now. He regretted that they hadn't barebacked. He'd felt the strong repeated release inside the condom when he'd been doggy fucked in the night, and he ached to feel the full flood of it inside him. Truth be known, he had wanted to wake in the morning with that cock working its way into him again—and he resented that it hadn't been there.

What was irritating him now was that Steve wasn't here to assure him that he hadn't been so complimentary on Philip's technique the previous night just to get the last ounce of passion out of him. He had said Philip had a good, hard cock himself, but he had said he'd have to assess how good a lay Philip was later. It was later now, and Steve had evaporated without comment. It wasn't good enough that Steve had told him he was a good lay in the heat of the fuck. Steve had been so detached and analytical before that. Philip wanted to hear Steve tell him he was the best when Steve was in his analytical mode.

The walls spoke of a legion of competitors and Philip was very much a competitor. He wanted to know how he stacked up with the competition. He'd made no bones about telling Steve he was the best. He wanted to hear the same from Steve.

The Esculpta cock ring lay on the dresser. Philip dressed, picked up and pocketed the cock ring as a souvenir of the experience, took the elevator down to Oxford Street, flagged a taxi back to the Grace hotel, stripped, and went straight to bed.

Later that afternoon, Philip heard a persistent knocking on his door. Slipping on a robe, he went to the door and opened it.

"Hello, I don't think we've ever met," Steve, leaning against the door frame, said. He was standing out in the corridor. Just in the gym shorts, athletic T, and flip-flops—no change from the bookshop or dressed any more formally than since that day, which was only the previous day, but seemed so much longer ago than that to Philip. Philip couldn't imagine how Steve had ever made it past reception. But then he'd been to this room in the same thing the previous day and had made it up here. That's how he knew where to come today.

"Of course we've met. You reamed me a new asshole last night. Just as you said you would, and I sobbed, just like you said I would. And then you left me."

"But it was a good sob wasn't it? And where did you go this morning? I went out to get us breakfast—there wasn't anything in the house to feed you. We used all of the eggs I had in the omelet last night, remember? And when I got back you were gone."

"Breakfast? You were coming back?"

"Yes."

"I don't know if I believe you. You said it was in your rules. Just the one day. That was yesterday, not this morning. If you've come for your precious cock ring, stay right there. I'll get it for you."

Philip thought of telling Steve to remain in the corridor and to shut the door while he retrieved the ring, but Steve already had moved inside the room. He stood just inside the open door, though.

"I'm sorry, I don't know what you're talking about," he said. "We've never met before."

Philip was incensed by the mocking smile on the man's face. Was there no end to the power games he played? "Of course we have. We've—"

"Shush," Steve hissed. "Go with me here. There are rules to this. I'm a first and only guy. I want you again. I want to fuck you again and again. But I have rules. I've got to have never met you before. I can't breach too many rules too quickly. But before we agree that this next fuck will be the first and only again—I hope to be followed by the next first and only—I wanted to give you this. I have my two sketches the rules tell me that I must have. This is a third. I've never done this before—done three sketches to keep. I hope you appreciate what that means."

Steve unrolled the sketch he had brought with him. It had been drawn from the photograph Steve had taken of Philip under him being fully fucked. "You told me I was the best.

And I'm telling you that you're the best I've ever had too. Every time you look at this, I want you to remember me—and to remember how totally I was fucking you at this time. How much you were enjoying it."

Steve fucked Philip from behind with Philip bent over the bed, spreading his legs as far apart as possible, spreading his buttocks with his hands as far apart as he could too, and panting and sobbing—and loving every stroke of it.

When they were done and stretched out against each other in the bed, Steve asked in a low voice, "When is your next flight out?"

"Tomorrow, and if I don't get some sleep before then I'll be in no shape to work the flight."

"I've been thinking," Steve said. "I have places in two cities. If you are on this route semipermanently, is there any reason you can't home base in Sydney rather than Los Angeles?"

Surprised, Philip turned his face to Steve, his mouth working but nothing coming out as he had no idea what to say. Steve saved him the embarrassment. He covered Philip's mouth with his, and turned his body toward the side so that he could slip his cock into Philip's now-reamed-to-fit ass in a side split. Once encased, Steve turned Philip belly to bed and used his powerful thighs to trap Philip's legs close together, tightening his channel impossibly on the buried cock.

Philip cried out in surprise, pain, and ecstasy. "God, that's too tight. I can't . . . oh SHIT!"

But Steve was already beginning to stroke deep. "You can and will . . . and will love every stroke of it," he commanded. "I want you as tight as possible."

Whimpering and moaning—but believing himself in heaven and mastered just as he liked—Philip happily settled down. Steve had remembered to wind the lions' head cock ring around the root of his cock—Philip could already feel the silver oblongs of the lions' heads on his rim, which meant Steve was all inside him. Philip hadn't had time to notice whether Steve was wearing a condom. Part of Philip hoped not—he wanted to feel the reward of those repeated strong ejaculations deep inside him—if only for this version of the first and only time.

For the Glory of the Earth

Ervin Walker hiked up to the top of the ridge of the White Oak mountain range as he did every Friday afternoon, weather permitting. He was standing there, looking northwest over the rolling south central Virginia farmland as he had done nearly every Friday from mid afternoon until almost twilight for the past twenty-four years since he had received the call. This was his time to meditate and to let the words he would preach come Sunday morning at the Pentecostal chapel down in Pleasant Gap sink into him. Somehow standing here and looking down into the valley beyond his small farm, his own little slice of heaven, was what gave him his inspiration.

He had been born on this farm and he planned to die on this farm. Others were talking of selling, some because they just could not make a go of it anymore. But his land had come to his family at the time of their freeing, during the War of Succession, and each first son of each generation of the Walkers since then had pledged to remain on the land and to do their work for the glory of the earth. Nothing was more important than preserving the glory of the earth and receiving the bounty gleaned there from days of plenty and fallow alike. That they had received more than their usual share of days of fallow for too long now was one part of the troubles on the land hereabouts, but only one part. It had been seven years. That meant something to Ervin, more apparently than to some of his neighbors who were close to giving up. He had the faith the seven years of famine would be followed by seven years of plenty. He lived by this knowledge, which had seen his family through many generations of troubles with the earth in the valley he now looked down into. His family had known to lay up a good portion of the bounty in the feast years to tide them over in famine years, and they thus far had managed thereby to hold a steady course.

Rain. What they needed was rain. And protection from the outside forces of evil that were descending on this valley. Ervin lifted his arms and looked heavenward, looking for signs of rain, praying for the rain. And, with a thought to the outside forces threatening the valley, he was also listening for that one word or phrase that always came to him late Friday afternoon. The word or phrase around which he would construct the simple message he would impart to the faithful few in his momma's chapel down in Pleasant Gap.

He stood there, for more than an hour, eyes closed, denying himself the glorious sight of his own farm descending from the ridge into the valley below. Denying himself the sin of knowing how prosperous he was compared to many of his neighbors and how fortunate a man of color such as he was to have been from a landowning family these past hundred and fifty years and more. Pushing out the sin of pride—and closing his mind to the other sin, the most powerful of those that plagued him but that he could not withstand—he rocked his solid, muscular body of a man not quite fifty and used to working the land hard with honest, manual labor, and he hummed and opened himself to the word.

When the word came, it was a single word this time, not a phrase, as it often was. It was the word "sacrifice." It entered his mind so strongly, with a thunderclap that tantalized, not promising rain, but marking the shift in fronts and the blast of dry heat, that Ervin knew this was the word he was meant to talk on Sunday morning. And it came to him with such strength that he knew that it was also the key to the valley's broader, more immediate problem. He didn't know how it was key to this, but he often didn't know the purpose of the word he was to preach while he stood on the top of the mountain range. Often fuller knowledge of what he was supposed to say and do came to him while he was doing his Saturday chores, working almost twice as hard on a Saturday as he did any other day of the week because there was to be no toil on Sunday. Sometimes the message didn't enter him until just as he was standing before the congregation on a Sunday morning to let it out of him.

The word had come earlier than usual. It was still daylight when he descended to the split-rail fence line marking the inner yard around the house, where the smaller farm animals and the tractor and old Ford pickup were kept. As he approached the farmyard, he felt his insides tensing up and that old sin tearing at him. There was nothing he could do about that, though. He had tried, but he could not deny that no matter how much he prayed or attempted denial. There were more pressing matters before him; this was a sin so great that he would need that and just that to concentrate on—someday. And now the temptation was overwhelming. He should never have taken Monte, Diamonte Moore, on. But when he had done so, that had been because of another call that came to him on the mountain top. The call that the young man needed his help, needed a chance to fulfill his own destiny.

But maybe it was a testing of himself, of Ervin Walker. If so, Ervin had failed the test. The young man was just too

153

attracting—and, the real downfall, too willing, too pliable. He gave himself without question, with no fuss, no reproofs, just as if it was most natural thing, when every fiber inside Ervin screamed out that it was not natural.

Ervin's eyes went to the young man as he approached the farmyard. Monte was at the wire fencing around the chicken house, on his knees and leaning over at the edge of the wire, repairing it where the chickens had pulled the wire out of the dirt at the base of the fence, and nearly had it separated to the point where they could escape the pen, little knowing that the fence was there to protect them.

The older man ached, as he always did, at the sight of the young man's bare back. Nothing aroused the juices inside the man more than the sight of those young, broad, muscled shoulders. Monte had come to him as an outcast in his last year of high school up in Chatham, where he had withdrawn from the school football team, despite high school football being the end all of everything in this region of the state, because, what was publicly discussed. Monte was drawn to working the land and raising and caring for animals. His teammates and schoolmates had derided him and shunned him—not because he was not suited for football, because he had a magnificently formed body and a talent for the game, but because he would not devote his full time to it—and because of the rumors about what he had done with his body.

Monte also knew what none of his classmates or the school's alumni who were so taken up with the success of the football team knew for sure, although some suspected. Monte knew he couldn't spend time in the school's locker room with other young men without revealing the secret he himself had only learned shortly after his eighteenth birthday when the football coach, Mr. Docrity, had given him a ride home from practice one night and stopped on the banks of Green Creek in a remote location and fucked Monte four ways from Sunday in the bed of his Dodge Ram truck. Monte hadn't minded the fucking. He hadn't struggled or questioned the coach; he'd just laid back in the bed of the truck and opened his legs for the coach to do what he wanted, locking eyes with the coach in a welcoming smile and no more than a moan and grimace and arching of his back and reaching around to grasp the coach's bare buttocks as Docrity's slowly entered him and began to pump. This uncomplicated, full surrender of Monte to the coach's lust inflamed Docrity and caused him to come back again and again for what Monte willingly gave him.

Monte wasn't one to make a fuss; he pretty much went with whatever the flow was as dictated by anyone in authority over him.

After two months of football practice and long rides home by the coach, Monte's teammates had started to razz him about what he was giving the coach. Monte, uncomplicated in his sexuality, would have told they what he'd given the coach, but Docrity had forbidden him to do that. The young man had been too conflicted by the directions in which he was being pulled to remain on the team. And while withdrawing from the team, he'd withdrawn from most of the rest of life as well.

Withdrawing even from Chatham wasn't totally Monte's choice. As rumors spread of what the coach was doing with Monte, it was Monte who took the pressure. The coach had taken the football team to state semifinals four years in a row. It wasn't the coach who was going to be taken to task. It had to be the student who led him on and robbed him of his resistance. And the coach wasn't going to stop fucking Monte by his own decision. Monte wasn't planning on giving up the coach either, but the second time he was taken into the shadows behind the school gym, beaten by his former teammates, and told to get out of town, he did so—as soon as he picked up his high school diploma.

Monte's shyness and ostracism had led his school counselor, a childhood friend of Ervin's, to approach Ervin about taking the boy in to explore his love for animal husbandry on a farm—a farm a good distance from Chatham—as soon as he finished school and until his classes at the community college in Danville, to the southeast, commenced. Little did the counselor know the temptation and perpetuation of an "issue" she was creating for both the young man and for Ervin.

She had never known why Ervin's wife had left him.

Ervin walked up behind the crouching Monte and placed a hand on the young man's shoulder. Having heard the older man approaching, Monte didn't flinch.

"I'm fixin' the wire so they can't peck their way out," he murmured.

"I see that you are, You're doing a fine job of it," Ervin answered in a low, hoarse voice.

Monte turned his head and looked up at the older man, a knowing look entering his eyes. Both of Ervin's hands were on Monte's bare shoulders and he moved them, gliding down to the young man's shoulder blades. The feel of the hard muscles on a young man's back was a fetish for Ervin, bringing out urges he couldn't resist. He stood back up, his knees now touching Monte's back, but stayed standing only long enough to unbutton his shirt and spread it apart. Then he bent over the young man's back again, letting out a low moan, and his bare chest closed over the muscular back of the crouched younger man, his taut nipples rubbing against Monte's shoulder blades. Ervin reached around with one hand and cupped Monte's chin and turned and raised Monte's face to him. Monte's lips opened to Ervin's. A growl deep inside Ervin's chest marked the feeble attempt he was making to deny his sin. His free hand went to palm one of Monte's pecs, his thumb finding and rubbing over the nub of Monte's nipple.

The young man's body trembled under the caressing touch of the rough toil-callused hands of the older, more experienced man. Leaving Monte's breast, Ervin's hand moved down Monte's hard belly, unbuttoned the fly of his worn jeans, and wrapped itself around Monte's engorging cock.

Disengaging from the kiss, but their eyes still locked on each other's, Monte gave Ervin a shy look, and asked, almost in a whisper. "You gonna fuck me again today before chores are done, Mr. Walker?"

"Come into the house now," Ervin answered in a hoarse, strangled voice. "The fence is secured good enough for now."

"You gonna fuck me good?"

156

"Just come into the house, Monte."

"Yes, sir." Obediently, without hesitation, Monte stood and followed Ervin into the house.

Ervin fucked Monte on Monte's bed. It was always on Monte's bed, not Ervin's. Ervin slept in the same bed his parents had slept in—and his father's parent's before that. It was the bed Ervin's mother had birthed him in and the bed both she and his father had died in—the bed Ervin assumed he would die in too. And maybe his son, Tyrone, after him, the son that Ervin's wife had taken away with her when Ervin was discovered to be having his way with Lamont Jackson a couple of farms over.

They fucked on Monte's bed. And they fucked the way Ervin liked it, Monte on all fours or on his belly, and Ervin crouched over his young, well-muscled back, kissing and biting the curves and contours of the young man's back and rubbing his nipples on Monte's shoulder blades, while he stroked Monte's ass in long, deep strokes. Monte panted under Ervin as the older man moved from loving caresses and holding his thick cock at the root and revolving it in Monte's channel, guided by Monte's gasps and murmurs of "yes, there, like that. Fuck me good, Mr. Walker," as Ervin snaked a hand around Monte's waist and stroked his cock to ejaculation.

Monte sexually relieved, Ervin continued stroking, progressively sinking into lust and beyond-control need. They ended with Monte, always all-out passionate and vocal, not holding out on wanting the fuck, crying out, "Ram me! Ram it hard. Yes. Again and again!" And, lost in the primordial fuck, Ervin did just that, pulling out of the younger man's canal with a cry at the end and barely getting the condom ripped off his shaft before he shot his load, in three strong bursts, across the small of Monte's back and collapsed on top of the young man's trembling body.

"That were a good fuck, Mr. Walker. Thank you kindly."

Ervin turned his head, not wanting Monte to see his pained expression, his humiliation of giving into his lust again—and being thanked for it.

Once Monte was into a fuck, he went as whole hog as any young, randy stud, wanting more of it, harder and deeper. And he could be a screamer for it. As casual as he was in giving it away, he could really turn a man on with how intense he was in the clutch.

Sometimes when Ervin felt he wanted the fuck more than once, he'd remain in Monte's bed and they would doze between takings. As submissive as he'd been to the coach's demands in the bed of his truck or the backseat of his car and grateful to Ervin for taking him in and permitting him to work on the farm for pay before his first year in community college—and feeling protected by having an older man who wanted to make love to his body—Monte uncomplainingly fell in with whatever mood or servicing request Ervin made. He never was the one to ask for a fuck, but he never denied Ervin when Ervin wanted it. He had never denied or hesitated with the coach, either, not even that first time.

On occasion, Ervin worried about Monte's pliability, but his own sin was so great that he didn't want to worry about it too much or for too long.

Monte never questioned Ervin's need to gain sexual satisfaction through him at all. The young man's greatest interest was in working on the farm and, specifically, with the animals. Watching animals breed—and sometimes the males trying to breed with each other—was taken by Monte as just the natural way of nature. He assumed that he would ask for sex from Ervin just in the natural scheme of nature if Ervin didn't ask it of him nearly twice a day, fully satiating the needs of even a young, vigorous man in his prime. And Ervin was thicker, could reach deeper, and could stroke longer than Coach Docrity had been able to do. Monte did wonder on occasion whether a younger man could do him even better, but he was in no particular hurry to find out.

He also wondered about being fucked by a white man—if that would be any different from being fucked by the coach or Ervin. He never thought about the morality of being fucked by any man—only about the pleasure he could get and receive from it.

During the day, Ervin could approach and fuck Monte almost anywhere where there was cover. He didn't like to do it out in the open, saying that he couldn't do it with the thought that his sin could be so openly observed from the heavens. But the cover of the shed they called a barn, or inside the pickup cab, or under bushes in the shadow of the house had all been taken advantage of when Ervin's lust got the best of him, which usually was when he saw Monte crouched over, showing the curve of his magnificent, young, hard, bare back.

At night, they always did it in Monte's bed, though. And when he was done, Ervin would return to his own bed, always alone. While moving between the beds, he would admonish himself for giving into his sin. But once in his parents' bed he gave not a whisper of his weakness. In his parents' bed, although a sinner he was, there was no inkling of his deepest, darkest sin. As long as he didn't do it in that bed, surely his ancestors knew nothing of his great failing.

* * * *

"I thought this was all goin' on cross county at the Coles Hill farm."

"EnergyFuture Incorporated is actually looking in several locations," the handsome man with the squared-away Marine look, blond buzz cut, and jeans and sport shirt tailored to fit in but still a bit too stylish for Danville, answered.

The question had come from the audience in the meeting room of the public library on the north side of Danville, Virginia. It was the first of the evening that had even a hint of critical question behind it, and Ervin was beginning to be convinced that the movie-star-handsome corporate representative booked to talk to this open meeting on Saturday evening had salted the audience with supporters of the plan to open up a uranium mine in his valley. Thus far the man, who was all smiles and glib talk and flirty looks at the grinning women present, had called on questioners by raised hands. This was resulting in softball questions from folks Ervin had never seen before to his recollection. And Ervin was pretty

159

sure he knew everyone living in the White Creek valley. This last question had been impatiently called out from the audience by one of the valley farmer's Ervin did know, Bill Kemp.

"What about the health hazards of uranium mining?" a woman's thin, crackly voice with a patrician Southern accent floated out over the audience. Ervin could hear a groan go up from many of those in the room he didn't recognize.

"We have plenty of literature on that laid out on the table here, Ms. Harrison. You are welcome to take any of it home with you. And you'll notice that Pittsylvania County's congressional delegation up in Washington has, to a man, written endorsements on those studies."

"Well, Bob, Mark, and Tim are all up in Washington, D.C.," Sadie Harrison called out in a dry voice. "I'm just a bit more interested in the health of those who will be living down here with all that radioactive uranium being brought up from our earth here abouts and refined right here. You did say it was to be refined right here, didn't you?"

The groan, reminiscent of the canned laughter tracts used in TV situation comedies from the previous century, rose again across the audience packed into the windowless library meeting room.

They have come prepared, Ervin thought. That man—Jack Carson, the representative EnergyFuture sent down from Richmond to charm folks into numb brains, to contain and nullify any opposition, and to get land purchases started had done his homework. He even had known who Sadie Harrison was and that she would be a major focus of his problem mitigating the opposition to what EnergyFuture—and Richmond—wanted to do here. She was perhaps the wealthiest person in the northwest corner of the Pittsylvania County. She was as old as the White Oak mountains and her family had been wealthy landowners here since the Revolutionary War. She herself had indexed that she knew everyone who was worth knowing when she had used the first names of the state congressional delegation representing this region in Washington. She also was known as a leading environmental and animal rights advocate in a county known for its

160

ultraconservatism and as a hunter's paradise. She was the major supporter of the county's SPCA, which she insisted that it maintain a no-kill policy.

As, smiling an "I'm not the least bit worried how this is turning smile," Jack Carson raised his arms to show that he wanted to tamper down the audience reaction before he gave a "reasonable" answer to Sadie Harrison's "obviously" impertinent questions.

Ervin stole a glance at Monte in the folding chair beside his to see what the young man's reaction to all of this was. Monte seemed to be wide-eyed and fascinated. His attention was glued to the handsome, confident-acting man standing on the platform at the front of the room.

"As I noted earlier, the refining aspect is very important for the local economy," Carson said, casting an indulgent smile in the general direction in which Sadie Harrison was sitting in the dimly lit room. "Your political representatives have lobbied hard with EnergyFuture to establish a mine in the White Creek valley area. It will bring several hundred jobs to this region."

"Jobs for folks in Pittsylvania County, or workers from elsewhere?" Lamont Jackson, one of the small-holding farmers a few holdings north of Ervin's farm and Ervin's erstwhile lover, called out. Ervin knew that Lamont was one of the farmers who was really hurting and probably would sell out to EnergyFuture if he could—and would probably be one of the first in line for a job with the company if it came here. Although this saddened Ervin, he could understand the financial spot Lamont was in. Lamont's wife hadn't been as forgiving as Ervin's wife had been. She took him for all he was worth, which wasn't much, when she left him.

Of course, it was Ervin's own sin that had led to Lamont's wife leaving him, just as Ervin's wife had left Ervin. That had been enough of a shock—especially having lost visiting rights with his own son—to Ervin that he had been able to deny himself for over a year, during which he lived a solitary life. And then Monte had come to the farm. Monte had not seduced him; he had merely done what Monte did—moved around shirtless, exposing his magnificent back to Ervin. And then, when Ervin's weakness got the better of him, merely lifting his tail to Ervin, as Ervin covered his back, and letting Ervin slide inside him.

"Both, of course," Carson answered. "We would hire in the county and bring in specialists from elsewhere if we could not fill those jobs with local hires. No matter where the workers come from, though, they would be bolstering the region's economy."

Lamont tried a follow-up question on just how many of the jobs would be open to locals and how specialized these jobs were, but Carson was already concentrating on locating the next questioner, and those sitting around Lamont shushed him down.

Carson managed to recognize the raised hand of one of the softball question pitchers, who droned off into a longwinded question that most likely was designed to put everyone to sleep. Instead of dozing, though, Ervin looked over at the large map chart that was an on easel on the platform beside where the company huckster—as Ervin thought of Carson—was positioned.

Ervin had come thinking he'd have to fight for his land, but seeing from the chart on the easel that this wasn't so had kept him more quiet on the question end than he thought he'd be. The chart showed that the boundary of the holdings the company was seeking to acquire came up to the edge of his farm but didn't encroach on it. From the pattern, he could see why this maybe was so. His farm lined up with the vast land holdings of Sadie Harrison—it was Sadie's family that had owned Ervin's once and thus the small section at the edge of Harrison land that the Walker family had been given. The lines appeared to have been purposely drawn to keep her property out of the holdings the mining company sought, evidently to try to keep her from fighting the acquisition. But if they thought that would satisfy or deter Sadie Harrison, Ervin thought, neither EnergyFuture nor the politicians and lobbyists supporting them in Richmond and Washington knew Sadie Harrison very well. Better that they had waited for the old woman to die. Of course she'd probably outlive everyone in the valley—out of sheer meanness.

Of even greater interest to Ervin in viewing the chart after he had recovered from the discovery that his own land wasn't in danger was the pattern of land already owned by the mining company and that yet to be acquired. The two categories were denoted by different-colored overlays. Viewing the chart revealed that it looked like a crazy quilt. It occurred to Ervin that the company would have to control most of the land and still had to acquire several key acreages owned by others to be able to have a mining operation at all.

He was snapped out of this reverie by another called out question from Bill Kemp, shouted out over the convoluted dissertation being given by the man Carson had recognized from the audience.

"What kind of mine is this going to be? Tunnel or open pit?"

"And what about the radiation problems of an open pit uranium mine?" Sadie Harrison called out. "Won't rain bring up the radiation, and the other weather hazards too—we've had hurricanes and tornadoes go through here. Even had an earthquake as recent as three years ago."

"The dangers are minimal at best. Everything is covered in these studies here," Jack Carson answered over the hubbub of those protesting one side of the issue or the other. "But I see someone from the library staff signaling from in back. I'm afraid we'll have to give up the room now. We will, of course, schedule more town meetings on this. We have appreciated the opportunity to tell you what a godsend this will be for this part of Pittsylvania County."

Several residents of the land affected tried to move forward to talk with Carson as the meeting was breaking up, but some of the others were there before them—some of the obvious company plants—and evidently were going to engage in filibuster conversation until there was no time for anyone else to talk with him.

"Let's go, Monte," Ervin said, turning to the young man sitting beside him. "It's obvious this is a put-up job.

163

Should've known. Makes me thirsty. Let's finish the day at the Roadhouse."

At hearing the name of the Roadhouse spoken, Monte came out of the trance he was in of watching the hunky-looking representative of EnergyFuture Incorporated continue to work the room. They'd serve him anything he wanted there, and it was a bar, out in the country off of Route 29 between Danville and Chatham, where the likes of Ervin and he could be comfortable.

Giving Ervin a big smile, he uncoiled from the folding chair and voiced a cheery, "Ready." Still, his gaze remained on the squared-away Marine type, Jack Carson, until he and Ervin had cleared the meeting room.

As they got into the truck, Ervin said, trying to make it sound off hand, "You looked at that white man like you could eat him. He's city and white, Monte. Not in the same universe with you. He's also a real pole cat, the likes of which you don't want to mix with."

"Ain't seen a white man put together that good is all," Monte answered. "Still, I wouldn't say no if he wanted to eat me."

It was all said so naturally. Ervin gripped the steering wheel hard. Ervin wondered if Monte would ever lose his innocence about sex. He hoped not.

* * * *

Ervin didn't give a second thought as to anyone else, certainly not anyone he didn't want to see, going on from the uranium mine proposal meeting to the Roadhouse bar, which was a good twenty miles north of Danville. The Roadhouse catered to men like Ervin—and now Monte—in the evening hours, men who enjoyed the company of men and who might leave the place with a man they didn't come in with. Later, after midnight, it was likely to get rowdy and there'd be some entertainment on the platform by the bar, most likely put on by the young black guy, Slick, who took care of the table trade earlier in the evening. There might even be some action in one or more of the back rooms down the corridor to the john.

The meeting had gone on longer than Ervin thought it would, so he and Monte were arriving at the bar near to 11:30, within the transition time for clientele. All Ervin intended to do was to have one drink there and go on home and, because he was so keyed up from the meeting, fuck Monte silly. He'd make Monte forget the white man at the meeting. He didn't want to stay until midnight mainly because he didn't like having Monte in the bar for the late-night crowd. Monte was like honey to the latter-shift men, who tended to be rough trade, truck drivers and construction workers from down in Danville. Ervin didn't want Monte getting sniffed around by men like this. Monte was of a pretty basic nature, and it was clear that he felt no guilt about having sex with men. Ervin was afraid that the late-night clientele would eat Monte up—and that Monte just might let them.

As willing as Monte was, Ervin was confident that there had only been the coach and him. Monte had no concept of what a gang bang by truckers could be.

Ervin was only half way through his drink, though, when he was given reason to stay on past midnight. Speaking of the devil, which Ervin had occasion to talk about from time to time, he was about to chug his drink and tell Monte to down his too so they could leave, Ervin not liking the look being cast Monte's way from a burly guy with big muscles and curly red hair who had been getting out of a semitrailer out front when Ervin and Monte drove up, when who walked through the door but Lamont Jackson. And behind him, already looking like he owned the place, came that EnergyFuture shyster, Jack Carson.

As soon as Carson saw Monte, he gave a big smile, which then turned, but only briefly, to more of a scowl when he saw Ervin standing alongside Monte at the bar. Ervin could see, out of the corner of his eye, that Monte was returning the smile.

Slick almost ran to Lamont and Carson to show them to a table and to pay particular attention to Carson. Ervin had to allow that Carson wasn't the hulkiest guy in the bar now, but he probably was the hunkiest one. In the phenomena that exists in instant selection in male-on-male cruising, most of the catchers in the room were casting eyes of interest on Carson, while most of the pitchers—who until now had been watching Monte—were eyeing him as possible competition. Slick was nearly drooling over him and couldn't get him anything he wanted fast enough.

Ervin knew that Lamont was one of the guys—it had been Ervin himself who had initiated Lamont to this life—but he was surprised that Carson was. Since the man was in this environment, though, there was no doubting by the way he cased the room, that he knew what kind of bar this was and why he was here—and that he could get any bottom in the room to lie down for him and open his legs to him.

But his eyes kept going to Monte.

Lamont didn't seem too happy to be here with him, but no doubt Carson had correctly gauged Lamont's leaning either at the meeting or earlier in land purchase discussions with him and had pressed Lamont to bring him here. He'd had time to lay Lamont between the meeting and arriving here, and Ervin saw no reason not to assume that he'd done so. It also seemed evident that Carson knew that they would be following Ervin and Monte here—and that Carson's primary interest was in Monte. Something in the disappointment Lamont showed told Ervin that, no matter what Carson had done with Lamont, the interest he'd shown in talking with Lamont was in Monte— that even as he was pumping Lamont's ass, he probably was asking him about Monte.

Ervin hadn't been aware of the buildup to this back at the meeting, but now, in hindsight, having Carson's interests pegged, he realized that Carson had been doing a whole lot of looking in Monte's direction. He already knew that Monte had done lots of looking at Carson, and Monte had been straight-up open afterward about his interest in Carson.

Ervin turned his face toward the bar, ordered another beer, and told Monte he could have one too. Then he put a possessive arm around Monte and Monte just sort of folded into him. Ervin didn't need the drink, but he wanted to invest a little time into signaling to Carson that Monte was taken. That's why they'd be staying longer in the bar than he originally had intended to.

He took a couple of peeks in the direction of the table that Lamont and Carson were sitting at and saw that they were deep in conversation—probably haggling over the sale of Lamont's farm—and that Slick was still buzzing around them. The next thing he knew, though, when he took a look, Carson was no longer at the table, and Lamont was sinking into his glass of beer and looking not the least bit happy.

Ervin looked around the room but didn't see the huckster from Richmond. He half expected to find that he was circling in on Monte even though Ervin still had the young man in a clutch, but he just wasn't around.

"Stay put here for a few minutes, and drink up," Ervin said to Monte. "I have to go take a piss, and we'll go on home when I get back."

"Sure thing," Monte said. There were some wooden puzzles scattered out on the bar top, and Monte was absorbed in trying to put one of those together.

The john was at the end of a corridor off the back through a doorway covered with a beaded curtain. There were small rooms off the corridor on either side on the way back that were rented out in fifteen-minute increments. Ervin saw, in passing to the back, that Jack Carson and Slick occupied one of these rooms. Carson was seated on the side of a cot and Slick was kneeling between his thighs and sucking him off. When Ervin returned from the john, he could see that Carson had proceeded to pull Slick onto his lap, both of them naked from the waist down, and was lap fucking the young man. Slick was revolving his ass on Carson's buried dick, and his tongue was lolling out of his mouth like he'd never been fucked this good before, which was hard to believe as often as he'd been spiked.

Good, Ervin thought. That will hold the fucker long enough for me to get Monte out of the bar.

But Ervin had a different problem when he pushed through the beaded curtain and out into the main room. Monte appeared to be gone already. His beer glass was empty and the puzzle he'd been working on was put together—Monte was clever in fixing things—but Monte wasn't in the room. Neither was the muscle-bound, red-headed trucker.

He found them out in the parking lot. The passenger-side door—the one toward the shadows at the back of the parking lot—of the semitrailer's cab was hanging open. The trucker, bare legged, was standing on the running board, facing the interior of the cab. Monte's construction-booted feet were wedged at the top of the door frame, front and back. His legs were bare otherwise as well. From the movement of the trucker and the grunts and groans, Ervin knew that Monte was getting fucked hard and fast.

He didn't intervene. The trucker was a lot bigger, more heavily muscled, and very likely much meaner than Ervin was. The trucker also was white and there was a filled gun rack mounted on the back wall of the semi cab, which Ervin clearly could see, and which the trucker could get to before Ervin could anywhere close to him. Ervin hadn't survived in this rural part of Virginia by taking risks and asserting rights. And he had no right to Monte, really. If the young man wanted a younger man than Ervin fucking him from time to time, even if he was white, Ervin didn't really see that he could kick about that.

And from the noises Monte was making, he was clearly enjoying himself. Ervin just wished that Monte didn't give it away so easily and naturally. Even there, though, Ervin, who was very much aware of his own sinning in this respect, wasn't going to be hypocritical about how easily Monte was prepared to give it away.

After the trucker was finished, he pretty much pulled Monte out of the cab and deposited him on the ground in a heap. He then pulled on his jeans and was zipping himself up as he walked around the front of the truck, got in the driver's side, and pulled the semi out of the parking lot and down the road, not even glancing back at Monte.

Ervin rushed over to Monte's side, but he could clearly see that Monte was moaning and had a big grin on his face. He was still humming and giving a little smile in the Ford pickup on the way back to White Creek valley. All that he said was, "He gave me twenty dollars, and he had a right good cock. First white man I've had."

When Ervin got him back in the farmhouse and on his bed, Monte allowed as how Ervin had a right good cock too—and that from what he'd experienced so far, black cock was a whole lot bigger than white cock.

Ervin didn't fuck him in anger. It was more with relief that Monte didn't show any change in opening up for Ervin after having it rough from a trucker and in a concern at how innocent Monte seemed to be and how easily he could be taken advantage of—and some anger at himself for not being able to resist joining those who couldn't resist fucking Monte.

A large part of the attraction to Ervin of Monte was the young man's earthiness—how naturally he took to the sex, how willing he was to celebrate it and to give and take without constraint—and how gloriously beautiful he was in his natural state. Ervin felt the same way about Monte that he felt about his own farm and about White Oak valley.

* * * *

Chock full of remorse but fully recognizing that the flesh wasn't going to lose its weakness anytime soon, on Sunday morning, in the old one-room schoolhouse in Pleasant Gap that his mother had converted into a church, Ervin gave an impassioned sermon on the word he'd been given on the ridgetop the previous Friday—sacrifice. He was just letting the word pour through and out of him as it would. He had little idea what he was preaching, and the five other people in the small room—the Lincoln sisters on the front row, whispering gossip to each other; old Jethro, dozing and his hearing aide turned off three rows back; and the spooning couple right on the back row—weren't trying very hard to follow him either.

169

In the middle of his gyrations, Ervin stopped dead in his tracks. For the first time he really paid attention to the word—to the word "sacrifice." None of the others seemed to realize he'd even stopped. The meaning of the word suddenly hit him—not the meaning for this sermon, but the meaning for what was going on in the life of the valley.

Pronouncing a quick benediction, with the Lincoln sisters suddenly becoming aware, in shock and guilty pleasure, that the service was drawing to a close—a full half hour earlier than usual—Ervin bowed to the faithful and nearly ran from the building and headed back to the farm to begin a series of phone calls, calling a meeting for that evening.

* * * *

Ervin and Monte were belly up to the bar at the Roadhouse in the hour approaching midnight on Monday night. Ervin had never brought Monte here before on a Monday night, and it didn't escape Monte that this was unusual. For the first time the young man seemed to be nervous being here. To a great extent the crowd there was composed of the same men who had been there Saturday night. That wasn't particularly a surprise, because Pittsylvania County was a sparsely populated rural one, and there are only so many men around such an area who were out in the open enough to come to the Roadhouse regularly. Lamont Jackson was there, as was Slick. Slick seemed always to be there. The trucker from Saturday night wasn't there, but Ervin figured he wouldn't be there—hoped he wouldn't be there; counted on him not being there, in view of how often Monte had mentioned how much he'd enjoyed being rough fucked half in and half out of the semi cab—because he wasn't a regular patron of the Roadhouse. Ervin figured he'd just been passing through on a long-haul transport.

Lamont was standing with Ervin and Monte at the bar. Monte was fidgeting, looking around the room, once again a major attraction, but not being able to hold eye contact with any of the men who obviously wanted him.

170

Along about 11:30, even Jack Carson was there, having come in, looked around, spied Monte and smiled, and then gone to a table to be slobbered over by Slick. Monte settled down a bit after Carson appeared and did give him shy smiles now and again. But the hand that picked up his beer glass still trembled like it never had before in the Roadhouse.

Not more than fifteen minutes after that, the fire sirens started going off, following the telephone lines up from Chatham. There was such a siren on the roof of the Roadhouse, but the signal was heard from up Route 29 before it got to the Roadhouse. Ervin and a couple of the other men were chugging their beers at the first sound of the distant alarm and preparing to race their trucks to the nearest fire house, which was in the small town of Dry Fork. Ervin was a volunteer fireman; Monte wasn't.

"I gotta answer the call," Ervin told Monte in a loud voice. "You need to catch a ride back to the farm with someone else. Lamont can take you." Ervin didn't wait for an answer. He pushed off from the bar and headed out to his truck.

Ervin had said that loud enough for the whole room to have heard him, it would seem, so he had every reason to assume that Lamont had. But the siren had just gone off on the roof, so there was competition for his voice.

Whether or not Lamont heard Ervin, about ten minutes after Ervin left, so did Lamont—without taking Monte. Monte had been looking over at the table where Jack Carson sat—looking back at Monte—and he didn't even notice Lamont leaving. He looked around and, not seeing Lamont anywhere, he looked back at Jack Carson's table. Jack Carson was smiling and waving for Monte to join him. Monte took a deep swig of his beer; breathed deeply, almost hiccupping from the nervous catch in his breath; and pushed off from the bar.

Half way back to Ervin's farm from the Roadhouse, Jack Carson pulled his EnergyFuture Land Rover off onto a lane leading to the banks of White Oak Creek. He cut off the engine and turned in the seat, facing Monte.

"You know I've had my eye on you since the meeting down in Danville," he said in a low, hoarse voice. "You're a right fine strapping young man."

"I 'spose," Monte said shyly, his legs spread and his arms hanging down between them. He was looking down at the floor mat between his legs.

"You haven't asked why I pulled off the road."

Monte didn't answer or look up.

"You're not the least bit curious why?"

"I reckon I know why."

"And it doesn't bother you?"

"I reckon not."

"You know what kind of bar that was that we were just in, don't you, Diamonte?" It didn't escape Monte that Carson had taken the time to learn his name. Monte hadn't given him a name.

"They call me Monte. Yes, I know."

"That man I always see you with, the scratch farmer, Ervin Walker. Is he your man? Do you lie under him?"

"Yeah, he's my man."

"I heard tell you got fucked out in the parking lot Saturday night by a trucker. That true?"

"Yeah. It was OK. He paid me."

"And this Walker guy. Did he know about it? Was it OK with him?"

"Seems like. He lets me make my own decisions, do what I want."

"Lift your head and look at me, Monte."

Monte did so, but he didn't only look into Carson's eyes. Carson's thick cock was rising up outside of his fly and standing straight up.

"You see how I'm interested in you, how badly I want you, Monte? Do you like the looks of me as well as that trucker? Or Walker? You going to make me work hard at this?"

There was a pause, and then, letting his held breath out in a long sigh, Monte said, "No, sir."

"No what?"

"No, I ain't gonna make you work hard for it. I knew this was what you wanted when you pulled off the road. I knew it when you offered me the ride home."

"I'll pay you fifty dollars for it."

"That would be right nice, thank you."

Carson leaned over and, putting his hands on either side of Monte's head, brought his face in for a kiss. The kiss didn't last too long, though. Carson obviously was anxious to get right to business. Without releasing Monte's face, coming out of the kiss, Carson just continued pulling Monte's face down to his lap onto his already-released, engorging cock.

After Monte had sucked Carson until the white man was close to blowing and had to push him off, they fucked in the backseat of the Land Rover, with Monte giving Carson his money's worth by straddling the thighs of the sitting older man, facing him, and riding Carson's thick cock.

Carson encircled Monte's body with his arms and nuzzled his face into Monte's shoulder as they cooled off from the fuck in which they had ejaculated nearly simultaneously, Carson filling up the bulb of a Magnum and Monte shooting off up Carson's flat belly. His pent up lust taken care of, Carson wanted to take more time playing. His lips went to Monte's nipples and Monte arched his back to accommodate Carson's play. They kissed now in long, breathtaking moments with plenty of tonguing.

"That was extra nice," Carson said as they came out of a kiss.

"You're extra big," Monte murmured.

"You cramping? You want to come off it?"

"No, not yet. I like you deep inside me. We can do it again, if you want. You don't have to pay more. I liked it. Your cock is as good as a black man's."

"God, you seem so natural and casual with it. Are you this way with any man who wants to fuck you?"

"Not just anyone. But the ones I want to fuck, yes."

"And you wanted to fuck me?"

"Yeah, since the meeting in the library."

"It's a turn-on that you take it natural like this."

"Why not? Animals fuck. We're animals, ain't we? It's the way of nature. If you want me and I want you, why not?"

"Why not indeed. And tomorrow you can let Ervin Walker fuck you too and you feel no guilt that I fucked you tonight?"

"No. Why? Mr. Walker, he don't own me. And he says he sees it that way too. Otherwise I'd probably not be with him. And it's only for the summer."

"Only for the summer? So you aren't tied to Walker?"

"No, I'm goin' to community college in the fall."

"I see. I'd like to see you again. You think Walker would let you be out for a night?"

"Uh, I'm not sure . . ."

"I'd pay you a hundred dollars for a night."

"Well, then . . ."

"I've got use of a cabin over on the Dan River below Boyd's mountain. Maybe in a week or two . . ."

"Why not right now?"

"Now's not a good time. I've got these land deals to work. Another couple of weeks and . . . oh shit . . . what the fuck!"

Monte had swiveled around on the cock, facing the front of the Land Rover. He had planted the heels of his feet in the floor of the vehicle and gripped the tops of the front seats with his hands and was pushing back and forth with his channel on Carson's cock, fucking himself hard and deep on the shaft. Immediately lost to the moment, Carson grabbed Monte's waist in his hands and helped with the push and pull as he threw his head back and howled to the ceiling of the vehicle.

"Cabin now. Cabin now," Monte was chanting in a mantra.

They were barely in the front door of the cabin, when Carson pushed Monte down on all fours on an oval braided rug, mounted him like a dog, and rode him for a half hour.

On the second day, when Carson's interest seemed to be flagging a bit, Monte begged to be fucked in the shower and then to have his wrists bound to the headboard and for Carson

174

to punish him roughly. Any time there was a gleam in Carson's eyes in response to something that could be done in sex, Monte wanted to do it. There was nothing that Carson could conceivably think of asking Monte to do that Monte wouldn't do.

Monte kept Carson in the Dan River cabin for three days, riding the cock and being ridden by the cock in every conceivable location and position and time of day or night.

On the afternoon of the third day, Carson asked Monte to go back with him to Richmond. There he could enroll in a community college that Carson would pay for, and Carson would set him up in a small apartment. Carson's wife need know nothing of the arrangement, Carson said. He had gotten away with such an arrangement before.

* * * *

The afternoon of the fourth day, Ervin had the hood up on his Ford pickup and was seeing what he could do about keeping the truck going through another winter, when he sensed he wasn't alone. He looked up and saw Monte opening the gate of the fence surrounding the farmyard. The young man looked hot and tired—as if he'd been walking for miles. And, as it turned out, he had been. Jack Carson had let him off out on Route 41, and Monte had walked the dusty dirt back road into the farm.

As Monte approached, Ervin came out from underneath the hood and turned toward the young man. Monte was only wearing jeans and was barefoot. Ervin was the same.

"You've come back."

"Yes."

"To pick up your things or to stay?"

"To stay through the summer. Like we agreed."

"You been with that EnergyFuture huckster, Jack Carson, all this time?"

"Yes, sir."

"Thought so. Haven't seen him around."

"Was it long enough?"

"Yes."

"Good."

"He treat you right?"

"Nothing to complain about. Got a nice cock and can ride all night."

"OK, then. Best you get under the spigot and wash down."

Ervin watched Monte as the young man went over to the spigot next to the horse trough. Monte unbuttoned his fly and stripped off his jeans. Then he bent over to get his head under the spigot.

A low growl came up from deep inside Ervin's chest and, trembling, he walked to Monte, stripping off his own jeans as he moved. His eyes were on the curve of Monte's naked back. That image was what aroused Ervin the most. And it had been four days of foregoing his needs, living the sacrifice.

Monte felt the strong hands on his waist, and he moved to the side, as they guided him, coming down on his belly on the rim of the nearly empty horse trough, letting his head drop down into the trough and grabbing the far rim of the trough with his fists, while Ervin kissed and stroked his back with gliding hands. There was no resistance in the young man whatsoever. It was like he hadn't been gone the three days and more. There'd be no apologizing—indeed Ervin couldn't imagine that there would be—and Monte was as ready to be spiked by Ervin as he ever was.

Ervin's hands glided down Monte's back from his shoulder blades to the small of his back, where they fanned outward to the young man's hips. Monte raised his hips as Ervin's meaty cockhead moved into the crack and dragged across the puckering hole, again and again, while Monte gasped and sighed.

"Yes," Monte murmured in a husky voice, "Put it in me. Fuck me, daddy. Be good to me."

There was no hesitancy, no resistance.

Ervin's hands tightened over Monte's bulbous buttocks and spread them as his cock head pressed against the hole and pressed into the cavity.

Monte gasped and pushed back on the cock, taking it inside him. "Ride me, daddy. Fuck me deep."

So natural; so giving, Ervin thought. No hesitancy in the young man. Freely giving and taking pleasure. So . . . earthy. It would be a sacrifice to give him up.

Then Ervin was inside Monte, stroking him vigorously and hard and singing his hallelujahs to the noonday sun above, not caring who or what saw them. Though this be sin, his mind screamed, he would make the most of it.

Thrusting again and again. Monte pushing his rump back onto the cock, crying for more of it, deeper and harder. The two of them coming in a gush, almost simultaneously, Ervin flooding Monte's channel deep, as the urgency had provided no opportunity for niceties. Monte arching back to him after the ejaculation, the two men kissing deeply, Monte whispering that Ervin could do it again, if he wanted. Monte not begging for it now, but not avoiding it either. Always ready, always open for it.

"That white shyster's cock as good as mine?" Ervin couldn't help himself from asking, looking for some shred of dignity from what he couldn't help doing.

"Naw. I figure yours is better," Monte said. "But his was good too."

After lunch, they both climbed up the White Oak mountain ridge, sat near to each other on a rock, and stared down into the valley. It was Friday, Ervin's day to open himself to the word for Sunday's preaching. He was too full of the moment, though, to meditate. He wanted Monte up here, looking around the valley, for a time—to see and understand what he had sacrificed for. Afterward, Ervin would send him back down to the farm and would mediate for a word. He would cheat today, though. He sometimes did, but he always pretended that the word only came to him after meditating up here. He already knew, however, that the word that would come to him today would be "thanksgiving."

177

"See how beautiful it is down there?" Ervin asked.

"Yes."

"Pristine farm land. Never developed as anything else but fields and meadows—for more than three hundred years—and maybe longer, by the Indians, before that."

They were both silent for a few minutes, their hands entwined.

"And, thanks to you, it will stay that way."

They were silent again, gazing out over the valley.

"Did you have any trouble getting that Carson guy to drive you away after I left on the false fire alarm I set up and Lamont left as planned too?"

"No, none at all. You managed with the land sales OK?" Monte asked.

"Yes, Sadie Harrison hauled out her checkbook. The three days that EnergyFuture shyster could have been making land deals but was holed up with you somewhere, Sadie was buying up from whoever wanted to sell. Lamont Jackson's already sold out and gone from the valley. There's no way that EnergyFuture bastard's going to get that land from Sadie. She's already arranging to put it in the nature conservancy, so not even death is going to help them."

"So, we got what we wanted?"

"Yep. EnergyFuture can't get enough parcels of land together now to put in the uranium mine here. Sadie rattled the government in Richmond and came up with information not contained in any of those pamphlets they gave us. Only an open-pit strip mine would work here, it seems. All that radiation exposed and going up in the air morning, noon, and night, and probably coming back down as far away as Danville and Chatham. Now if they want to do their mining here in Virginia, they'll have to go back across the county to that Coles Farm tract. And that can be an underground mine. Still dangerous, but not like they wanted to do here."

"I'm glad you got what you wanted and the valley will stay as it is," Monte said.

"I hope it wasn't too much of a sacrifice, son," Ervin said. "I didn't know of any other way to get those three days out ahead of the Carson snake. I knew it had to be by sacrifice. I hope that brute wasn't too rough on you. I hated asking you to do that for us—keeping him occupied to give Sadie time to buy the land out from underneath him. But what we did here, we did for the glory of the earth. Can't do no better than honor the earth, my momma always said."

"Naw, it was OK," Monte said. He turned away from Ervin, so that the older man couldn't see him smile. "One thing I thought of while I was gone, though," Monte said.

"What's that?"

"I think rather than going into Danville for community college in the fall, I'll go up to Richmond. I think prospects there might be better than down here."

"Whatever suits you, son."

"You would be OK with that?"

"It will be a sad day when you move on, of course. But you have been a sin that I must work on. Not your doing, of course, other than being here. My weakness. You've made such a sacrifice for this valley. It will be my turn to make a sacrifice too. Not today or tomorrow, of course. But, yes, going to Richmond will be a good idea; you should find friends of your own age there. And I've ever said I have no hold over you, that you can do what you like."

"I think I'd like that . . . going to Richmond. I got a friend there who says he'll put me up while I'm going to college." Monte had to stay turned so that Ervin couldn't see how hard he was smiling about just how much he thought he was going to like that. As sacrifices go, it had been a pretty easy one—a lot more enjoyable than he'd thought it would be. That Jack had a cock as good as most black man's, even if it wasn't quite as good as Ervin's.

Snow Trap

Boyd had been leery of the arrangement from the very beginning, but he hadn't said anything to his father about it. His father seemed so happy about having found Vic two years after Aaron had died. Boyd would much rather it had been anyone other than Vic. He wished it had been someone Boyd hadn't known before his father met him. When he was being honest with himself, Boyd realized that he had fancied Vic for himself—for quite some time.

That last year at the Union Hunt private academy on the James, west of Richmond, had been a testing one for Boyd. He'd known since he was ten what his father's leanings were. Boyd's mother had split a couple of years before that. Boyd didn't think that had been because his father, Karl, was gay. He thought his parents were what were called swingers at the time and that his mother just wanted to swing out farther—and wasn't much interested in being a mother. Whatever the case was, she disappeared and left Boyd and his father in Richmond alone. Karl seemed to have been trying to lead a normal-looking life, but Boyd was only ten when Aaron appeared on the scene and Boyd's revelation came that Karl would be switching to being his mother now and that Aaron was going to take on the role of father—even in Karl's bed.

But it wasn't really like Aaron had come into the world of Boyd and his father. It was more like Boyd and his father appeared on Aaron's scene, because Aaron was older and richer than Karl was, and father and son moved in with Aaron in his larger house in Richmond. The only part of this that left Boyd feeling insecure, strangely enough, was that Karl didn't give up the family home and they regularly used it too, so Boyd never had a feeling of permanence with Aaron.

Early in Boyd's senior year at Union Hunt, Aaron had unexpectedly died from a heart attack, and Karl and Boyd moved back into the old family home. Karl sank into a depression that turned Boyd increasingly to his teachers and counselors in school for guidance and fathering. For several months, the fathering was picked up mainly by his swim and tennis coaches. Vic Peterson was in his first year as tennis coach, and that's where Boyd got most of his attention. They were still in their fall tennis schedule when Boyd began to realize that he was beginning to have an attraction to the tall, blond, and muscular Vic, not yet out of his twenties, that went beyond respect and fatherly advice.

And Boyd fancied that interest was being reciprocated.

Boyd didn't have any prejudices against a man being with a man—his father had lived with another man since Boyd was ten, and Boyd wasn't blind to the sexual relationship the two men were in. Aaron and Karl slept in the same bed and Aaron topped Karl, sometimes rather noisily. Karl made no effort to hide this from his son. And Boyd didn't have any defenses against accepting that he could go that way himself, not that he had any such attraction to either the significantly older Aaron or to his own father.

In expressing his own similar interests Boyd didn't feel any constraints as far as Karl was concerned; they'd talked it out and Karl couldn't very well object to Boyd saying he thought he was gay when Karl himself was so openly gay. But they'd agreed that, for the good of all concerned, Boyd would wait until he was eighteen before he'd make any moves in that direction. Boyd had decided initially, though, without discussing it with his father, that it was Vic he was waiting for.

Karl had attended the fall tennis team banquet. He was starting to come out of his depression earlier in Boyd's senior year and had come to some of the tennis matches. Boyd was the team's star player and Vic and Karl talked several times about Boyd's promise and were working together on putting together a college athletic scholarship for Boyd. By the beginning of spring practice, they had found him a berth at the nationally second-ranked University of Virginia. It had taken a lot of time together for Karl and Vic to achieve this, a time in which Karl came out of his depression and started to become close with Vic.

All was good, Boyd decided. It was probably just a "discovery" crush he had on Vic and there were other guys he could just as well start with. Seeing the effect Vic had on his father's depression, Boyd saw the coach as a possible replacement for Aaron in Karl's life. He saw the relationship in such a light, because on more than one occasion, he had come home unexpectedly and heard the two men fucking in Karl's bedroom. Most of these times the bedroom door had been ajar and Boyd had seen the two on Karl's bed, with Karl on all fours and Vic crouched over his hips and doggy fucking him.

Vic had a great body and was a muscular and handsome blond. Boyd didn't always pull away from his vantage point at the door. His attraction to the tennis coach had advanced through the year, and Boyd looked at the two men fucking more with interest and a wish that he was in Karl's place than in any judgmental way.

It was pulling Karl out of his depression, so Boyd didn't have any problem with it—other than whether it would change his own relationship with the tennis coach. It didn't seem to, though. The coach was as attentive to him and his development of his tennis technique and the progress of his studies and what he had to do to satisfy all of UVa's entrance requirements as he always had been.

Everything was fine until the eighteenth birthday party Karl threw for Boyd in late June at the beach house Aaron had left Karl in Nags Head, North Carolina. The school year at the academy had just concluded, the tennis team had won the state championship for private schools, and Karl invited the team to Nags Head to celebrate Boyd's birthday.

The team and coaches were stripped down to bathing suits and moving between the small pool on the deck at the rear of the beach house and the surf at the edge of the beach beyond. All of them were beautiful hunks, including the two tennis coaches, who had gotten to the lower ranks of the tennis pros before finding that the income from teaching tennis at private schools was more assured than trying to make it to a second round in a regional tennis tournament.

Karl was down on the beach helping to set up a volleyball net and most of the rest of the team and the coaches were down there too. Boyd had been in the pool at the house and had come out of it and was standing by a lounge toweling himself off when Vic appeared at the French Doors into the kitchen area.

"Come upstairs with me a minute, Boyd," the coach said. "Got you something special for your birthday."

"Sure thing," Boyd answered. "Soon as I dry off."

"Where to?" Boyd asked as they mounted the two flights of stairs to the first of two levels of bedrooms. Vic had put his suitcase in Karl's room earlier in the day, leaving Boyd to wonder what the accommodations would be. But since Vic's luggage was in there, Boyd assumed that's where they were headed.

"All the way up, to the crow's nest," Vic said. "Nice and private. Nobody will disturb us there."

The crow's nest was a small, square room, with windows on all sides, at the very top of the house. The best view of the beach was from here. The only furnishings in the room were built-in padded benches around all four sides and an oversized ottoman in the center.

As soon as they got to the top of the stairs into this room, Boyd looked around for whatever present Vic had stashed up here. But he quickly found out that the present wasn't something stashed up here. The taller, more muscular, and more powerful coach embraced Boyd from behind, pulling Boyd's back into his chest. One hand went to Boyd's chin, which Vic cupped and turned to his own face. The other hand slid down the front of Boyd's Speedo and cupped his balls and the root of his cock.

"Coach!" Boyd exclaimed.

"You're legal now," Vic growled. "We both know you've wanted it for some time."

He took Boyd's lips in his in a possessive kiss. Boyd struggled against him, but ineffectually, and slowly gave in as the kiss mastered him and his cock engorged to the touch of Vic. He couldn't deny that it was what he had wanted for some time. He just knew it wasn't right, that they shouldn't be doing this. It was his father, Karl, Vic should be paying attention to.

But Boyd's want betrayed him.

When Vic pulled away from the kiss, Boyd's face followed him and Boyd's lips opened to Vic again, hungrily seeking Vic's mouth. The coach laughed and then pushed his tongue into Boyd's mouth again and curled Boyd's tongue into his mouth, where he trapped it and sucked on it.

When Vic felt the young man relax in his embrace, he came out of the kiss and ran his hands all over Boyd's body, caressing bulges and exploring crevasses. When Boyd's "you shouldn't" murmurs died down into sighing and mewing, Vic turned Boyd and laid him down on his back on the ottoman.

"Don't fight me in this, son," he murmured. "We both know. We've both had to wait. But I'm going to fuck you now, and you're going to love it."

He pulled Boyd's Speedo off his legs and went down on his knees between Boyd's thighs as he spread them apart. Boyd gasped and moaned as the mouth came down over his cock head.

"No, no, it's not right. We shouldn't. We can't. Oh, shit, ohhhh," Boyd groaned as the coach gave him head with his mouth and started worrying Boyd's hole with his fingers.

He was standing over Boyd, between his thighs, and squeezing lube on his sheathed cock when Boyd lurched to the side, grabbed his Speedo off the floor, and with a "Just can't do it," tumbled down the stairs.

It was later, after all the partygoers had departed and they'd eaten dinner, with Vic acting normal and Boyd trying to hide his tension in front of his father, that Karl made his announcement. Vic and Karl had left Boyd in the living room watching a match on the tennis channel while they went to Karl's bedroom and fucked. After that they both reappeared in the living room for a nightcap.

"We have something to tell you," Boyd's father said as they both came into the conversation area in front of the TV and took a seat, side by side.

Boyd turned and looked at his father, trying to avoid looking at Vic, who had a very pleased with himself and confident look on his face. He waited Karl out on what he had to say.

"Vic is moving in with us," Karl said. "It will be like when you and Aaron and I were together."

No, Boyd thought. It won't be like that at all. Aaron never tried to fuck me nor did he ever suggest he wanted to.

"Oh, OK," Boyd answered.

Karl got up to retrieve the Scotch bottle in the kitchen, and Vic turned a smile toward Boyd. "We're going to have a great time, the three of us," he said. "I know it will take some getting used to, since I was your tennis coach and all, but you and I both know what we want. Earlier, up in the crow's nest . . . I understand you think you're not ready, but you showed that you wanted me. We'll be together in the same house. There will be opportunities. There's no reason for your dad to have to know anything about it."

Boyd got up, went to his room, left a note on his father's dresser to the effect of just now remembering having promised to play tennis with friends near their home in

Richmond early the next morning and that he decided he should go back to Richmond tonight—and let his father and Vic celebrate their new arrangement alone. Then he quietly avoided the living room in exiting the house and was off to get onto Interstate 64 toward Richmond.

For the rest of the summer, the three cohabitated in the Richmond house, but Boyd made sure he never was alone with Vic when his father wasn't there.

For Vic's part, he appeared happy taking care of Karl and just said a couple of times when Karl wasn't right there that "it was going to happen" and that he could wait for it. It would then be all the sweeter for both of them when it did happen, he said. When he felt frisky, he asked if Boyd remembered how Vic's cock felt in his hand and if he ever dreamed of it inside him. He'd laugh and Boyd would turn away, embarrassed.

But, yes, Boyd never lost the memory of the feel of Vic's cock or the want to have it inside him. Boyd was no longer a virgin. He'd lost his male-male virginity, out of frustration, to the friend he'd gone back to Richmond to play tennis with. As chance would have it, this older friend had had the exact same eighteenth-birthday gift in mind for Boyd that Vic had had.

Boyd almost gave it all up to Vic in early December in Boyd's dorm room at UVa. Vic had visited the university a couple of times in the fall, meeting with Boyd's new tennis coach and making sure that Boyd was settling into the team. On each previous occasion Karl came with him—but not the second Saturday in December.

After tennis practice at the indoor courts at the university-owned Boar's Head Inn west of the town, Boyd had gone back to his dorm, showered, and, with a towel around him and standing beside his desk, had picked up the note pad where the university tennis coach had written some notes for him on the day's practice matches. He heard a noise at the door and looked up to find that Vic was standing there. Vic moved into the room and shut the door behind him and muttered, "It's time."

This time Vic got his cock inside Boyd. As before, Vic moved quickly to Boyd, embraced him in overpowering arms, whipped the towel off, and brutally possessed Boyd's lips and stroked his cock until Boyd was moaning and relaxed in his arms.

When Vic's cock entered Boyd's ass for the first time, Vic was standing by the bed, and Boyd was stretched in front of him down onto the bed, his weight on his shoulder blades on the surface of the bed. Boyd's knees were hooked on Vic's hips, Vic's hands were gripping Boyd's buttocks cheeks, and Boyd's arms were stretched out from his sides, his fists digging into the edges of the mattress.

Boyd was murmuring ineffectual objections, but upon the second stroke of Vic's cock deep inside him, Boyd began to move his hips with the fuck, and he threw his head back and howled, "Oh, shit. O, fuck. Daddy, daddydaddy!"

By now Boyd wasn't the least bit inexperienced. He had been seduced and fucked by an upperclassman the first week of classes, increasingly suffering from want for the man fucking him now, a man Boyd had been trying to think of as off limits. And since that upperclassman there had been three others inside him—all of them, including the upperclassman, more than once. All of them lost enough to him to continue to be sniffing around him.

There was nothing more Boyd wanted emotionally and physically than this fucking Vic was giving. But the guilt of it just would not go away. This was supposed to be his father's man; he couldn't do this to his father.

On the sixth stroke, Boyd was clutching at Vic's buttocks and digging his nails in, holding Vic's crotch close in between his thighs, but he was sobbing and muttering a mantra of "we can't!" On the ninth stroke, he had his fists on Vic's belly, pushing him away, and then he rolled away from Vic and off the side of the bed. When he came up on his feet, he had a pair of jeans gripped in a hand. He was out of the door and had escaped into a nearby unoccupied dorm room and shut and locked the door before Vic had been able to adjust himself and come out of his room. Boyd heard Vic moving around in the living room of the five-bedroom suite for a few minutes but then all was quiet.

Boyd waited another half hour. Then he came out of the room and, seeing only a suite mate sitting in the living room and declaring that no older man was there or in Boyd's room, he went to his room, hurriedly packed a bag, dressed warmly, and hopped on his motorcycle. He couldn't stay here until he knew that Vic had left town and he couldn't go to Richmond where Vic undoubtedly would head from here. He had a key to the Wintergreen winter resort mountain house at the top of the Blue Ridge that Aaron had left his father.

It was nearly a two-hour drive on his motorcycle up the mountain. By the time he got to the base of the mountain, it had begun to snow. Before he reached the house, which was far down a winding and dipping lane off the main road up the mountain, he had had to get off the bike and push it. The snow already was accumulating. It was dark when he entered the house from the garage, where he'd stashed the motorcycle, and he had to rev up the heat. After turning it up, he went to the bedroom that was designated as his, climbed under the blanket on the bed, fully clothed other than the wet jacket and trousers he left on the washer in the garage, and was asleep in moments. He knew it would take a couple of hours for the chill to be taken off the temperature in the house.

He slept through to the next morning. When he opened his eyes and looked through the undraped windows all he could see was white. He got out of bed and went over to the windows. White everywhere; deep snow. No sign of clearing on the road below the house. It looked like it was nearly a foot deep. The blessing was that there still was electricity, but just as he said that, the electricity went off as well. The house had barely warmed up enough to be comfortable as it was.

There were large fireplaces in the living room and family room and he hurriedly laid and lit fires in those. They would keep much of the house warm. There was a propane gas stove in the kitchen, and he put coffee on that to perc.

With a sigh, he returned and went into the bathroom off his bedroom, did his "thing," and took a shower, taking

189

advantage of the water in the hot water heater still being hot. Coming out, he went to his bureau and took out a pair of briefs from the clothing he kept at the mountain house. He was pulling jeans out of his closet when he smelled it. The smell of strong coffee.

The coffee called him, and he padded down the hallway to the living areas.

Vic was sitting on a stool at the kitchen island, drinking a cup of coffee. He was naked. On the countertop in front of him was a pile of condom packets and a can of spray lube.

"It's getting cold in here," he said in a calm, matter-of-fact voice. "I think it's going to take rubbing our bodies together under the covers on a bed to create heat."

Boyd took off for the front door, with no plan other than escape. He got the door open and snow that had been a foot deep tumbled across the threshold before Vic reached him, pulled him back, slammed the door shut again, and then slammed Boyd down on his belly on the living room carpet, in front of the fireplace. Holding Boyd in place with strong hands gripping his waist after he'd stripped Boyd's briefs off, Vic came down on his chest on the back of Boyd's thighs and Boyd felt a wet tongue working its way into his ass crack.

"Raise your butt," Vic commanded, and, with a moan, Boyd raised his buttocks enough for Vic to pull his cock and balls through between his thighs so that he could work the asshole, cock, and balls together with his mouth and fingers.

"Isn't this romantic? Right in front of a cozy fire," Vic muttered. Then he laughed.

Boyd moaned his frustration, bucking and writhing until Vic instructed him to lie still, and Boyd did so.

"Raise your butt more. Present your hole to me. It's beyond time. I'm not going to wait any more."

With a whimper, Boyd went up on his knees and raised his buttocks.

Vic laughed. "You want it, don't you."

Boyd's answer was a gasp and a groan as Vic crouched over his hips and entered him. The thrust was accompanied by the electricity going back on. Boyd turned his head from where

190

he'd been staring, glazed-eyed into the fire to look into Vic's face. What he saw told him that Vic wasn't going to be put off this time. Then Vic began to pump.

"Please, please," Boyd whimpered.

"Please, what? You made me wait too long."

"Please . . . fuck me, fuck me, fuck me!"

"About time, you little fucker. You've been a real tease." Vic brought his chest down on Boyd's back, reached for and gripped the young man's wrists, and stroked hard and deep until they both had ejaculated.

Vic fucked Boyd from the rear, bent over the arm of a living room easy chair. Vic fucked Boyd on Karl's bed under the covers when the electricity went off again, with Boyd on his back and his legs being held raised and spread by Vic. Vic fucked Boyd in the shower after the electricity had reconnected and the water heater heated up, with Boyd's back against the stall wall and his knees hooked on Boyd's hips. That night after dinner, Vic fucked Boyd on Karl's bed again kneeling between Boyd's spread thighs, pushing his knees under Boyd's buttocks, and pulling his channel on and off the cock.

Afterward, the two stretched against each other in the darkness of the room, Boyd wrapped in Vic's arms, Boyd asked him. "How did you get up here? In the snow? I can't see that anyone . . ."

"That's right, we're trapped in the snow up here. Well, you are. I'm just where I want to be. And I'm going to fuck you silly, make you completely mine before the snowplows come through."

"But how did you . . . ?"

"I dropped in from heaven," Vic said, and then he laughed. "I'm your saving angel."

He was lifting Boyd up on his knees.

"Please, Vic. Enough. Haven't we . . . enough . . . ?"

"Lift your ass. Present your sweet hole to me."

Boyd cried out in surprise, frustration, and pain . . . changing to uncontrollable passion . . . as Vic thrust inside him and started to stroke hard and deep.

Vic was lying on his back, limbs akimbo, and snoring, when Boyd carefully pulled away from him and rose from the bed. As much as he had wanted Vic to fuck him, it still wasn't fair to his father. It was just too complicating of all of the relationships involved. He shouldn't be letting Vic do this.

How did Vic get here? Boyd had to know. Maybe it was a way for him to get out from under this—if he had the strength to pull away from the amazing fucking he was getting.

He slipped on flip-flops and went out into the corridor. He went into every room down the hall, checking out the view from the windows. Snow and more snow. It had started snowing again, but at least the electricity seemed to be holding now. He truly was trapped up here in the snow. Nothing but a sea of white from the windows and French doors in the living area. He went out to the garage. Nothing but his own motorcycle in the double garage. This was the last place for him to look. But then he remembered that the house had a third garage—the third one being through a door at the other end of the garage. He went over and opened the door.

The snowmobile was standing in the center of the garage. Boyd walked over and checked it out. Plenty of gasoline in the tank. Ready to go.

"Take it if you want."

Boyd's head snapped up, and he turned his head toward the door into the other garage. Vic was standing there, naked, his cock erect again, his body gloriously muscular, perfect, powerful.

"It's your choice. You can take the snowmobile, go down the mountain, and continue with your life as it is. Or you can stay here and let me fuck your lights out until the snow clears. I can handle both you and your dad. I'll give him what he wants and keep him happy. He's happy now, you'll have to admit. And if you stay here I'll give you what I know you want. I can keep you happy too. Which is it to be?"

"You're just with my father to get at me," Boyd whispered.

"That's not being very fair to your dad, Boyd. He's hot enough to want too. It runs in your family. Sure I've wanted to fuck you since I arrived at Union Hunt and found you on the tennis team. But I wanted a lot of guys I saw, and when I saw your dad, I wanted him too. I've got a lot of lovin' to give."

Vic could have gone on, saying how he liked the two-for-one idea of getting both father and son and that it didn't hurt a bit that Karl's previous lover had left him a fortune and both a beach house and a mountain house—and that snowmobile there, as a matter of fact. He decided to keep it to what Boyd was struggling over—what he, Boyd, really wanted was what it came down to.

"You wanted me from that time too. Tell me you didn't. You've pulled away from me a couple of times, but not before you made your 'want' clear to me. You gonna pull away from me again? Did you come up here to escape me or to escape what you know you want? Being up here together could be a blessing. We can use these days trapped by the snow to burn off the heat of our passion for each other so that we can control it better when we get back to Richmond. Or we can both smolder down there and make clear to your dad that something is wrong. If you're thinking of your dad, think about that. It's too late now for me not to be involved with your dad."

Boyd lowered his head, not answering. Not saying he was staying—but not saying he was going either.

Vic walked over and lifted him up in his arms and slowly walked into the house. "I'll stop and let you down any time you want before we get to the bedroom. When we get there, though, it will be too late. You will have already made your choice."

Boyd lay on his back at the foot of Karl's bed, his fists gripping the bottom edge of the mattress on each side, his legs snaking up to where he hooked his heels on Vic's shoulders, using the leverage of his fists to counterpunch the thrusting of Vic's cock, as he cried out, groaned, and grunted at the pounding, pounding, pounding of his lover's cock.

He turned his head toward a window and noted that it was snowing out there in earnest. Good, he thought.

Arabists' Literary Weekend

The man was thin and wiry, a regular beanpole, but he certainly knew what to do with his cock, which was also long, but not thick. It was a surprise, but an arrested surprise. Justin didn't quite know what to make of it, this encounter he originally had thought would be a total bust and then had hopes for and now was completely confused about. Peters was nearing his ejaculation, Justin could tell. Justin had had a weak one already, but it wasn't anything close to what he had wanted and, there for a short time, had anticipated.

Justin was on his back on the bed in his rooms in Oxford, grabbing for the rails of the brass headboard overhead, bruising his knuckles as the headboard hit the wall in the rhythm of the fuck—disappointed at having to do the grasping himself, but taking what arousal he could get from the bruising of his knuckles. His knees were bent and his feet gripping the mattress, giving him leverage to counterpunch Peters's penetrations. Peters knelt between Justin's thighs, his hands gripping Justin's knees—much too lightly for Justin's tastes—and rowed the knees back and forth to the rhythm of his fuck. Pulling them in as he drew his hips back and slid out of Justin's channel and pushing the knees apart as he glided in.

Glided in. Glided out. All very civilized.

Although the man was hitting all of the right spots, he was being much too delicate to fully arouse Justin. Justin was doing what he could: positioning his knuckles where they could get bruised, counterpunching to encourage thrusting, talking the want of punishment, trying to arouse anger by brutally twisting Peters's nipples when he could reach them. It wasn't happening.

There had been some hope—not only because of where Peters had taken him before coming back to Justin's rooms at the university but also because when Peters had stripped, there, surprisingly, had been those barbed-wire band tattoos around his biceps. Not just tattooing on an Oxford don, but also signals of BDSM inclination. A hopeful, but apparently empty sign of something rougher under the academic exterior.

As Justin laid down on his bed and opened his legs, he had reached over and pulled the lower drawer of his nightstand open, showing the collection of restraints, ball gags, tit clamps, ball stretchers, and the flogger. But, although Peters must surely have seen them and, when he'd first bottomed inside Justin's channel, he paused and ran fingers over the most recent welts on Justin's torso and thighs, he had said nothing—and done nothing beyond taking a gentle hold on Justin's knees and beginning a slow, long stroking action. Justin wasn't sure he'd even call it an action. As Peters was working that long, promising cock inside him, Justin had taken a hit from an amyl nitrite popper bottle and settled back on his elbow ready to watch the root of the cock pistoning into him and aiding the buildup to fireworks.

But there hadn't been any fireworks, any glorious punishment.

Peters had gotten off, jerking several times and then pulling—gliding—out, ripping the now-white-slug of a condom off and rubbing his moist cock head on Justin's lower belly while telling Justin what a good lay he was. But for Justin, there hadn't been any more than a little precum squirt when he was frantically working his own cock, expecting and wanting so much more.

And then Justin was alone. Peters hadn't even suggested another assignation. Justin rolled over to a sitting position on the bed, opened the upper drawer of the nightstand, and took out a pack of cigarettes and a lighter. He sat up on the side of the bed, lit a cigarette, and punished himself mentally by going through an assessment of the evening. It was the best punishment he was going to get out of the evening.

He'd had a hell of a time finding even one gay bar in Oxford. He was here from Stanford as a visiting scholar, an Arabist. He knew they weren't all straight here. In the short time here he'd already observed how randy they were for men in the rooming lodges and he'd already been spiked himself hard and deliciously brutally by a fellow Arabist student and robust rugby player named Thomas. Thomas had been the most satisfying fuck Justin had had here as yet. The beefy young florid, sandy-haired ruffian must have been an expert horseman. He both was a horse himself and rode Justin hard, spurring him on with frequent applications of a riding crop.

It had been Thomas who told him the nearly impossible to believe—that there was only one gay bar in or around Oxford, the Plush Lounge, and that it was pretty lame. The best night there was Saturday, although "best" was disappointingly relative.

"I go to London when I want entertainment. When I want tail, I stay right here. There is plenty of that to be had in the university rooms. You, for instance, are very nice tail indeed." He was following with his fingers the welts he had raised on Justin's buttocks and building up to another ride.

So, having heard that Saturday was the least tame night at Oxford's Plush Lounge, that was the night Justin had gone there. And indeed it seemed as tame to him as he feared. It got a little interesting, though, when an Arabist tutor, Peters, entered the lounge, where a loud band and pulsating strobe lights tried to make up for the lack of a crowd. He scanned the room and, seeing Justin at the bar, raised his eyebrows. Justin raised his half-full stout glass to the tutor, and the tall, thin man fairly glided over to the bar and onto the stool next to Justin.

After a couple of drinks, Peters had confirmed that this was the only gay bar within miles of Oxford, and Justin had been constant in voicing his disbelief this possibly could be so.

As the buzz from the drinks increased, the discussion got more pointed.

"Do you really understand what sort of bar this is or are you just bored and slumming?" Peters asked. "You have a divine body, by the way."

"Yes, like any other establishment of its kind, bored men come here to hook up and get bored, I would think," Justin said.

"That doesn't really answer the question—which is you, specifically. Could you have gotten those jeans any tighter, by the way?"

Justin laughed. "Yes, I came here because I knew it was a gay hookup bar—not much of one, though, it appears."

"Well, one never knows about Americans who come here," Peters said, snuffing out his cigarette in an ash tray shaped like a set of buttocks and turning full toward Justin. "They seem to have the silliest notions about what we do and have in stores and establishments here. But say, young man," Peters plowed right ahead, "Do you take cock?"

Justin's mug stopped half way to his lips and he peered at Peters over the top of it for a quarter of a minute. Then he continued with the swipe and took a long swig, put the mug down on the counter, and moved his hand to Peters's thigh.

"It depends on the cock."

"Go ahead, be my guest."

Justin move his hand to Peters's crotch and ascertained that the staff was one of the "keeps on going" kind. He smiled in Peters's face, not moving his hand from the bulge between the thin man's thighs.

"Satisfied?" Peters asked, giving Justin a level stare.

"Do you think you would be satisfied with me?" Justin responded. "Do you want to check?"

"Those jeans leave nothing to speculate about, and I am far less interested in cocks than in holes. But, oh, yes, dear boy. You are the best thing in here. And you are the best fresh thing I've seen at the university this term."

"Then perhaps," Justin answered.

"Would you now? Through those beaded curtains in the back corridor . . . if I was to tell you about some of the other choices underground here for young men like you, depending on your interests?"

"That would be closer to a yes," Justin said.

"And if I took you to one of your choice afterward?"

Peters stood against the wall, far back in the darkened corridor beyond the beaded curtain, where many another tryst had been consummated if the scattering of spent condoms on the floor could be trusted. Justin was draped on the front of the tall, thin academician, hanging from his neck from hands clasped behind Peters's head, Justin's feet flat on the wall and spread at the sides and level of Peters's chest, Justin's trousers and briefs on the floor below and Peters's were around his ankles. Peters was grasping and separating Justin's buttocks with the palms of his hands, and Justin, using the leverage of his feet, rode the long cock as both panted and pursued their individual fleeting pleasure.

Afterward, Peters had raised an eyebrow when Justin told him what sort of underground club he would like to visit, but he took him to one in an English basement of a seedy tenement off a main drag that advertised itself in a dimly lit red-on-black sign as the Club S. Peters told Justin that the initial stood for "satyr."

Justin received his first real arousal of the evening, seeing a young man tied to an X frame on a small stage and being flogged before he was fucked from behind by a big bruiser. And then when Justin invited the tutor up to his Oxford rooms and the invitation was accepted, Justin thought the night would turn out well. Peters's reaction to the performance had seemed to match Justin's, and he'd sat on a stool, with Justin gathered into his spread thighs and run hands into Justin's clothing and played with both Justin's nipples and his cock, pinching the nipples as the bruiser on the platform stage thrust inside the channel of his bound, blush-bottomed captive.

As Justin sat and smoked his cigarette after Peters left his room and reviewed the night, he still couldn't quite figure out why it hadn't given him what he wanted.

With a sigh, he rummaged around in the lower nightstand drawer, pulled out a leather cock ring and ball stretcher combination and a slapper crop. Taking another hit from the popper bottle, he laid back on the bed, groaned as he painfully laced his balls into the stretcher and splitter until the balls were tight, separated orbs pulled far away from his groin, and then moaned and writhed and stroked his cock to an ejaculation. His eyes watered as he mercilessly slapped his extended and tightly bunched balls with the crop.

It just wasn't the same arousal value if he had to do it himself, though.

* * * *

When the invitation came for a weekend gathering at Philip Hardesty's country home in the Forest of Dean to the west in Gloucestershire, Justin was both surprised and impressed. Hardesty was *Mr.* Arabist at Oxford. Although his reputation was part of what had drawn Justin to take the Oxford fellowship, Justin had known that he probably never would meet Hardesty, just those around him who basked in his light. Joshua Ramsay, Justin's own tutor, had been the one to deliver the invitation.

"Oh, by the way, Justin. Since you have transport, perhaps you could take along the other students who have been invited as well. It will be the three students and then the Arabist seniors who will be there."

Justin was delighted to agree to that, especially when told that one of the students would be that rough rider, Thomas. The other one was Leonard, a somewhat timid young man, who was small of stature, as beautiful in face and physicality as any woman, and, Justin had heard, a favorite of the more aggressive and rough tops at the university.

Who knew what mischief the three of them could find in the Forest of Dean during a weekend, although Justin quickly dispelled that from his mind. The payoff this weekend would be in hearing the senior Arabists speak of whatever things of the Arab world the informal discussions would lead them to. The main topics were to be Arab literature, but Justin knew from reputation that the talks would range much further and could, he hoped, touch on his own specialty, below-the-surface sexual practices in the medieval Arab world. Justin's research had told him that some of the current BDSM practices and equipment dated from this source, and these were possibilities he sought to verify—not least with the hope of discovering practices that had gone dormant in subsequent centuries.

Coleford Hall, the country home of Philip Hardesty, set high above the Severn River, was both famous and infamous in the lore of the Forest of Dean. Set on a Saxon site, it had been a place of worship—pagan worship of the most licentious nature some said—in Norman times. The foundations of the main section of the house, the existing structure being Jacobean of the early seventeenth century, dated much farther back, to the fifth century. The "modern" wing dated only back as far as the late seventeenth century. Extensive catacombs had been set in the Norman period, though, and the appendages of the current manor house appeared to follow the footprint of the original Norman cellars. Even older than all of these, though. was a Roman temple site set at the edge of the extensive lawns on the hillside above the Severn. The manor

201

house at one time must have had extensive vistas of the river valley, but now it was blocked in by tall and ancient trees that gave the house an aura of being tucked away in total isolation from the outside world.

The three students arrived in the late afternoon and were assigned to second-floor—which Justin had to remind himself was the third floor in American terms—chambers in a wing running between the back of the Jacobean manor house and the stable wing. Justin was assigned to his own room and Thomas and Lenoard to an adjacent, larger one. Dinner was set in an hour's time in the dining room on the Jacobean manor's first floor, where the only other room was the large library in which the group would meet for their discussions. The ground floor of the Jacobean manor was taken up with three stone-floored chambers, the central entrance hall, with the stair hall running behind it, a former parlor, which was maintained as a museum of the house's history, and, on the opposite side of the entrance all, the former dining room, which was left unfurnished as a memorial to the four Royalist officers who had been trapped there by the Roundhead forces of Cromwell during the English Revolution and who had fought to their deaths in that room. The bloodstains on the stone floor had been meticulously preserved.

Justin spent the hour before dinner studying the discussion agenda for the evening, while, if what he could hear was indicative despite the foot-thick stone walls in this wing, Thomas spent much of that hour riding Leonard's ass in their chamber. Justin's own ass twitched at the thought, and he hoped that Thomas had brought his riding crop.

The presence of the Arabist seniors at dinner was humbling to Justin. Not only were Philip Hardesty and his own tutor, Joshua Ramsay, present but there also were the notable scholars James Stowell and Timothy Coleson. The one guest who gave Justin pause was Charles Peters—the man who Justin had so recently had a sexual encounter with, starting in the Plush Lounge. Peters made no unusual comment of foreknowledge upon introductions, which Justin was thankful for, but a knowing look transpired between the two.

The five seniors sat in a circle of easy chairs surrounding a low table piled high with books that all were Arabic literature in both the original and English translations that the scholars would occasionally dive for, separate from the rest, and wave over their heads as they made points that often were arcane even to Justin. Justin was the only one of the three students, sitting outside of the circle in straight chairs, to be making much of an effort to follow the discussion. Thomas alternated expressions of boredom and of a cat having caught a mouse, and Leonard maintained the expression of ever being the caught mouse.

But Justin listened to as much of the dense and erudite conversation as he could, reveling in being this close to scholars who were so passionate and glib about a literature largely ignored by much of the world and also by being in a musty, wood-paneled library with dusty overstuffed chairs, rich mahogany tables and bookcases, oriental rugs on the floor, and a full surround of old and moldering books. The smell was musky, not at all unlike the smell of a brutish man in heat. Justin was in heaven.

"Any discussion of this sort must start with that Arabian nights in reverse Sudanese classic, Tayeb Salih's *Season of Migration to the North*," the slightly bent, grayish James Stowell with the ferret face tossed out as an opening gambit as soon as the scholars, varied drinks in hand, had settled in their easy chairs.

"Utterly ridiculous," the hunky youngest among the scholars, Timothy Coleson, favoring his Egyptian mother in his dark beauty more than his English father, countered, with a snort. "If it's the Arabian Nights literature where we must start, it must be with Anton Shammas's *Arabesques*."

"Why would we want to start at the Arabian Nights literature at all," Justin's tall, slender fuck friend from a previous encounter, Charles Peters, interjected. "And should it not be Philip who introduces the subject?" With this, he turned and cast a worshipful gaze on Philip Hardesty, their host and their seniormost.

"I believe Philip has said that we cannot start anywhere but with Naguib Mahfouz and the Cairo Trilogy," Justin's own tutor, the short, slightly rotund, hirsute and decidedly Jewish Joshua Ramsay said.

"Mahfouz has his own *Arabian Nights* work," Coleson countered doggedly. "We could segue into his other works from that topic. We have not recently delved farther back into the base than Mahfouz's early twentieth-century themes in the Cairo Trilogy."

Justin perked up with eagerness. The Arabian Nights tales were thinly disguised erotica, and this would be a splendid place for the discussion to start as far as he was concerned. And he was all for pushing back to the medieval period.

All eyes turned toward Hardesty for a verdict—all except those of Leonard, who had eyes only for Thomas, and the olive-skinned hunk, Timothy Coleson, who had turned his dark, fluttering eyelashes in Justin's direction, openly assessing the young American scholar in what Justin understood as an open invitation to getting better acquainted. There was some hope for Justin's Oxford nights, the thought. There was a look of cruelty in Coleson's eyes.

Hardesty, the most imposing figure in the room in stature, bulk, and presence, spoke in a low, rumbling voice that, probably on purpose, made all lean in his direction. "Of course the discussion must start with the Nobel Laureate, Mahfouz, and, in deference to our young colleagues, Thomas and Leonard, we will discuss from the Kenney English translations." Hardesty inclined his head toward the two students in the outer ring and gave an indulgent smile. Leonard looked up, startled, as if he wondered whether the master was asking him a question. For his part, Justin smiled and beamed inwardly that Hardesty had known that he was fluent in Arabic.

"We only have the weekend, so, with Mahfouz, the Egyptian Dickens, we can reach a depth into Arabic life and mores in the first half of the last century quickly and efficiently. Beginning with *Palace Walk*, we are given detailed images of the life and family of the prosperous wholesale grocer, Al-Sayyid Ahmad Abd al-Jawad, at the beginning of the twentieth century. I hope that no later than noon tomorrow we can reach the disintegration of the family unit and the values it holds to on the surface into a modern Egyptian state, influenced by English decadence. For this we will need the third book of the trilogy, *Sugar Street*, and the follow-up novel *Midaq Alley*. And then, as you like we can move on to such lesser lights and less both lush and succinct looks into an Arabic world with Shammas and Salih. Mahfouz's *Arabian Nights* can be used as a segue into eroticism in the opposite direction than you are proposing, Timothy."

He'd said the last somewhat dismissively, and both Coleson and Stowell were cowering and blushing a bit.

As the discussion commenced, Justin leaned forward, listening for any mention of Ahmad's philandering son, Yasin, for signs of Mahfouz's subtle introduction of sexual mores of the time on a normally taboo topic for literature of the 1950s. He was even more interested in discussion of the youngest son, Kamal, as his own readings of Mahfouz had led him to believe that Mahfouz was hinting at the forbidden male domains of the Cairo coffee shops as places for rich merchants to assess and bid on the attentions of young men, something Justin had encountered in underground writings on Arab life in the nineteenth and early twentieth century, but not something he had discerned thus far in Arabic literature. If there was an Arabic author brave enough to even hint at this custom, his tutor Ramsay had told him, it would be in the brave and subtle works of Mahfouz.

Late into the evening, the men were served cups of sweet, sludge-like Turkish coffee, with Hardesty making sure that the students were included in contrast to when the liquor was floating around the inner circle earlier in the evening. The discussion became so esoteric and the coffee was having more of a sedative effect than a stimulant. Even Justin's eyelids began to droop. Leonard was already sound asleep and gently snoring, and Thomas's head kept lowering and being jerked back up, with longer and longer intervals of lowering.

At last Hardesty released the young men with the setting of a time for them to reconvene in the morning that had Thomas groaning, and a servant guided the three young men back to their bed chambers through a series of corridors.

Justin had no idea whether Thomas and Leonard were doing any funny business—and only briefly speculated on whether Thomas would come to him—when he was drifting off to sleep, his mind sifting out the nuggets of possibilities on his interests that had been embedded in those parts of the scholars' discussions that he could understand.

Tomorrow he was determined to ask a few questions to see if he could loosen the senior scholars' tongues more directly on the question of sexuality in early periods in various parts of the Arabic world. He wanted to push them back into the medieval period and loosen their tongues on male-on-male sexual practices—and on any references to bondage and sadism. It seemed that whenever they had gotten to the brink of such a discussion, they had moved away from it—but that they all had more inside their font of knowledge that they could share. Joshua Ramsay had told Justin that there probably would be something for him to learn this weekend, and he'd given Justin a very guarded look when he did. Justin just knew it had to do with sexual taboos in earlier Arabic periods.

* * * *

Groggy, his world spinning slowly, arms and legs dangling, Justin was carried down the stone staircase into the dungeon. He was naked, and one of the black-cloaked figures carrying him was already kneading and separating his buttocks cheeks while the other one had one hand encasing his cock.

Justin's head was lolled back and he saw, as if in a hazy dream, that Thomas and Leonard had already been brought down into the rough stone-encased room with the lit torches attached high on the walls of the pentagonal chamber. Leonard was bound facing a rough-wood X frame, and one of the three black-robed figures already in the dungeon as Justin was brought down, the tallest and most bulky of the figures, was flogging Leonard with a multistripped black-leather whip as the young man writhed, threw his head back, and cried out in gurgling and babbling tones that reverberated around the walls of the chamber.

Thomas was on his back on top of a leather-padded pommel horse-type device with platform wings on the side. His arms and legs extended down the four legs of the device and were bound to the appendages at the wrists and ankles. His thick cock was standing up in maximum erection, stroked by the hand of one black-robed figure, who also had a hooded head lowered on Thomas's chest, where he was chewing on Thomas's nipples. Another black-robed figure was crouched where Thomas's bare ass jutted over the end of the horse and had a hooded face buried between Thomas's buttocks cheeks. Thomas was moaning quietly, not in any apparent distress.

The two figures who had carried Justin down from his bed chamber after pulling him out of his bed in the dark of the night, strapped the young man's forearms in leather cages hanging from an overhead apparatus, and snapped similar cages on his ankles that were connected to ropes. Justin was facing the X frame as he was being bound to the overhead bar, and he saw the reason Leonard's cries were subduing into muffled groans as the tall figure, having turned the flogger over to one of the figures manhandling Justin, forced a ball gag into the young man's mouth.

The front of the figure's robe was parted and Justin marveled at the massiveness of the man's cock, as the figure had proven to be a man. The man encircled Leonard's waist with a massive arm and raised the hand of the other arm to Leonard's chin and forced the young man's head back, arching his back. The arm under his waist pulled his legs and hips away? from the X frame, and Justin narrowed his eyes and his nostrils swelled in arousal as the man's gigantic cock slowly worked its way deep into Leonard's tight channel and began to plow him.

One of the figures was standing close behind Justin, and his arms came around Justin's chest. The figure's leather-gloved hands ran up to the American's pecs. Justin cried out in surprise and heavenly pain and arched his head back as the hands on his breast closed clips on his nipples and pulled on them, pinching and distending Justin's nipples. The figure stood back, and the flogging of Justin's back and buttocks and thighs, with the flogger that was being used on Leonard when Justin was carried down the stairs, began. Justin cried out his ecstasy and immediately went rock hard.

He looked over to the pommel horse-like device to find one of the black-robed figures crouched over Thomas's pelvis, kneeling on the platform wings running out from Thomas's hips. He was fucking himself on Thomas's cock. Another figure was moving around the device, prodding and caressing Thomas's arms and legs and torso until he had positioned himself at Thomas's head and, removing the young man's ball gag, pushed his cock into Thomas's mouth.

The figure fucking Leonard let out a roar and let loose of Leonard's body, which slumped against the X frame, and stepped back from the frame. But almost immediately Leonard's small body was being lifted back up by one of the figures that had carried Justin down into the chamber. And then another cock was being pushed up into Leonard's channel. It was a very long, but thin cock. Justin identified it as that of Charles Peters.

Justin's legs were now being lifted off the floor, the limbs streaming behind him, and spread. The ropes attached to the cages binding his ankles were being pulled taut to some bar overhead. Philip Hardesty—for Justin had already identified the tall figure with the monster cock who had first taken Leonard as the senior Arabist and their host, who naturally was taking his privileges of being first—was standing between Justin's raised and spread legs at his back and was entering Justin's channel. The throbbing cock was thick to the limit of Justin's capabilities, and he was grateful that Hardesty was first. The rest were likely to be easier to take after the reaming of this cock.

At the same time Hardesty was snapping the flogger on Justin's back and thighs, although he stopped this as soon as his cock was fully encased and, grabbing Justin's waist between his hands, was pushing and pulling Justin's channel on his cock.

The other figure that had brought Justin down from his bed chamber was standing in front of him, his robe open now to his naked body. The body was beautifully formed and muscled, the skin an olive color. The youngest senior, the half Egyptian, Timothy Coleson, Justin realized, as the man crouched down under him and took Justin's cock in his mouth. Justin jerked and screamed as the man crunched Justin's balls in a strong hand grip and then began to lace leather straps with weights around them, extending them to the floor.

Justin moaned and groaned and cried out his ecstasy. Even in the haze he was in, induced, he reasoned, by whatever had been in that Turkish coffee the students had been given to drink, Justin was having just the attention he had sought since he'd come to Oxford.

The cock of the figure behind Justin jerked and Hardesty was barely able to pull out before he ejaculated in large glumps of cum up Justin's back. Justin's legs were being swung back up in front of him and raised and spread from his body. Coleson rose up from the attention he'd been giving Justin's cock and Justin had only a glimpse of the man's cock sheathed in leather covered in smooth metal studs—almost identical to the ancient Arab contraption Justin had seen in a museum several years earlier and that had set off his hunt for similar devices in early Arab use—before the cock was plunged up into his channel and Coleson pressed his forehead on Justin's, stared into Justin's eyes, and commenced a whispering commentary on the pleasure he could see in Justin's eyes from the punishment being applied to his canal.

Panting and groaning, Justin took Coleson's mouth in his in a mutually applied brutal kiss and ejaculated in three strong spoutings up Coleson's heaving belly.

* * * *

Justin was awakened, lying in his own bed, to the tune of an alarm clock that gave him only a half hour to be at breakfast. He met a pleased-looking Thomas and a frightened animal-aspected Leonard in the corridor, and they went down together to the country kitchen on the ground floor of their wing without daring to say anything to each other. All had been in a haze the previous evening and none could be positive that anything had happened other than a vivid dream, although Justin felt sure of what had transpired—because he welcomed it.

They ate breakfast quickly and quietly, barely finishing before a servant arrived to guide them back to the library through the labyrinth of oddly angled corridors and raised and lowered levels from wings added to the manor house haphazardly over the centuries.

The five seniors were sitting in the easy chairs in the inner circle as they had been the previous evening. They were just starting, Justin surmised, as they had just been served coffee and were once again debating where to take up the discussion.

Hardesty turned to Justin as the three students took their chairs in the outer circle.

"Joshua tells me that you may have some questions on the period Mahfouz writes about in the Arab world, and in Egypt in particular, young man."

"Yes, I do," Justin answered, emboldened by the experience of the previous night, even though no one present was speaking of it or giving even a hint that anything untoward had occurred. "I am studying the below-the-surface sexual mores and practices on the Arab street in this period. In particular, the underground of male on male relationships. I had seen references to coffee houses and—"

"Ah, yes, a worthy topic for today," Hardesty said.

"And in particular bondage and sadism between Arab males—and the antecedents of that," Justin interjected.

Hardesty speared Justin with a piercing gaze and then rewarded the young American a wink, which was the closest reference Justin was going to get of the activities of the previous night. "Perhaps then we should start with the *Black Book* of Hamat Reyyes, in the Blumingdon translation," Hardesty murmured, drawing all gathered in the room to lean forward in their chairs to hear him, as he turned back to the inner circle.

This time even Thomas and Leonard were enthralled with the ensuing discussion.

That night was a repeat of the previous one, except that Justin spent his time split between being flogged bound to the X frame and being bound on his belly on the horse and fucked from behind with his balls in a parachute ball stretcher—his balls tightly bound, separated, and extending to the floor—and Thomas and Leonard took their turns on various other equipment.

This time Justin had only pretended to drink the Turkish coffee and was totally awake and enjoying every stroke of the attention being paid to him.

He wasn't invited to weekend at Coleford Hall again during his term at Oxford, but thereafter Charles Peters wasn't shy in visiting him in his rooms—he'd explained that he had held off in the first encounter so as not to spoil the mutual pleasure to be had in the Coleford Hall dungeons—and made full use of the toys Justin kept in the lower drawer of his nightstand.

One night, several article manuscripts were forced, one by one, under his door, the contents of which put Justin into a pleasurable sweat and reaching for his engorging cock. They all were written in the unmistakable prose of Philip Hardesty.

And then there was Timothy Coleson. Justin was to learn, in private sessions at Oxford, that Timothy Coleson knew far more about medieval Arab bondage and sadism practices than anyone else could image that he could know—and that he had a very interesting soundproof basement in his Oxford home.

Friday Nights with Lenny

I stepped back from the sidewalk, hugging my arms close to my sides, and leaned back on the wall at the corner into the alley, raising one leg, knee bent, and my cowboy booted foot flat against the wall. The hole in the sole of that boot was worn clean through and the cold of the wall wasn't as cold as that of the sidewalk pavement. Besides, it was a good pose for the purpose. While still watching up the conveniently one-way street for slowing cars, I cupped my hands over my mouth and blew. The breath came out in steam and, I'm sure, made it look like I was smoking a cigarette. I decided that was rather cool for the pose I was taking.

I needed a heavier jacket than this leather vest. A bulky jacket wouldn't work as well, but if I froze to death, it wouldn't matter what I was wearing. Winter was coming on. I definitely needed a warmer jacket than this.

I heard the slamming of a metal door back in the alley, and in a few moments I heard his lumbering steps. Just like clockwork at this time. I'd decided a long time ago that the guy must work someplace back there that stayed open late. Wherever he worked, it fronted on the street behind me and I hadn't had the curiosity yet to check it out.

"Hi," he said, as he hit the head of the alley. A big-boned guy somewhere in his thirties. Always looking hangdog when he came out of the alley. But it was after 1:00 a.m., so that was understandable. A big lug. Clumping feet, big hands, a head with hair that had a mind of its own. Cauliflower ears and a bent nose. He looked like he'd been in a lot of fights—but not fights of his choosing because he had sort of a teddy bear demeanor. But not fights that he'd lost either.

I said "Hi" back as he passed and huddled my arms into my chest again, looking up the street, not at him.

I'd been staked out here since late summer and we'd only gotten to the "hi" stage. Of course, I only saw him here once a day, if even that. Sometimes, if I was lucky, I was someplace else when he came out of the alley. I did look forward to the "hi," though. It's about the only thing anyone said to me that wasn't just demanding something they wanted.

I watched him lumber up the street, and I had turned my head, looking for slowing cars coming from the other direction, before realizing that he had turned and come back at me.

"You look cold," he said.

I turned my head, surprised. "My fur coat's in a storage vault in Palm Springs," I said.

"Mine is too," he answered with a little laugh. "In a storage vault somewhere. Just can't remember where the storage vault is. But seriously, you look cold and like you need to warm up someplace. You got a place?"

"Yeah, my mansion's back there in the alley. The second cardboard box on the right."

I wasn't being snotty on purpose. I couldn't be seen standing and talking with someone who liked like he might be a john but wasn't while a real one might be just about to cruise by.

"You hungry?"

"I'm always hungry."

He stood there for a moment, in silence, like he was thinking something over. I desperately wanted him to move on, but he was the only guy who said "hi" to me, so I reined myself in. There weren't any cars moving on the street anyway.

"What the hell," he said. "I had a good night. Thursdays are always light. And I'm not feeling like eating alone. My place isn't far from here. It's warm and I got plenty to eat in the Kitchen. Come on up and I'll fix you something to eat and you can warm up before coming out on the street again."

"Well . . ." I couldn't think of a way to say no without hurting his feelings and I'd gotten used to hearing that "hi." He looked like such a teddy bear. And there weren't any cars cruising down the street.

"You look like you could use a shower too. When was the last time you had a shower? You got any clean clothes back there in that cardboard box mansion? And I could throw these in the washer and dryer while you have a meal. Come on. Winter coming on is a lonely time, and there's nothing on the television late Thursday nights I like to watch."

"Well . . . . OK, thanks. Give me a minute." Still looking frantically down the street for the hint of a john promising a better opportunity, I backed into the alley and headed for my stash.

We were walking the couple of blocks to where he said his apartment was and he was slowing down while we walked and not saying anything when he abruptly stopped by the door of an all-night bodega.

"Just a minute," he said, his voice a little nervous. "I remembered I needed something in here. I'll be just a sec. You can wait out here."

I watched him out of the corner of my eye as he entered the mom and pop store. He was acting nervous enough that I half thought he was going to hold up the place. But he went down an aisle and stopped right where I sometimes stopped in this store. With a knowing little sigh, I turned and propped my back on the support column next to the bodega window, lifted my cowboy boot with the biggest hole to the wall behind me, hooked my thumbs in my jean pockets, and looked up the street while he picked out what brand of condom and lube he wanted.

I knew how I was going to pay for the shower and dinner. I had gone naturally into "the pose," because there always was a chance that something more promising would be cruising by in a flashy car.

At the street door to his apartment building, not much more than a tenement, he stopped and turned to me and, in an earnest voice, said, "My name's Art."

That put us past the "hi" stage. "I'm Jimmy," I answered. I'm not Jimmy, of course, but it's good enough with johns—more often than not more than enough—and a lot easier for them to remember than my own name.

His place was small, but clean, and actually had a separate bedroom, with a brass headboarded double bed, and bath, in addition to the room that served as living room, dining room, and kitchen. It was toasty warm, though, which made all of the difference. And he had a compact washer-dryer unit and was washing the clothes I had been wearing and fixing some dinner as I showered.

He'd shyly looked away as I'd taken my clothes off, and I had to clear my throat for him to reach out a hand to take them. I made no effort to cover myself. I knew he intended to fuck me—that he was just slow in working up to it.

After the time I'd spent out on the street, the apartment was actually a bit more than toasty warm, and when I came out of the bedroom after my shower, I was just wearing low-rise jeans and a flannel shirt over my shoulders that I didn't bother to button. I hadn't put on any briefs or socks and shoes, either. I knew the score here.

His eyes went big when he saw me pad out into the living room, and the skillet he held in his hand wavered for a moment. But then he smiled and said, "Spaghetti OK? From a can? I'm not much of a cook."

"Spaghetti's fine," I said.

"I do have some Chianti to go with it," he continued. "If you . . ."

"Yeah, that would be good. I'm old enough."

He smiled a little smile and I saw him relax noticeably. I knew what he'd actually been asking.

We didn't talk much over dinner. We both sat at the table with the chairs reversed and our arms reaching over the backs like we were in some sort of macho man mode—denying what we both knew we were going to do afterward. I wasn't much for chit chat, and I could tell that he was nervous. Probably had never picked a rent boy up off the street before. Half way through his meal, he looked up and saw that I had wolfed my food down and, without asking, got up and opened another can of spaghetti. He was walking on eggs and doing everything he could to be nice to me. Very much the teddy bear. Big and lumbering and looking like a bouncer in a club, but a shyness and gentleness in him as well.

Time to put him out of his misery.

"So, are you going to fuck me now?" I asked after my plate was clean and my Chianti glass empty, doing my best to keep anything out of the tone of my voice that would be hurtful to him.

"I . . . I . . . ." He looked almost frightened.

"It's OK. I saw what you bought in that bodega. I expected it. Unless, of course, you don't like men."

"Uh . . . I don't know what . . . what you get for . . ."

"You're giving me more than enough," I answered. "You're being very nice to me. I'm good with a fuck . . . if you're interested. So, are you going to fuck me now?"

217

"Yes," he said in a small voice as if it was a revelation to himself, "I'm going to fuck you now. Shall we . . . should we . . . ?"

"On the bed's fine with me. Or the floor if you don't want to use your bed that way."

He sat on the side of the bed, his thighs spread, and I was standing, facing him, between his legs. Before he had collapsed on the bed, we'd both been standing there, plastered against each other and rocking back and forth while he kissed all over my face and neck and brushed my shirt off my back. I pulled his T over his head and took the measure of his bulging, hairy pecs, and then ran my hands down his torso and unzipped him and fished his cock out. He was horse hung. God, maybe more than horse hung. What's bigger than a horse's dick? An elephants? The bigger-than-life proportions of the rest of him held true with his equipment. I held him, needing two hands to make the effort worthwhile, as he engorged and went into a frenzy of kissing down my neck and mouthing and sucking on my nipples as his butt slowly descended to the mattress and his lips went down to my belly.

I had let loose of his dick on his way down, and just placed my hands on his head and ran my fingers into his hair.

He tongued and sucked on my belly, making little guttural sounds deep inside him, with one hairy arm encircling my waist and the hand of the other one working hard on the buttons of my jeans fly. That open and spread, his mouth went lower and swallowed my cock and started to give me slow head, while I worked my fingers in his coarse, mussy hair and arched my back.

I wasn't used to a john taking this much time with me. Of course a lot of this was him working himself up to doing something he'd probably rarely done before.

I let him suck me for a good ten minutes until I felt I couldn't take any more without coming—he seemed content to continue working the cock in his mouth and he seemed to be gaining expertise there with each passing minute—and then, slipping out of his mouth, I went down on my knees on the floor between his thighs, took his cock in my mouth, and started showing him what an expert blow job was like.

I was more interested now. The guy's cock was huge. I'd become jaded with the homeless rent boy stuff to the point that it took a really thick and long cock to impress me, and this was one that I knew would stretch me to the limit and let me know I'd been fucked.

I placed a palm on his belly and gently encouraged him to lie back on the bed, wanting to convey that we were going to be doing this for a while, and then I gripped both of his wrists in my hands, to give him the symbolic sensation that he was mine and under my control now, and I sucked on. He lay docilely back on the bed and shuddered and moaned.

When I stood up, deciding he was engorged and throbbing enough, I held our cocks together for a few minutes, stroking them lightly and looking down into his face. His expression was one of lust and wonder and more than a touch of fear. I knew that, at that moment, he wasn't sure what was going to happen next. Was I going to push my cock into his hole? It was right there. He was in position. I could tell that he wasn't sure who was going to get fucked—and that he was so far gone that he would have taken it if I'd nailed him.

But then I reached over for the plastic bag on top of his night stand and took out the box of condoms and opened it. He had gotten Magnums. At least he knew what he needed. I wondered, though, for a second or two whether there was a size larger than that.

When I was rolling the condom down on his cock and spraying it with lube, I could see any fear in his eyes was being pushed out by the look of arousal and anticipation.

He groaned and grunted and reached for my waist with his big hands as I straddled his torso with my knees right there next to his thighs and with his legs over the side of the bed, and, holding the root of his cock in a hand, working my channel down on the staff.

Once he was bottomed—which was one hell of a job for me to accomplish—he seemed to begin thinking in terms of him being the big man and me being not much more than a boy. He also showed that he had stamina. I started the rise and fall rhythm, but increasingly he was using his hands to lift and lower me on the cock. Slow at first, and he murmured, almost apologetically, "Am I hurting you? Should I—?"

"Do it. Fuck me harder, fucker," I hissed through clinched teeth. "Make me feel it."

He answered by jerking me up and slamming me down on the cock, harder and harder, faster and faster. With me flopping around on top of him, letting him control the frenzy of the fuck.

It was a monster cock, filling and stretching me, and I came quickly, spouting up his belly.

Taking that as a signal to take full control, he turned and moved both of our bodies up onto the bed, placing me on all fours, crouching over my hips, and fucking me hard, deep, and fast in a doggy fuck, until spasming and jerking his cock out of me and ripping the condom off, he ejaculated up my back.

He collapsed to the side on the bed, turning me as well and pulling me into his belly. We lay there, both panting, him nuzzling his scratchy chin into the hollow of my neck.

"I'm sorry. I lost control. I'm—"

"Do it again," I growled. And I meant it. I hadn't been touched like this for some time.

I remember being aware that light was coming in the bedroom window. It was daylight already. We had been fucking for how long? But not that long if you took into account that it had been after one thirty when he picked me up and we'd messed around a lot before getting to the bed. I didn't normally overnight with johns. We usually fucked where that wasn't possible, and it was usually wham bang good-bye. This wasn't really overnight, though. The guy worked someplace where it was practically the night shift. It probably almost always was getting light before he went to bed.

This wasn't anything like overnight. Nothing special at all, I thought, as I drifted off to sleep. Nothing special here at all. Warmth for a few hours, a nice big cock, and a nice guy really, but nothing . . .

When I woke we were both still stretched out on the bed, on our backs. But not touching. Art was sitting up against the headboard, a couple of pillows propping up his back. He was smoking a cigarette and looking at me. His cock was in full erection.

"What time is it?" I asked, rubbing my eyes.

"Ten in the morning—but still early for me . . . for us. Go back to sleep."

"What is this?" I asked, reaching for and enclosing his erect cock. "This isn't sleeping."

"I was thinking of you. How sweet you are and what a great fuck. But I brought you up here . . . not thinking to . . . at first . . . well, when I first asked you if you wanted to come up. What are you doing?"

What I was doing was turning over on top of his thighs, my face next to the erect cock, my arms running up his torso, palms laying on his hairy pecs, the pad of my index fingers on his nipples.

"I'm going to give Willy what he wants and then I'm going to put him—and you back to sleep. You need your sleep."

His voice was thick and low. "I can't let you . . . you're not just giving it away, I know. I can't expect . . ."

"You're going to let me shower again and you're going to feed me breakfast, aren't you? Even if it's in the afternoon. You aren't going to throw me out on the street again right away, are you?"

"No, I'd never throw you out," he murmured, and then, in a guttural voice, "Oh, shit. Oh, fuck."

I had swallowed his cock and was giving him slow head. He writhed a bit under me and told me it was time for me to pull off him so he could fuck me, but I held him there and sucked on him until he'd ejaculated in my throat. Then I laid my cheek on his stomach, with his cock under my chin, and we both found sleep.

The next time I woke, the clock on the nightstand showed 1:15 in the afternoon. He'd said his shift started at 4:00 p.m. He worked in a music club called the House of Blues as the bartender and the manager most of the time. He'd be the bouncer too, he said, but it wasn't usually that sort of club. He'd worked those clubs—which I could tell from his battered face—but, he said, had gotten tired of that sort of stuff.

He wasn't in the bed. The shower was going. I leaned over to the nightstand and fished for the box of Magnums. There were fewer left than I would have thought.

He had his back to me, standing in the shower, when I entered the bathroom. I wrapped my arms around him. He gave a jerk and a low, guttural sound when he realized I was rolling a condom on his cock. I'd encased his staff in both hands—it took both of them—and had started slow stroking. He'd gone hard immediately. While, still standing behind him, helping the cock fill out inside the condom with one hand, I soaped up every surface of his skin with the other one.

After that he took charge, turning me in the small shower and lifting me and settling my channel on his cock. With my shoulder blades against one wall and my knees bent and my feet flat on the opposite wall, he palmed and squeezed and separated my buttocks cheeks with those big hands of his, crouched between my thighs, and fucked me under the stream of hot water, to a mutual ejaculation.

At breakfast, after a silence during which I put away three fried eggs and a mess of bacon, he said, "I want you to stay here, with me, not out in that alley. At least until you can find something better. It's getting too cold for you to be out there."

"You'd let me turn tricks during the day and stay here at night?" I asked, looking up at him and raising my eyebrows.

"If that's what you want. But it would be OK if you stayed here—just with me. I know I'm not—"

"You're just fine. And your cock and your fucking are more than fine. Your eggs could stand a bit longer on the grill and more salt, though."

We both laughed; he nervously.

"What do you say? You stay with me, and I'll take good care of you."

"You wouldn't ever say anything if I just didn't show up for a while?"

"No, I wouldn't. Whatever it took to get you warm and dry and well fed."

"And riding your cock?"

"Yes. I won't lie to you. I'm smitten with you. And, to be blunt, you *are* for sale."

"I don't know. It wouldn't be a great deal for you and I couldn't ask you to give me money. I'd have to turn tricks to get some money."

"You could work where I do," Art said. "We need someone to bus the place and to serve tables when we get busy, which isn't often. You could go and come with me, and you'd be warm. Come with me tonight. Hiring is my decision. We can bring your stuff into the club when we get there and just bring it back here after we close. We can set it right over there, ready to go whenever you wanted to take it. You could take it and leave whenever you want. What do you say?"

"Sounds like a sweet deal," I said, half meaning it, half feeling a bit trapped. "You must really want me bad, though."

"I do. You know I do."

What the hell. He was a nice guy, this place was nicer than my cardboard box in the alley, and he had a cock to die for. I wouldn't have chosen being a rent boy if I didn't want to ride cock.

* * * *

"He sounds good, don't he?"

I turned my head at the sound. I'd been so mesmerized by the smooth saxophone playing, though, that I hadn't heard what Art said. I gave him a glazed look.

"I said he makes a good sound with that saxophone, don't he?"

"He sure does," I answered. Beyond good. So good, it made me go hard. Smooth jazz got to me that way.

Art was behind the bar at the House of Blues, cleaning glasses, getting himself ready for the crowd that would appear later in the night. The club didn't normally start to fill up until nearly eleven, the peak was at midnight, and it was deserted again at closing time at one. Mostly regulars showed up—and then just for an hour or two to get their fix. It was Friday night. Lenny's night to shine on the saxophone, with piano backing. Other nights Lenny was playing somewhere else. He was so good that Friday night was the big night at the House of Blues.

I was standing in front of the bar, drying the glasses as Art washed them. He'd noticed I'd stopped drying as soon as Lenny started playing.

He'd come in only about ten minutes earlier, right before his first set at eight. A young blond guy, probably a college student, and probably rich from the looks of his preppy clothes, had come in with him. The piano player, Thaddeus, who provided the regular backing throughout the week, had started playing an hour earlier. Lenny just sauntered in, the college guy following him, and slouched onto the stool next to the piano, took the sax out of its case, and worked his way naturally into the tune that Thaddeus was playing. The blond sat at a table in the first row, leaned an elbow on the table and his chin on his hand, and listened, instantly transported.

Just as I was. I had never heard music that smooth and sexy before in my life.

Lenny was supposed to play forty-minute sets with twenty-minute breaks backstage, which Art told me he sometimes stretched out to as much as an hour and got away with it. There was really no management that showed up here outside of Art, and Art didn't have time to keep track of what the musicians were doing. Thaddeus, an ancient, substantially sized very, very black man, didn't seem ever to take breaks, though—as long as Art regularly walked over with a fresh beer for him.

At the first break of this Friday, Lenny got up from his stool and stretched. It was then that, without his sax hanging from his neck in front of him, I got my first look at him. He was butt ugly—at least on the first look. But looking at him longer brought everything into balance and he suddenly was charismatic and arousing. He was of above-average height and was lean and wiry. His arms were well-muscled and so lean that I could see the blue of the veins popping out and running close to the surface—at least on one arm. The other one, his right, was covered with a swirling, multicolored tattoo that ran down to his wrist and then v'd down on top of his hand to swirl around his middle finger. His fingers were long and sensuous. He wore a tight muscle T-shirt that v'd deep in front. His pecs bulged prominently as did his crotch in his tight, worn-nearly-white low-rise jeans. He had a gold chain choker necklace, and he was as bald as a billiard cue.

His face was craggy and he looked exactly like someone who had been singing the blues for years. In stark contrast, his eyes were a milky blue and whenever they fell on me, I nearly melted on the spot. So did the college student when Lenny looked at him.

After he'd stood up, I saw him look at the blond guy and incline his head and then turn and walk back to the beaded-curtain covered doorway at the back edge of the small stage. The blond stood up from his table and followed Lenny into the back.

Not more than fifteen minutes later, Art sent me into the back for another tray of glasses. The door was open to the break room as I passed and I was so surprised by what I saw that I stopped, withdrew into the shadows across the corridor from the door, and continued to look, trying to figure out what was going on.

Both Lenny and the blond were naked, facing each other, and straddling a bench. The blond was leaning back against a wall, his shoulder blades on the wall. His hips were rolled up so that the small of his back was supporting his weight on the bench. His left leg, the one toward the door, was bent and his foot was on the floor. The ankle of his right foot was hooked on Lenny's shoulder. He was lithe but looked like an athlete, well muscled. Definitely pampered.

The tattooing I'd seen on Lenny's right arm extended all the way down his right side. And he was as lean as I thought, and hard bodied.

I'd seen plenty of guys fucking before—and preparing to fuck—but this scene caught my attention because of what Lenny was doing with his hands—and with their cocks. Their cocks were docked and Lenny was holding them with his left hand. When I looked closer I saw that they were connected. There was a metal rod running from inside Lenny's piss slit to inside the blond's, and Lenny was slowly moving his cock back and forth, piss slit fucking them both with the metal rod. I'd heard of this before—it was called sounding—but I'd never seen it. And never would have imagined it could be done like this with two guys. I saw a cloth laid out on a small table at the other side of the bench and that other rods, which I knew were called wands, were laid out on that. And not just wands. A hypodermic syringe was laying on the cloth too.

The tattooed middle finger of Lenny's right hand was slowly finger fucking the blond's ass channel. The blond had a bottle of poppers in his hand and was taking a hit like every minute or so.

I was feeling myself go hard just from the wildness and unexpectedness of the scene and couldn't focus on what to concentrate on, the sounding of the cocks, Lenny's tattoos, the expression on the blond's face, or that tattooed finger appearing and disappearing in the blond's hole.

I managed to break away though when I heard Lenny say it was time to go out and do another set but that the blond should stay there and wait for him. I ran and got the tray of glasses and rushed back to the bar with them before Lenny could get his clothes back on. Art gave me a long look when I got back, I'm sure wondering why I was gone so long. But he didn't say anything. Art always wasn't saying anything, not rocking the boat.

You can bet that I found a reason to go into the back when Lenny's next break came up.

The blond was stretched out on his back on the bench, pretty much gone to the world, his head propped up against the wall behind him and his arms dangling off the side of the bench. Lenny, naked again, was straddling the bench, facing the blond. The college guy's thighs were spread and resting on top of Lenny's thighs. Lenny's cock was inside the blond's passage and he was moving his hips back and forth in the rhythm of the fuck. One of his hands was encasing the blond's hard cock, which had a sounding rod running down into the urethra channel.

The syringe I'd seen earlier was on the floor next to the bench.

As I watched, Lenny pulled the wand out, chose one of a bigger size from the cloth on the table, and slowly ran that down into the blond's piss slit. The blond moaned and I saw his cum burble up around the sides of the wand and dribble down the sides of his cock.

I turned and fled back to the club room, where the crowd was beginning to thicken. I stayed busy the rest of the evening and did what I could not to think of what Lenny had been doing to the blond college guy in the back room.

If anything Lenny's saxophone sounded sweeter and sexier as the night progressed.

I was busy helping Art clean up after closing, so I didn't see either Lenny or the blond leave. But along about 1:15 in the morning, I was taking trash out to the dumpster in the alley when I saw a flash car stop at the head of the alley. Out of habit, I went out to the street to see if it was a john looking for me. It was a new red Camaro. I bent over and stuck my head in the open passenger window.

Lenny was sitting in the driver's seat. "Well, don't just stand there; get in," he said.

* * * *

I was flat on my back on an upholstered bench in a living room high up in a high rise, with full-wall windows on two sides. My wrists and ankles were spread over the sides of the bench, reaching to a thick carpet and tied to the legs of the bench.

Lenny had said it was for my own good.

His thighs were under mine and he was facing me, straddling the bench. He was naked. He had an impossibly

227

long, if not terribly thick cock, which was laying in the crease where my thigh met my groin on one side and was curled over onto my lower belly.

I watched, trembling, and babbling a bit as, holding my hard cock upright with one hand, he slowly inserted the wand into my urethra canal. I moaned and then groaned as he slowly twirled it. His own cock was hardening as he worked mine.

"You'll be fine," he murmured. "I know you're interested in it. You came with me willingly, knowing I was going to fuck you. And I saw you watching me do this to Ben. I knew you wanted it too."

"Please," I moaned.

Releasing my cock with his hand but leaving the wand in my cock channel, he moved his forearms under my thighs, raised them a bit, moved his pelvis closer in between my thighs, and penetrated my channel with his now-rock-hard cock. I held my breath as he moved up inside me, and arched my back on the bench and let my head drop over the top edge.

The focus of my senses was split between the sensations of the cock way up inside me and the wand buried in my own cock.

"Oh, god, fuck me. Fuck me, fuck me," I whimpered.

And then he did. At great length. Without a condom. Bathing my insides deep when he came.

Lenny lived by his own rules.

* * * *

I didn't walk back into Art's apartment until after noon on Saturday. He was sitting at the table, in the same clothes he had worn the night before, with a newspaper in front of him. An ashtray overflowing with butts sat next to an empty coffee cup. He didn't look up at me when I first walked in. The expression on his face was more sad than angry or anything else. He looked tired.

I went into the kitchen area and opened the refrigerator. He was the first one to speak.

"You haven't eaten? I'll fix you something."

"Haven't eaten, no. Didn't have any money."

"Sorry. I can give you what you earned yesterday . . . and can pay you right away for any days you work."

"I'd like that. I'll fix myself something. And I was thinking that maybe I'd do more of the cooking around here for us. I think I probably can do it better than you can."

He perked up at that—and I felt even more like a heel than I had when I was walking up the stairs, wondering what I'd tell him about just leaving before closing and not coming back all night.

"I brought your stuff—your sleeping bag and your other stuff," he said, gesturing over to the space in front of the radiator. "I pulled out the clothes and they've been washed, dried, and folded and are layin' over there on the end of the sofa. You need more clothes. And a coat . . . for the winter. You need to shower?"

"No thanks, I'm good."

I took a swig from the milk carton and chewed off a section of a cheese slice. It had gone quiet and I looked over at Art, who was sort of hunched down into himself again. I'd told him something he didn't want to hear by telling him I didn't need a shower. It told him I'd been somewhere other than the alley I'd come from. It told him I'd been with a john, that I'd been someplace I could get a shower. Not quite, but I didn't want to tell him who I'd been with. God, I felt like a bastard. I put the milk carton and the unfinished slice of cheese back in the refrigerator.

"Art."

"Yes?"

"Can you take me to the bedroom. I need you to take me to the bedroom."

He fucked me standing next to the bed, me lying on the bed below him. It was all him. I wanted him to know that it was all him. He was standing, facing and hunched over the side of the bed, his hands gripping me on each side where my buttocks curved down into the small of my back.

My weight was on my shoulder blades on the surface of the bed and my arms extended out on the surface of the bed, my fists clutching at the bedspread, bunching it up and releasing it in the rhythm of his pumping. My cheek was against the scratchiness of the chenille bedspread, and I was crying out how big and stretching he was and how much I was loving his dicking. And I wasn't lying.

My legs were wrapped around the small of his back and he was pulling and pushing my channel on his cock with the strength of his hands.

Afterward we lay stretched against each other, me on my side inside the embrace of one of his arms. I traced his solid, big-boned nakedness with the tips of my fingers, moving up to his face and his lips. My own lips replaced the fingers and we engaged in what probably was the first long, lingering kiss we'd had. I could feel him shuddering and a sob escaped him from around my lips. I moved a hand down his torso and buried my fingers in his pubes and rubbed and pulled lightly on his thick, curly hair down there. I could feel that he was reengoring. He started to turn over me, to cover my body and then remount me. But I gently pushed him back onto his back.

"Shhh, be still," I whispered. "There's plenty of time for that. You need to sleep now. I'll take care of you and then you sleep."

He sighed as I handed his cock and began to slowly masturbate him.

"You're so good to me, Art," I whispered.

He made a low, guttural sound. His pelvis was starting to move in rhythm to my jacking. But my jacking wasn't enough for him. He turned, coming over on top of me. I surrendered to him. It was what he wanted. I spread my legs and raised my knees, placing my feet flat on the surface of the bed. He was between my thighs, his big, hardened cock poking at my lower belly. I reached over to the nightstand for a condom packet.

"One thing is for sure," I said, as I reached between our body and rolled the Magnum on.

He huffed a "What?"

"We're going to need more condoms real soon."

His answer was to start working his cock into me, while he embraced me closely and buried his face in the hollow of my neck. Panting hard and trying to spread my legs farther apart and raise my buttocks more to him, I turned every ounce of my attention to trying to open to him. It was like this each time, working hard to open to the hard thickness of him. And I loved it each time.

Then he began to pump and I lost all thought of anything.

Thinking came later as I sat at the table, eating. I'd left Art asleep at last on the bed, a smile on his lips.

My thoughts were convoluted and went back to the night before. In Lenny's king-sized bed beside the full-wall window overlooking the lights of the city. Lenny's back was propped up on pillows against the headboard of his bed with his legs stretched out in front of him, his arms embracing me as I lay stretched out on top of him, pointed to the ceiling.

Most of his long cock was up my channel. It may have been the longest one of any man who'd had me. We were both looking down the line of my trembling torso, with me panting shallowly, by his instruction, as he slowly twirled the third, larger wand into the piss slit of my cock with the same hand that he was holding it erect with.

With every fiber of my being I was concentrating on holding steady, when I wanted to yowl and set my hips in motion in response to the filling penetration of two of my orifices.

"You're good with this," Lenny murmured. "A natural. You wanted it bad, didn't you?"

"I heard about it," I answered. "I was curious, yes. I've tried most everything."

"And this. Good is it?"

"When you do it, yes."

"Nothing more possessing, one man of another, than this."

"Yes." I moaned as he slowly twirled the wand out and reached for a thicker one. A few moments of heavy breathing from both of us and deep moaning from me, as the fourth

231

wand worked its way in. His cock was throbbing inside me, and hard as a rock. This was as arousing to Lenny as it was to me.

"Now, right now, you are fully mine."

"Yes."

"From what Art tells me—and more from what he doesn't say—you are a whore."

"Yes."

"You going to be my whore?"

"Yes."

He laced his legs through mine and raised up and out, giving him leverage to start pumping up into my channel with his cock.

I felt his thumb press at my lips as he began to pump me with his cock. I opened my mouth to the thumb and started sucking on it, as he moved it in and out. He possessed me and was fucking me in every orifice. Complete, total possession. I felt the release of my cum rising up around the embedded wand and flowing down the sides of my cock, into my pubes. He ejaculated not long afterward in a strong spurt deep inside me. No condoms for Lenny. He lived on the edge.

I woke up on the bed in the morning, naked and sore all over. He'd fucked me twice more in the night. I was alone, but it didn't take long to realize that what woke me was the sweet sound of the saxophone.

I showered and dressed. He was still playing when I came out into the living and dining area. His apartment was so much more than Art's was—more of everything and more in every way. But I wasn't really comfortable in it. Everything was just too expensive looking, too slick. I didn't think of it at the time, but it was as too slick as Lenny himself was.

He was sitting, naked, on a dining room chair next to a glass-topped table. His body was beautiful—not in a bodybuilder's way but sensual, hard, reflecting a hard-living life that went with the blues sounds he was pulling out of the sax. I ached for him to fuck me again, to play me like he was playing that sax.

On the table beside him was a hypodermic syringe and a small glass bottle. The bottle appeared to be empty.

Lenny didn't even know I was there. I didn't bother to go into the kitchen. I walked to the entrance to the apartment and closed the door quietly beyond me. Lenny wouldn't have known if I had slammed it.

For a while I didn't know where I was going, but my feet carried me back to Art's apartment.

* * * *

I was so deep into remembering this as I sat at Art's table that I only slowly was aware he was standing in the doorway to the bedroom, dressed, his hair wet from the shower. The look he was giving me was unguarded, and I instantly felt the heel again from the love and desire I saw in his eyes.

"Guess it's about time for me to go to work again."

"If you'll give me a few minutes, I'll shower and dress and go with you," I said.

He beamed at me. "We got time to stop and buy you some more clothes, if you'd like."

"Yes, I'd like that. And maybe we can stop at the bodega and get a couple more boxes of those Magnums."

He beamed again.

We were happy and domesticated through the rest of the week, settling down into a pattern. And I'd been right. My cooking was a lot better than his was.

* * * *

Lenny was crouched over me, his weight borne on a hand propped next to my head, as I lay flat on my back on the padded bench in his living room, my hands clutched and digging into his biceps, my heels digging into the carpet on either side of the bench, toes, tense, pointed up. His other hand was between our bellies, cupping both of our docked cocks, the cocks linked by a metal rod penetrating both of our piss slits.

233

He was slowly rocking his cock back and forth, narrowing the distance between our bulbs of the exposed metal, forcing more of the wand into each of our cocks, fucking both of the urethra channels.

I was panting and watching his eyes closely, only now and then casting a gaze down my torso to the two docked cocks. He'd told me what the goal was. There was still two and a half inches of rod to be seen between our bulbs.

"It usually takes forever for a guy to learn to take this," Lenny murmured. "You learn fast. You love this. My own little fuckin' whore."

He rose up momentarily, reaching for a bottle of poppers. "Here, take another drag on this," he said, waving it under my nose. When I had, my eyes followed the bottle back to the surface of the adjacent table, where the wands were laid out on a table. Next to them was the hypodermic syringe and the other bottle. I shuddered in fear of that.

Lenny went back to moving his cock, swallowing more of the wand at his end, penetrating my urethra canal more with the wand at the other end. I felt the tip of my bulb kiss the tip of his. With a little jerk I came. And so did he, our cum colliding and mixing. He wrapped an arm around my waist, raising my pelvis to his, his continuing to sway back and forth, sending the wand connecting our cocks shimmering. My torso was arched back toward the surface of the bench, my head thrown back, my arms dangling at my side. His lips went to the hollow of my neck and then descended to my nipples.

Swaying back and forth, back and forth. I had had cum in reserve and gave it to him now. The same with him.

"Nice" he said, stopping and holding. Then, "I'm taking you to the bed now and fucking your lights out."

"I can't stay the night," I murmured. But he wasn't listening to me.

That was the first thing I'd said to him too that second Friday night when I was putting the garbage in the alley dumpster along about 1:15 a.m., as Art and I were closing up the House of Blues.

The red Camaro had shown up at the head of the alley and I'd dipped my head to the passenger window and told Lenny, "I can't stay the night."

Art and I had had a good, solid week of settling in when Friday night rolled around again and it was Lenny's regular gig to play at the House of Blues.

He'd brought the blond college kid with him and, once again, the kid had followed Lenny beyond the beaded curtain into the back of the club after Lenny's first set. And once again Lenny took his sweet time on his break and the blond didn't come back into the main room with him.

And once again Lenny's playing was mesmerizing. He played just like he was playing for me and was playing my body as smoothly and sweetly as he was playing that sax. Art just let me moon. He knew I'd make up the work time during Lenny's breaks and that this was only once a week.

I have no idea if Art knew that it had been Lenny I was with the previous Friday night or not. All I know is that Art said nothing, showed nothing other than a bit of concern in the way he saw me mooning over Lenny and his music. I don't know, maybe if Art had shown more jealousy . . . but then maybe not. I knew I was like a skittish colt, ready to break and run back to a life on the streets the first sign of possessiveness from Art.

Which was kind of funny, really. That's what attracted me to Lenny. His complete possession of me.

I got busy toward 10:00 p.m. and didn't see whether the blond guy came back out to the main room the rest of the night.

On Lenny's bed that night, he was on top of me, fucking me from behind, and I was belly to the bed, when he went up on his knees between my thighs and pulled me up on my knees in front of him. I could vaguely see our reflection bouncing off the window overlooking the city. He was holding me against his chest with one arm embracing mine.

I watched—and whimpered—as he reached over beside us with the other hand and picked out a wand—thicker than I'd taken before—and, cupping my hard cock, began to work the wand into my piss slit, twirling it as it descended into me. Then he pushed my torso down again, so that I was on all fours, and began pumping me seriously with his cock. His hand was still cupping my cock and holding it so that, as my body lowered more from the onslaught of his ass fucking, the bulb of my cock pushed into the surface of the bed—or, rather, the end of the wand did.

As his strokes pushed my hips down lower, the wand was slowly penetrating deeper into my urethra canal. Lenny took his hand away and I was then forcing the deeper penetration myself. When it occurred to me that I was now fucking my own cock with the wand, I was overcome with arousal and ejaculated. Sensing that I had, Lenny laughed and came inside me too.

He pushed me all of the way down on the surface of the bed, with his body covering mine.

The last thing I remember saying before I drifted off to an exhausted sleep was, "I can't stay the night."

I woke up Saturday morning to the sound of soft sax music from the living room. I turned over on my back and realized from the swollen soreness feeling in my cock that the wand was still in it. Just the thought of that made me start going hard again. I rolled onto my back, grasped the bulb at the end of the wand, and, slowly, started to pull it out. I moaned at the feel of it moving inside. I'd pulled it three-quarters of the way out when, without thinking, I slowly twirled it back down to half way. I arched my back from the pleasurable feel of it. Out . . . and then back in. Out and in, out and in. I was groaning and moaning at the forbidden pleasure of it. When I pulled it all of the way out, it was to leave my ejaculation unimpeded.

I lay there, thinking what a slut I was and knowing that I repeatedly had said I couldn't stay the night, knowing that Art would be sitting at the table in his little apartment, smoking cigarette after cigarette, pretending to read the newspaper, probably doing my laundry, and worrying about where I was.

With a sigh, I rolled out of the bed, took a shower, dressed, and walked out into the living room. As before, Lenny was lost to my presence, making love to his saxophone, the syringe and empty drug bottle next to him on the glass-topped table.

* * * *

When I walked into the apartment early Saturday afternoon, Art was sitting at the table again, but he was eating his breakfast. He was wearing a robe over pajama bottoms. No overflowing ashtray, no mauled newspaper. I'll admit there was a twinge of concern in his eyes, which gave me a twinge of guilt. But he was none the worse for wear. I had been gone overnight on a Friday and had come back to him. He was trustful—and simple enough—to believe I'd come back to him the next Saturday morning too. I had, of course, but this level of trust in him gave me a little concern.

Which was ironic, as I was the one causing the concern.

"You missed the excitement of last night."

I gave him a hard look. I hadn't missed any excitement last night. Lenny had given me just about more excitement than I could handle. But I could see that Art wasn't being sarcastic.

"What excitement?"

"One of the customers—that young college kid who followed Lenny around like a puppy dog. Right at closing I found him in the break room at the back of the club."

"Did you have to roust him out?"

"No. He was dead. He'd OD'd. On heroin, the medical examiner thought likely. Back there in the break room sometime during the evening. He was naked and everything, his body just lying on that bench back there, stiff as a board."

"God, the cops and everything came?" My mind was racing. Lenny. Did he know? Had he known all that time he was sounding and fucking me last night. And offering me poppers? And with the hypo needle next to us. And the one next to him this morning?

"Yeah, they did. And they want to talk to as many of the people in the audience we can identify and Lenny too. They didn't show much interest in talking with Thaddeus, though. I told him that I'd never seen Thaddeus away from the piano. The guy must have a cast-iron bladder or bag or something."

"Me?" I asked, still in shock and not listening to much else Art was saying.

"They don't know about you. And there's no reason they need to unless someone else mentions you. I thought with what you'd been doing before and all—"

"Thanks, but I've never been picked up," I said. "I hadn't been out on the street all that long."

Art smiled a little smile like this made him happy.

"But it's fine with me if they never hear about me," I added.

I didn't know the blond from Adam, so I didn't have too much grief to spare on him. But Lenny. Now I was scared of—and for—Lenny. I wouldn't go with him again.

"You hungry?" Art asked.

"Yes, but I'll fix something."

"Need to take a shower."

I hesitated, knowing I'd just had one at Lenny's place. "Yeah, that would be nice. But you look like you haven't had yours yet yourself. Maybe we could do it together."

I fucked myself on his cock, with him standing against a wall of the shower and me draped on his front, fists locked behind his neck and hanging off him, my feet leveraging off the wall out wide from his waist, and pumping my channel on his cock.

We had to stop at the bodega for a couple more boxes of the Magnums on our way to work that afternoon. And the rest of the week went just fine. I could feel myself in the groove and the panic of being in a groove like this dissipating with each day.

I'd had a scare and a brush with something I couldn't control. But now I was in control. If the cops didn't get at me and wear me down, I'd just bypass Lenny from now on. Let him spiral down by himself if that's where he was headed.

* * * *

238

Late, late Friday night, the two of us facing each other, both straddling the padded bench in his living room, our foreheads touching, sweating, each of us watching our own cock and that of the other, the two almost touching, as we each sounded ourselves. Lenny was way ahead of me in wand thickness. His looked like a baseball bat.

"Here, let me," he whispered. He took hold of my cock and pulled the wand out. Then he pulled the much thicker wand out of his cock and pressed the end of it at my piss slit.

"No, Lenny, I don't think . . . it's much too thick."

"This will help you."

"Oh, god, no Lenny. I don't."

But the needle was already piercing a vein in my arm. "Just a little. Just enough to relax you, to loosen you up. To help you take this. I want to see this in my little whore."

"No, Lenny, no . . ." The drug was already working on me. The room was swirling around me. I leaned back on my elbows on the bench and watched that seven inches of baseball bat beginning to be inserted into my urethra. I felt the thickness of it and yet again I didn't. I was floating and laughing. No cares at all as, inch by inch, the wand disappeared into my cock slit.

"Nice. Fucking time." There was an edge of excitement in his voice.

Lenny was standing, still straddling the bench and lifting my pelvis up to him with hands gripping my waist. My torso was arched back toward the surface of the bench, my weight on my shoulder blades, and my arms dangling uselessly down the sides of the bench. I was looking at a smiling, almost leering, Lenny up the line of my arched torso, beyond my erect and throbbing cock with three inches of wand showing—but now not even that. I could feel myself drawing the wand inside me. Maybe only two inches showing now. How long had it been? Six, seven inches? Oh, shit, oh, jesuzzz. Not more than one inch now. My cock hungrily swallowing it. Lenny in double, triple now. Smiling, his cock penetrating deep, deeper. Pumping me, pumping, pumping, pumping. I'm laughing, crying out to him how wonderful I feel, how I want him to fuck me forever.

Lenny's fingers gripping the last half inch of the wand as he fucks me. Drawing it almost all the way out. Pushing it back in. Twirling it. Out, in, twirl. Out, in, twirl.

"My little whore," I hear him say.

Out, and I watch my cum splash all over his belly . . . his bellies . . . there are multiple of them.

I feel him come too, in a flood, the flood of all time. I'm laughing.

"To the bedroom," the three Lenny's say, in unison and harmony.

Fucking, fucking, fucking. All Friday night long fucking me. Lights flashing on and off, all colors, all night long. The bedroom window wall melting and the bed floating out over the city. And then . . . nothing.

The mother of all headaches when I woke up Saturday morning. In Lenny's bed. No saxophone music to wake me this morning. I rolled over, placed my feet on the floor, waited for a few minutes to gather my strength and intent, and then shakily stood and gingerly padded to the bathroom to take a shower.

No shower today, though, not here. Lenny was curled up on the floor of the bathroom, a syringe beside him, dead as a doornail.

I couldn't pull on my clothes and get out of there fast enough. I literally ran the ten blocks to Art's apartment and busted through the door. Art was sitting at the table.

"God, Art, I need you. Take me to the bedroom and fuck my brains out. God, I need you."

Not asking any questions, not then, not later, Art did just as I asked.

No connection was ever made. I couldn't be happier to be settling down with Art and working with him at the club.

The sleeping bag and a dwindling pile of my "stuff" from my earlier life are still sitting there next to the radiator, symbols of a choice I still can make.

I'm happy with the choice I've made, though. I didn't get a winter coat until the next winter. You don't need a winter coat in bed. We did, though, have to find a cheaper and higher volume supplier of Magnums than the bodega near the House of Blues.

Experiencing Partnered Sounding

(An Essay)

I like to write edgy gay male stories, but I'd never even heard of the sexual act of sounding before someone remarked on a gay story site that they had trouble finding such stories. I looked the term up and was both intrigued and shocked, wanting to include sounding by one man of another in a story but having no context I could put it in. I usually write from the emotions, and I didn't think I could do justice to the sounding experience in a story without having had the experience myself. I mentioned that to my steady male lover at the time, a university exchange student from Lebanon, Samir, who had been sent from Beirut by an former lover specifically for me to mentor at the university in exchange for regular, dominating sex. To my surprise, Samir said he had been sounded back in Lebanon and knew of a tattoo artist in this university town who did soundings.

I left it at that for a couple of weeks, afraid to pursue the issue, but my muse increasingly pressed me to write about sounding. I had been challenged to do so. The tattoo artist had rooms above his shop. He was a wiry, bald, but hard-muscled guy, probably in his late thirties, who was a walking billboard for his craft. I normally would not have chosen someone like him to have sex with, but he had something I wanted to acquire, and there Samir was, egging me on. He seemed as excited for me to have the experience as I was to learn of such a strange experience.

The tattoo artist told me that the key to sounding was that I remain absolutely still through the experience so that no internal damage was done—that after my urethra canal, running down my shaft, toughened to the experience through multiple use, the worry of damage would lessen. I was trembling. I had no plans at that point to have more than the one experience so that I could write about it. Seeing that I already was trembling at the mere idea of it, the tattoo artist said that the best position for me would be sitting on his cock in his lap, with my extremities immobilized.

I told him I was worried about giving up full control, and his answer was that that was the whole point of one man sounding another. I would have to be submissive to his every command. And as preparation he would need to fuck me first and take full control of me. That I would have to be completely submissive to him; if I couldn't fully submit to him, he wouldn't provide the experience.

With Samir watching, I let the man bend me over his bed and fuck me from behind. As he did that, he gave me commands of positions to take and responses to make with my hands and channel muscles. He commanded that I hold the urge to ejaculate, and I did so, with difficulty. When he was satisfied that I would follow commands immediately, he showed me the sounding rods, saying he would use no more than two of the smallest ones on me in this first experience. Then he explained what he was going to do with them, in detail. I almost backed out at that point, but Samir was giving me encouraging looks, and I didn't want to disappoint Samir, who had set this up at my request. Once again the tattoo artist said I'd have to remain completely still, but that I didn't have to hold off ejaculation. I could let it flow; I would just have to combat the urge to jerk while I did it if a wand was inside the canal.

He said that if I waited for the wand to be extracted, though, the experience of ejaculation would be explosive and I could jerk freely—and probably would want to. When we had both cooled off, he sat in a straight chair, commanded me to kneel between his legs and service his cock with my mouth, which I did, and to roll the condom on him when he was hard and spray his cock and my channel with lubricant again, which I did. Then he pulled me onto his lap and cock, facing away from him. He worked his knees between my thighs and forced my legs wide apart, immobilizing them. He had Samir pull my arms around to his back and handcuff them, immobilizing them as well. He lifted and lowered me on his hard shaft until he was satisfied that he was in complete control of me. I had gone hard in the process.

He then had to repeatedly tell me to relax, hold still, and breathe naturally as, holding the bulb of my now-hard cock erect between two fingers of one hand and squeezing it to open my piss slit, he slowly pushed the silver sounding wand with a slight bulge at the end into my urethra canal and fed it down into the narrow canal. As he did so, I could feel his cock throbbing inside me, and I could tell that he was as keyed up as I was. He kept murmuring encouragement in my ear as I laid my head back in the hollow of his shoulder and whimpered at the feel of the hard steel penetrating down the length of my shaft, telling me how nice my cock was and how well I was

245

doing. At length he told me the wand was in four inches, that he was going to extract it and replace it with a thicker one, and then that he was going to fuck my cock with the thicker one.

I gasped as he slowly pulled the rod out, and I almost ejaculated then. I trembled almost uncontrollably as the larger wand entered the canal and he stopped and murmured to me to relax, hold still, and breathe naturally. He was hard as a rock inside me, and I was concentrating as much on his cock inside me as on the wand. He was breathing heavily now, as much into the experience as I was.

He told me that the thicker wand was deeper than the first one had been, but he didn't say how much deeper. He said then that he was going to start fucking the channel with it and that, although I could flow with the wand in, perhaps I'd want to warn him when I was about to come and he'd pull the wand out. He said the ejaculation I experienced from sounding would be like no other and that it might be best, especially the first time, if the wand was out, because I'd probably want to jerk and shudder as I spouted. He began moving the wand up and down, slowly, in the canal, and it did feel very much like fucking. He twirled it, and, emitting little gasps and working hard to maintain control of myself, while lost in the new sexual sensations I was feeling, I felt myself ready to blow, and told him I was about to. He extracted the wand as I shot out onto the carpet, now free to shudder almost uncontrollably—and doing so. He was right. The ejaculation was extraordinary. I felt my whole body collapse into itself and go weak and trembly like a bowl of Jell-O.

Telling me how good I'd been, he stood, bringing me up with him, took two steps to the side of the bed, bent me over the bed again, and fucked me to his ejaculation. Afterward he put his mouth to my ear and whispered to me that he wanted me to come back to him for more. It didn't sound so much a request as it did a command, though, which frightened me.

I admit that I did go back to him a couple of times, enjoying the experience each time with progressively thicker wands and wanting that special ejaculation, but I eventually stopped it as having been something to experience but not to practice regularly—afraid more of the control aspects of it than of the physical act. Fundamentally, I didn't want the tattoo artist to control me, and he would do so as long as I came back to him—and I would likely sink deeper and deeper into his control the longer I let him dominate me this way. The man who had initiated me into male-male sex had controlled me totally and used me mercilessly, and I didn't want to give up that much control ever again.

After the third and last session with the tattoo artist, I did let Samir, who dominated me and who I totally trusted, sound me a few times himself, and I felt a closer connection with him when he did it than I'd felt with the tattoo artist. With Samir, the familiarity and trust level permitted us to come almost simultaneously. Also, Samir continued practicing this on himself in my presence before we fucked, increasingly so when he knew I was aware of the practice, and it was arousing to me to watch him work himself with the sounds.

During that first session, the tattoo artist offered to sound Samir, who was willing, so that I could watch the effect on someone more experienced and able to take thicker wands longer and deeper. And from those experiences, I felt able to write stories about sounding. My first effort was *Dark Angel Sounding*, which has become my gay male best-seller—and probably my most controversial work—and which, having had the experience, permitted me to write the sexual act as one of domination, submission, and total trust—and as medically safe if done properly. It remains for me a "darker fetish," and I usually write it that way in my stories that include that sexual act.

Porn War

The song "Kisses Sweeter than Wine" sprang to my mind, because that was what his kisses were. As far as I could tell in the dimly lit Blue Moon resort hotel room in Las Vegas, he was a young hunk, no older than I was. Most of the men in the room were older, a few probably twice or more my age. None were complete throwaways, but he was prime among them. And he had latched on to me as soon as I'd entered the room, probably the last to arrive of eight or nine or twelve. It was that murky in the room. The rest of them already naked. Most of them already humping.

We stood, rocking together against each other in instant high heat, and kissing—those sweeter-than-wine kisses—as he pulled my clothes off me. We all wore face masks, which, along with the dimness in the room, supposedly would make it difficult to identify each other during the meetings of the conclave the next day when we were clothed—but surely not impossible.

He certainly couldn't hide his mop of blond hair or his magnificent build or his extra-long cock completely even in clothes in the light of day in a Las Vegas hotel meeting room. And if he touched or kissed me again, I'm sure I would know it was him.

I could recognize Marty Doans without any trouble. Muscle solid, but a bit squat, nearly bald, and bordering on pudgy—and very, very hairy. I could identify him primarily, even with a face mask, because he obviously was holding court. I'd never seen him naked before, and although I'd heard about him having a super-thick cock, I couldn't see this now. He was sitting on the side of a bed, one of two queen beds in the room, with another man kneeling between his knees and servicing his cock. Which is why I couldn't see it. Two men were on the bed behind him, fucking, and Marty had a cigar in one hand and three or four fingers of his other hand up the ass of the man doing the fucking behind him.

Marty was the organizer of the conclave and a big-name publisher of pornographic e-books. You got your books under his gay male imprint and you could quit your day job.

My books were under his imprint, and I'd never had to have a day job.

So, yes, I knew Marty, of all the guys in this room, even with the mask on. And I also knew the squirrelly little guy who came with Marty, Peter Knoles, who, though obviously wanting some of what others were getting, was nervously flitting around the room from coupling to coupling, but pulling back almost immediately because Marty wanted something or Peter was afraid Marty would want something and someone other than Peter would supply it. Last I saw of him on this night, he was standing at the wall trying to adjust the temperature because Marty complained about it being too hot in here.

Of course it was hot in here with a dozen or so guys in high heat.

I didn't know whose room this was. Probably either Marty's or Peter's. The invitation delivered under my door shortly after I checked in earlier that afternoon just said, "If you're really a player, and we're not talking cards, there will be more of this in Room 103 at 11:00 p.m." The invitation had included a fifty-dollar bill.

The sweeter-than-wine hunk had me straddling him on the bed Marty wasn't using himself. The hunk was on his back, my knees were buried in his pits, and I was arched back, grabbing an ankle with one hand and his cock with my fist, while he sucked me and I slowly face-fucked him. He lifted my torso to vertical after a period of good moaning and servicing, raised my hips a bit more, and brought them forward so that his mouth and tongue could get to my asshole. The underside of my cock was thumping on his forehead and he was bringing me to a boil so fast I hoped I wasn't going to be leaving anything sticky in his wavy blond hair.

He'd already asked me if I took cock or gave it, and my answer of "both, but more of the taking," had pleased him immensely. I knew then that I was going to be fucked by a long cock. In truth, from the atmosphere of the room, I knew I was going to be fucked by more than one. By Marty, for sure, if this was his party. He'd asked me for it before, in New York, but I'd never given it. I'd always managed to fend him off with a plausible excuse. I sure was going to be giving it tonight.

Didn't matter to me tonight. I was walking along the edge on a vodka high already, and I didn't mind doing research for my books and being gifted with new plotlines.

I went to arch my back again, but couldn't, because I realized that there was a chest behind me, a chest obviously sporting a studded leather harness. And two beefy, hairy arms encircling me, one holding me in place and the other possessing my cock, slick from the attentions of the sweeter-than-wine hunk. The new arrival had leather bands with studs on them on his wrists, and his arms were tattooed. The hard cock at the small of my back wasn't anything to sniff at.

Between the hunk working my ass with his tongue and the leatherman working my cock with his fist, it wasn't long

251

before I gave the hunk a facial. Sorry about the hair, I thought. A protein shampoo. My ejaculation signaled the leatherman to move me back and set me on the hunk's long, curved cock—it took an eternity for me to slide down that pole—and then he moved around to kneel over the hunk's face and receive attention for his own ass and for me to bend down and suck his cock. He didn't take that position for very long, though. He moved back to behind me, embraced me with one arm, and stuck a popper under my nose with his other hand.

"Inhale this good," a growly voice whispered in my ear. "You're gonna want it. We're gonna go for a DP here."

I moaned and inhaled. I kept right on inhaling—and moaning and groaning—as the leatherman slowly worked his cock in on top of the one the hunk already had buried inside me. The hunk held still with his while the leatherman began to slow pump me. They came almost simultaneously inside me.

My world was spinning from the popper, so I didn't much care or feel very much pain. I did do a lot of groaning and grunting, though.

I think I was only semiconscious, but I was awake enough to realize when the leatherman was pulling me off the hunk and carrying me over and setting me in Marty Doan's lap, facing him, and on what I found was a very thick cock indeed. I just let my shoulder blades fall back onto the tops of his feet and my arms dangle on the carpeting beside me, as Marty began pulling me on and off his cock. The leatherman knelt down and gave me another pull on the popper before sliding his cock down my throat.

I woke I have no idea how much later to the flush of a toilet in the bathroom off the hotel room. The lights were off in the room, but a weak glow of sun was coming in from around the edges of the curtains on the windows and the light was on in the bathroom. The bathroom door was open. I saw a naked, fat, hairy rump standing in front of the toilet. I heard a second flush.

No one else was in the room. My arms were pulled above my head, my wrists bound to the headboard with restraints. My legs also were spread and restrained at the ankles, with leather leads running down to the bottom corners of the bed. The leads on the legs weren't pulled tight. There were a couple of pillows under the small of my back, elevating my hips. And I saw a small collection of toys—dildos and beads—laying on the bed beside me. I had no idea if these had already been used or were waiting to be used.

It all seemed familiar. I wondered if I'd written this scene before. My predecessor under my pen name, Brent, certainly had.

As Marty walked out of the bathroom and toward me, he was adjusting a wide, studded leather band around the base of his cock. He also was stroking himself to an erection.

"Hey, what're you doing?" I asked.

"Wrong question," he muttered. "It should be what have we been doing? Good of you to join the party again. There for a while it was like fucking Raggedy Andy. Too bad you weren't more awake. The part of you that was was enjoying it."

Without further ado, he hopped up on the bed, crouched in a half stand between my spread legs, and reached down and grasped my waist in strong hands. He pulled my pelvis up to his, shifting my weight onto my shoulder blades with my torso arcing down to the head of the bed. He thrust his thick, studded cock inside me and began to pump. Feeling no pain or even difficulty in taking his cock with added studs, I realized that my channel had been reamed well open, with no opportunity to tighten up again for however long I'd been in this room.

Whatever.

I turned my cheek to the side and moaned. He was fucking me good. I just wouldn't look directly at the gnome he appeared to be in this stance. He was fucking me really, really good, in fact.

But the restraints and the toys had me a bit worried.

"Um, Mr. Doans . . . Marty . . . just because I write gay male BDSM doesn't mean I practice it."

"You do now," was his response. "Do you want me to stop?"

"No, not particularly."

"You need another shot of the poppers?"

"Depends on what else you're planning on doing."

"I'll take that as a yes. Before I do it, I'll give you another shot or two. You'll want it."

At the front of my mind was the knowledge that Marty Doans could either make or break a gay male porn novelist.

Before he untied me and sent me back to my room, with another $100 in my jeans pocket, to shower, breakfast, and show up at the conclave only an hour late, I discovered that, no, he hadn't used all of those toys already.

* * * *

Before facing the first session of the conclave, an annual meeting of gay male porn writers, held pretty much in secret wherever Marty Doans's Bent Stallions Publications made arrangements, I felt I needed a real drink. It wasn't that far from noon. I saddled up to the bar of Las Vegas' Blue Moon resort hotel, a gay guy's only place, and asked for a Bloody Mary double. I'd met Marty before, face to face, in his New York offices when my lover, Brent Davenport, the original Jasper of the Jasper rough sex novels fame, died and I had to establish that I had written Brent's last three manuscripts—his highest-return best-sellers—myself. But I'd never been to one of Marty's conclaves, although I'd been invited before.

The main reason I'd never come was that Brent had been in a war of traded barbs with one of Doans's other best-selling authors, the gay male Romance novelist going by the pen name Niles James. The bitterness was such between them that, if they had ever met at a venue like this, the fur would fly.

I had only come to this conclave because I had been asked to come as a paid speaker—and was assured that Niles James would not be attending. Once here, though, I saw his name on the attendees' list. Well, I would just have to do my best to avoid him. I had half a notion to take off my "Jasper" name tag and go in as someone else—but I was a paid speaker in that name, so I guess I'd just have to find out who the old codger was—he had to be old if he was a contemporary of Brent's—and stay clear of him.

When I went to put the Bloody Mary on my room tab, the bartender checked his computer and said, "Your account has been linked to the Room 103 account, Mr. Jasper. You may just cite that room for charges from now on."

Marty, I thought. This was beginning to look like a setup, like I was lured here for Marty to use. He'd made clear before that he wanted me, and I'd only barely been able to outrun him—until now, well, until last night, of course. I'd thought that last night would do it for him, but now he was slowly owning me. I downed the Bloody Mary, ordered another one, and, that one in hand, soared into the meeting room.

A panel session on the difference between erotica and porn—an argument I had no time for; what I wrote was what I wrote—was in full cry. I took a seat toward the back and looked around. There were maybe seventy people there. I wasn't a bit surprised to see that well more than half of them were women. Brent had had a major burr under his saddle about the false genre of women writing "just pretend" or "how we'd like to fantasize our man" stories read mostly by other women. I had come to share his disdain for this quite large share of the gay male porn market, but like him, not too vocally because many women buying and reading that fake stuff were also buying ours, even though we thought of ourselves as writing for the actually actively gay male.

Over half of the men present were well into their fifties and sixties. Although I felt a bit sorry for them writing what most of them weren't actively engaged in now, I respected that most of them—probably all who dared come to a conclave such as this—had once been active and were now writing from memories they wished to remain captured and arousing them for as long as possible.

Only a few of the men present were young, as I was, or not much beyond forty, and probably writing from active experience. Not that I could say that much of what I wrote was from active experience myself—or was before Marty started taking me under his jaded wing the previous night. I had enough gay sex, just not that much that could be classified as BDSM. I now certainly could write BDSM stories better, the specialty Brent had known best and written most—with the knowledge of experience. At least light BDSM. I was willing to bet that it was from this core group of younger men here that Marty had chosen his invitation list for last evening's party in his hotel room. And I wondered if more active and intimate sessions were in store during the three-day event. I wouldn't be surprised if they were the only reason Marty even held these conclaves.

I scanned the room several times, trying to pick out who Niles James might be. I couldn't very well avoid him if I couldn't identify him. At the next break I asked the older man I'd been sitting beside if he knew who Niles James was and could point him out to me. He did and could and pointed over to where a pudgy cross between Orson Wells and Truman Capote older man was talking with a well-built young blond guy.

"That's him," the man said. "Writes great Romances. The best-selling author in the Bent Stallions stable."

I bristled at that claim, but I remained polite. I had marked James's looks so that I'd remember to stay away from him, but my attention had already gone to the young blond he was talking to. I was sure just from watching him move and assessing his build that he was the sweeter-than-wine lover I had started with last night—and would have been more than pleased to continue with. Now him I would make no effort at all to stay away from.

I turned to ask the man if he knew who the blond was, but he was gone, and Marty was bearing down on me. I was to have the privilege of lunching at his table, at which he had gathered a bevy of twittering women authors of gay male Romance. It was not lost on me that Marty was introducing me to many disparate forms of sadism.

* * * *

The porn war between Jasper—as initiated by Brent Davenport—and Niles James was of the most bitter sort. It was born from a love-hate relationship. Brent and Niles had been lovers. They met as writers, with Brent writing mainstream sci-fi short stories for a pulp magazine and Niles already writing his gay male Romances for another publication of the same pulp magazine conglomerate. This, of course, was light years before the advent of the computer, let alone the e-book, which had caused the porn novel industry to burgeon because a buyer didn't have to worry about what to do with the book after he'd read it—or that much while we was reading it. Although Niles wrote Romances, he practiced BDSM and introduced Brent to the practice before Brent ever thought of writing that genre. It was Marty Doans, a young BDSM adherent of Niles's, who both encouraged Brent to switch to writing gay male BDSM for his startup Bent Stallions publishing effort and came between Brent and Niles sexually.

And it was Marty who tore Brent away from Niles and who egged on the two in competition with each other as writers and who, gleefully, started and nurtured the porn war between the two. He touted and promoted them both as "the" best-seller in his stable and encouraged and exaggerated the professional animosity between the two. It didn't take the two long to buy into the hype themselves.

This manufactured animosity was a palpable source of energy in this conclave, I clearly could see from the first session I attended. Nearly every side conversation I heard concerned the porn war between Marty's two standards and the fact that this was the first time that anyone had seen both Jasper and Niles James on the list of speakers. That neither name was applied yet in the schedule of sessions and the key concluding session time slot was not filled in yet only added fuel to the fire of anticipation.

If this was Marty's doing, I'd have to give him props as a consummate showman. Even I didn't know for sure what session I was to be impaneled on. The invitation to speak had suggested that I talk about the rules of BDSM in writing, which

I found to be laughable. There were no definitive rules for BDSM in either doing it or writing about it, I believed, after having picked up writing it upon Brent's demise. There were, of course, clubs of it with rules of their own, but I had found that there was a whole range of application of the genre in both practice and stories and that a varying readership could be counted on for falling into this range.

My own BDSM writing thus far had been a toned-down version of Brent's and more heavily geared to bondage and milder toys and full enjoyment by all concerned. I would be the first to admit that I had little personal experience in the heavier BDSM arena and would be writing Romance myself—which only added to my resentment of Niles James dominating that aspect of the gay male market—if given the choice. I did enjoy a rough kind of sex, though, and I had been taking Jasper's work more in that direction. The fans of Jasper hadn't seemed to be complaining about that, at least yet—that I knew of.

Brent had not practiced BDSM techniques with me— well, beyond some of the tying up practices. By the time we met, he had softened and was actually quite romantic with me in our love-making.

I had accepted the invitation and the topic and had proceeded to put together a talk on the various techniques, equipment, and toys of BDSM in the gay male world and on how they could be—were being in Jasper's writings—applied to pornographic writing. I would just ignore the word "rules" altogether unless it came up in the question period. And if it did, I knew there would be a knock-down-drag-out fight in the room no matter what I said I believed about it.

As we went into the afternoon session, still without a topic for that last session or a mention of either me or Niles James as session speakers, I became increasingly convinced that I had been given a fake topic and wouldn't be speaking on the rules of BDSM at all, but rather would be paired with Niles in some sort of cat fight to conclude the conclave.

In this I was proved to be quite right.

My eyes kept going to the puckered-lipped, obviously self-satisfied pile of blubber who had been identified to me as Niles James and who sat simpering in the front row of the other section of chairs in the meeting room in the middle of a harem of equally simpering female writers. And as my eyes bored into him, I was aware that others were looking at me too, apparently having zeroed in on my "Jasper" nametag and already in delicious anticipation of what Marty obviously was planning.

When I couldn't take any more of this, I rose and slipped out of the room—I had sat as far back as I could find a seat—and went to the hotel reception desk.

"Is there an appropriate bar I can go to around here?" I asked. "Not in this hotel." I already was taking my name tag off as I asked. I wanted to be away from all of this for a while.

"The Men's Paradise bar is just a couple of blocks west on Western Sahara. Kind of a dive, but there's a play area in back, if that's what you're interested in. A little early, though. They just opened at 4:00."

"Sounds fine, thanks," I said. I was just looking for a drink or two away from here, but I wasn't bothered if it was the kind of place that had action in the back. If it was on the rough side, it was close to where I had been in my early days.

* * * *

I saw him as soon as I entered the dimly lit, nearly deserted bar—my sweeter-than-wine blond hunk from the previous night of sex in Marty's room.

I saddled up to the bar beside him, ordered a beer, and turned to him. He was looking down into the bar top rather than at me, although I had seen him glance up when I entered and then look away quickly.

"Hi, my name is Tim," I said. "I think we've already had a bit of sex. Maybe more than a bit."

He looked up at me, his expression a mix of embarrassment, interest, and amusement. His smile was much too glorious to have been partially hidden behind a face mask. He didn't deny we'd had sex.

"For real? Your real name is Tim?"

"Yep. That I cannot deny."

"In that case, I'm Julian. I admit that I've been looking for you today, but didn't see you at the conclave. Both of those sessions were insufferable, though, and not finding what I was looking for, I came out of that gaseous balloon to soak up my disappointment."

"Anyone tell you your kisses are sweeter than wine?" I asked. "Not to mention that you have a terrific body and a great cock."

"So that would make us twins?" he asked, with a laugh. "Gotta admit I was thoroughly enjoying you before that leather guy pulled you away. Nothing half that good again before Marty shooed us all out of there to have you alone to himself. You weren't looking all that conscious when I left. I was a little worried for you, especially when I couldn't pick you out in the crowd today."

"No, I slept through most of Marty," I answered. "Sure would like to take up where you and I left off, though. I'm told they have accommodation for that beyond that doorway over there covered with a beaded curtain."

The room was small and pretty grungy, but it had a quite adequate six-foot-square vinyl ottoman in the center of it that the bartender who took Julian's money wiped down when he'd shown us to the room. It was Julian's money, because he insisted on being dominant and calling the shots, which was just peachy with me.

When we'd been left alone, Julian got right to business, and I let him work, as I had enjoyed letting him take the lead the previous night. We did the sweeter-than-wine kiss thing, rocking against each other, as we stood beside the ottoman, stripped off each other's shirts, and unbuckled and unzipped each other. Julian retrieved both of our dicks and worked them against each other, while he slowly arched me back, bending me over the ottoman. I let him do as he wanted, holding his head between my hands, keeping him in the honeyed kiss.

When he'd bent me to where my shoulder blades felt vinyl, he pushed me up onto the ottoman until my head flopped over the end. He moved around to the head of the ottoman, and I found myself opening my throat to the slow stroke of his cock while he leaned over me and ran his hands over my torso as far down as running his fingers into my pubes and tantalizing the root of my cock. I went right hard for him, which was a good sign to me that he was what I wanted and would scratch my itch. He eventually returned his hands to cover my pecs and worry my nipples.

When he felt the time was right, he pulled out of my mouth, turned me onto my belly, my head still flopping over the end of the ottoman and my arms dangling off the sides, and lay full on top of me, moving his body slowly on top of mine, listening to me moaning softly. He took his time. I spread my thighs a bit and his cock fell into the crack and I felt his cock slide down along my entrance. He lifted his hips, sliding back up to my entrance. Then down and then up and repeating until he felt me shudder in his embrace. If I could have trained my rim to catch his bulb as it passed and suck it into me, he'd already be fucking me.

"Yes, yes, fuck me," I murmured, as I raised my hips to him, presenting for him. But he was taking his time. After a bit of pressure work on my rim with the bulb, he started moving down my body, kissing me on the back as he moved. He had an arm around my waist and he pulled my rump up even more into the air than I had raised it, wanting him to enter me.

His tongue and mouth went to my hole, and I groaned my pleasure and need. He pulled my cock and balls through my legs, having nudged my thighs to spread their stance further. He sucked the cock and balls, giving equal time to those and my hole, as I writhed under his attention and whispered the mantra of "fuck me, fuck me, stick it in, please fuck me, now, please."

And then he did just that, going into a crouch over my hips and folding his body over mine, and slowly, but relentlessly, entering and entering and entering me. I shuddered and trembled as I felt him throbbing and moving inside me,

261

fully possessing me. Not terribly thick, but terribly, terribly long—reaching for my tonsils. Fucking deep. Then shallow; then deep again.

His arms were wrapped around my chest and he rose up on his knees, bringing me with him. One of his arms lay diagonally up my chest. The hand of the other one was stroking my cock in rhythm to his stroking inside me, a stroke that paused and then picked up in a different rhythm and speed whenever I felt I had the measure of it, making me gasp and gulp and beg for more, deeper, faster, harder.

He cupped my chin with a hand and turned my face to his for a sweeter-than-wine kiss that went on almost forever . . . until, with a lurch and a muffled cry, I shot out over the vinyl. I felt his encasing arm pull back from me then and I fell forward on my chest on the cum-slickened vinyl. He crouched closer over my hips, grabbed my waist with his hands, and pumped me harder, faster, deeper to his own ejaculation.

We returned to the Blue Moon separately, after paying extra to use the bar's shower, Julian showering before me, me still lying in a pool of cum and moaning when he was finished. The supper had already started before I reached the resort hotel. Marty's table was fully seated—thank god, I thought. But it was somewhat disconcerting to see that Julian was seated there, and looking fresh and somewhat disinterested. Who would have guess that just a half hour earlier he had his long cock up my ass? Also seated at the table was the pudgy Niles James. A bevy of old maidish women were fawning over him. Understandable, I thought. He did write that insipid Romance. But then I admonished myself. I rather enjoyed his Romances, I'd have to admit, especially the ones of recent years. I never admitted to Brent that I read them, of course.

I didn't realize before I sat down at one of the few empty seats at another table, though, that it put me right next to who quite evidently had been the leatherman who DP'd me the previous night. I wouldn't have known him from Adam—at least until I zeroed in on the studded wrist bands he was wearing and got a peek at the leather harness under his half-open shirt—but he certainly remembered me. I spent half the meal removing his hand from my thigh and even my basket and listening to him whisper in my ear what he wanted to do to my body. Some of that sounded rather enticing, though, and I didn't have much to say when he pointed out that the last time he groped my crotch, I was hard.

Sometime during the meal I discovered that he wrote leather and biker books, which came as no surprise, but also that he read my—or, more correctly, Brent's—BDSM and rough sex books and was dying to take me for a solo ride, test out positions and tie ups Jasper wrote about, and compare research notes. He even told me, in hushed tones, that he had a whip he'd named Jasper.

He followed me back to my room after dinner, which I didn't realize until I already was trapped in a dead-end hall. The only thing that saved me from a research session, which I'll have to admit I was half tempted by, was that I found my pass card wouldn't work on my hotel room door. I turned and breezed by him, with the explanation that the key didn't work, and he was so nonplused by that, only half believing me, I'm sure, that he didn't impede my passage.

"You are no longer in that room," the hotel desk clerk cheerily told me. "You've been moved to Room 103, and your luggage has already been transferred. Just a minute and I'll prepare you a new pass key."

"Marty Doans again," I exclaimed. I said it loud enough that the leather guy, who had followed me in disbelief out to the reception desk, overheard and immediately vanished. I smiled at the thought that he probably was one of Marty's authors too and knew better than to mess with someone Marty was being possessive with.

I seethed through the two evening sessions, paying little attention to what was being said and looking over at the leatherman occasionally and frowning my "I'm not in the mood anymore" warning. Although he continued to eye me, all it took was for me to look annoyed at him, and he turned his eyes elsewhere.

That night I was reminded that the Blue Moon was a full-service gay male resort. When I entered Room 103, I immediately noticed the sling suspended in the middle of the room from four chains attached to a strong hook screwed securely into a ceiling beam. The sling hadn't been there the previous night and the room had been too dimly lit and filled with teeming naked bodies for me to have noticed special amenities like strong ceiling hooks.

I was contemplating the why of the plastic cover—more of a kid's swimming pool effect because of the lip around the sides—that was under the sling, when a naked Marty emerged from the bathroom and had me undressed and in the sling, with my arms and legs running up and bound to the four corner chains, before I could think of a reason why he shouldn't do it. My attention was riveted on the impossible thickness of his cock. Brent's cock had been impossibly thick. I actually liked impossibly thick cocks.

I told him something of this after I'd finished screaming at the tit clamps he applied to my nipples.

"We don't have to do it this way, Marty. You've got a thick cock. That's enough for me to give you a good time in a fuck."

"I'm startin' to get complaints on your writing, Jasper," he said. He always used my pen name. To him, I *was* Jasper. "Buyers are beginning to notice that Jasper doesn't have the BDSM zing he used to have—rough sex, yes, but you need a refresher in some of the finer techniques and toys, I think."

Refresher? I thought. Heavy BDSM was Brent's bag, not mine. There was a reason I wasn't writing heavy BDSM. But then, as Marty, already inside me and pounding to beat the band, started jerking on the leads to the tit clamps and I resumed some minor screaming again. I recognized that I certainly was getting experience in what he wanted me to write. I wouldn't have trouble writing how pinched and pulled nipples felt like from now on—or how, mysteriously enough, they were, in fact, connected to the arousal of my cock and to my enjoyment of a thick dick working my channel.

I spouted for him. And it wasn't long before I learned what the plastic cloth with the rim under the sling was all about either—when he came inside me, pulled out of me, fisted his cock, and lifted it over my belly.

I'd never actually included water sports in anything I'd written before. But I guess the point was that Brent, as Jasper, had. And that Marty wanted this sort of stuff to be included in Jaspers books again.

I got the message.

* * * *

Peter Knoles, Marty Doans's flighty assistant, was hopping from one foot to the other in front of me the next morning as he handed me the final schedule for the day's sessions, the last day of the conclave. As he got me to accept it, he skipped back a few extra paces from me and almost went into a fetal position, as if I was going to swat him like a fly.

After I looked at the schedule, I certainly felt like doing so—but only because Marty wasn't there himself. Just as I feared, the last session was now titled "Porn War," and Jasper and Niles James were the sole listed panelists.

I could have spit bricks and was building up the effort to do so, when I heard a surprised exclamation of "Shit!"

I looked up and into the wide-open eyes of Julian, who had just appeared in front of me. He was staring at the nametag on my shirt.

"You. You're Jasper!?" he both exclaimed and quizzed.

I looked at the nametag on his shirt. It said "Niles James."

"Shit!" I said.

"But . . . but . . . you aren't old enough," he said, being the first to recover.

"Neither are you . . . to be Niles James," I retorted.

"The original Niles died. Marty wanted to keep the franchise going and he liked my Romance writing, so I took over as Niles James."

"And the original Brent died and Marty had me take over Jasper," I said. I didn't reveal that Brent had been my lover as well. When you're shopping for a new lover, you don't

265

necessarily tell the prospects about the earlier ones—beyond telling them enough to know what you could do. Julian definitely already knew what I could do—and what I would do for him, which was anything he wanted me to do.

"Well, you do Romance just as well as you write it," I said, maneuvering from the sticky situation to more amenable ground.

"You know we're supposed to be sworn enemies," Julian said.

"Yeah, I know. That's pretty much what the schedule of this afternoon's session says. So, what do we do? Cut out again? Leave 'em hanging?"

"I can't afford to do that," Julian said. "I need this gig."

"Me too," I answered.

"Then let's give them what Marty wants. Let's tear into each other in the conclave session and then go off and hide and fuck while they think we're in mortal combat somewhere."

"Sounds good to me," I was quick to agree. "But it'll have to be your room. Marty had me moved in with him."

"He's giving a press interview now. Switch your luggage to my room while he's tied up with that. He'll never find you there. Tomorrow we'll duck out when no one's looking and figure out how we can be together more. I live in New York."

"So do I."

"Sweet."

I smiled, thinking of wine and his kisses.

When I got to Marty's room and opened the door, I shuddered at what I found. The sling was gone, but chains with wrist restraints now hung from the hook in the ceiling. And on the bed was a flogging whip. I gave brief thought to whether Marty had named the whip. I loaded my suitcase and got out of there as soon as possible.

But I had to admit that Marty was right. If I was going to continue to be Jasper, I was gonna need more experience in what Jasper wrote about. Marty lived in New York too. Guess I just wouldn't avoid him and his research sessions. It could only make my writing better.

And he did have a very thick cock.

~

About the Author

Habu is one of the pen names of a former supersonic spy jet pilot, intelligence agent, male model, movie actor, and diplomat. A wild youth in South East Asia was spent enjoying whatever sexual opportunities came his way, and much of his gay male writing is about recalling incidents from those days and inventing ones he'd perhaps have liked to experience. He now leads a very quiet and ordinary happily married family life.

An American, he is a published mainstream novelist and short story writer under another name and in another dimension of his life. He has written or cowritten (with Sabb) approaching 1,000 published short stories and over100 published erotica e-books, primarily of gay fiction but also memoir, straight fiction and ménage fiction. His hand and creative writing can be seen in stories and books by habu, sr71plt, Dirk Hessian, Shabbu, and Stephen Kessel—among unrevealed others that might surprise readers. The fictionalized

GM memoir *Flying High, Diving Deep* is loosely based on his life experiences. He can be found at the adults only gay male site BarbarianSpy, which he shares with Sabb and Dirk Hessian.

You can send feedback about this e-book directly to habu, or send general feedback on this e-book to BarbarianSpy.

Our authors always like to receive feedback, and appreciate it when readers post reviews at Goodreads, and other sites.

FOR LITERARY HEAT

Not all books listed below may currently be on release.
BOOKS BY DIRK HESSIAN
Xtreme Erotica
The King's Men
Shores of Tripoli
Prophecy of Noto
Pretender's Fate
General Erotica/Romance
Fire Down the Valley
Constantinople
The Beautiful Way
Blue and Gray
Colonel's Treasure
Beginning of Time
Labyrinth
BOOKS BY HABU
Gay Erotica
Memoir Faction
Flying High, Diving Deep*
Xtreme Erotica
Second Coming
Vortex: Sacrificed by Curiosity*

Dark Angel Sounding *(included in Sounding:Ultimate Control)**

Control)*

Sounding: Ultimate Control (Print Only)*

Sounding Five (E-book only)

General Erotica

Romance

Four Coins

Lower Than the Heart

Brambleton

Gotta Keep Trying

Finding Amnad

Platres Conclave

Other Novels/Novellas

Gilded Cage

House on Park

Anything for Ambition

Dance of the Ravishers

Hard Knocks U*

My Neighbor's Spa

Man's Man: Tales of a High Priced Gay Hooker*

Trip Money

Clint Folsom Mysteries Compendium Volume 1*

Death to Blonds - Stolen Judgment (Clint Folsom

Mystery)

Clint Folsom Mysteries Compendium Volume 2*

The Indian Doctor

Sailorboy

Home to Fire Island

Choke Hold

Gay Erotica Anthologies

Tails in the Tropics

Tails in the Med

Rough Riders*

Grab Bag 1*

Grab Bag 2*

Grab Bag 3*

Grab Bag 4*

Grab Bag 5*
Beyond the Beaded Curtain*
Habu's Christmas Balls
The Sporting Life*
Fetish Galore!*
Literary Gay Erotica
Cairo Surrender*
The Handyman*
Homeward Bound
Journey to Mirage*
Menage Erotica
13 Ways for Halloween
Luther*
The Indian Prince
BOOKS BY SHABBU
Finding Jason
Dirty Pool
Operation Black Jade
Cigars!*
Angel in the Barn
Gayly Complicated
Despoiling David
The Tree of Idleness
I Met a Man
The Interview
Rough Road to Happiness
BOOKS BY SABB
Hiring in Hollywood
The Legend of Holleystone Grange
Surprise Encounters
She is He
Wrong Man
Loyal to his King
Barbarian Tales - Book One - Traveler's Tales*
Barbarian Tales - Book Two - Journeys Begin*
Barbarian Tales - Book Three - The Inheritance*
Barbarian Tales - Book Four - Road to Persepolis*

~

* indicates the book is available in paperback and e-book.